ASHES OF BETRAYAL

DAVID J. GATWARD

WEIRDSTONE PUBLISHING

Ashes of Betrayal
by
David J. Gatward

 Created with Vellum

To Miles

Grimm: nickname for a dour and forbidding individual, from Old High German grim [meaning] 'stern', 'severe'. From a Germanic personal name, Grima, [meaning] 'mask'. (*www.ancestory.co.uk*)

ONE

Bob 'Thumbs' Ackroyd wasn't so much sailing three sheets to the wind, as being dashed about in a storm, barely clinging onto the last remaining splinters of his tired ship's shattered mast.

He'd headed out late afternoon with every intention of having only a couple of pints, perhaps three at the most, but then he'd bumped into Charlie Fletcher, and everything had gone very rapidly downhill.

It was easy to blame Charlie, because Charlie had a face on him that needed blaming for something. Anything would do really, Bob thought, as he stumbled around in the dark, trying to remember his way home.

Charlie's face always looked guilty, like he'd always just been up to no good and couldn't quite believe he'd not yet been caught. He carried a glint in his eye with all the bravado of a proud, and very stupid, jewellery thief, happily showing off the diamonds he'd just pinched. And that smile, the way it curled just enough to show broken teeth and allow a filthy laugh to escape? Bob had lost count of the number of times he'd seen folk have a go at slapping it off the man's ruddy-cheeked face.

Bob was very aware that he and Charlie were both old enough to know better than to drink so much, and had been for decades now, but neither of them cared, and by now, it was too late to even try and change. They'd known each other since primary school. A friendship forged in the unforgiving crucible of the playground was a precious thing and he valued it above all else.

Bob remembered how, when they'd hit their sixties, they'd promised each other that it was time to slow down, that perhaps stealing wheelie bins and letting down car tyres wasn't becoming of gentlemen their age. Then their sixties had faded and into their seventies they'd stumbled, promising this time that yes, they would give it a rest now, stop wandering the streets in the early hours singing songs that would make a soldier blush.

Now they were eighty, Charlie a couple of months ago, Bob this very night. That was why he had ventured out after all, and kept it quiet from Charlie, in the hope of entering his eighty-first year on Earth with some attempt at decorum.

Oh well.

'Oi, Thumbs! Over here!'

Charlie's call from somewhere in the darkness ahead was punctuated by the wheezing of an old man's lungs, somehow still managing to keep him alive despite the cigarettes, and the constant thuds and thumps as he stumbled along, using walls and fences to keep himself upright.

Bob was tired. He wanted to go home. Charlie, though, clearly didn't.

'What?' he called ahead. 'What is it?'

'This! Come here! You're not going to believe it!'

'Not sure I can be arsed, Charlie,' Bob replied, leaning against a wall, very aware of the excitement in Charlie's voice. 'Reckon my bed's calling.'

'Is it bollocks, like! Get your arse over here, come on, lad!'

Bob took a deep breath, sighed, and pushed himself onwards.

'This'd better be worth it,' he muttered, but the sound of barely muffled chuckling ahead didn't fill him with much hope that it was.

Bob thumped into Charlie before he saw him, and they both tumbled to the ground, two old men rolling around on a back-street pavement like brawlers, which, had they not been so drunk and floppy, would've no doubt have broken a bone or two.

''Bloody hell, Bob!' Charlie moaned from beneath him, as Bob did his best to heave himself back up to his feet. 'Did you not see me?'

'Of course I didn't see you!' Bob replied. 'It's the middle of the sodding night, there's not a star in the sky, never mind the moon, and my eyesight's so bad now I'd be hard pressed to see you in the midday sun on market day!'

Eventually back on his feet, Bob reached down to grope for Charlie and help him up.

'Watch where your hands are going,' Charlie said. 'Drunk I may be, but you're still not my type.'

With Charlie now on his feet, Bob asked what it was that he'd been so desperate to show him.

Charlie's chuckle slipped into the moment once again, and Bob watched him raise a pointed finger.

'Look!' he said. 'Up there! That window.'

'What window?'

'That one!'

'There's a lot of bloody windows, Charlie...'

'The open one! That one!'

'Why the hell would I want to look at an open window?'

'Just shut up and listen!'

'What? Listen? Why?'

And then he heard it.

'Bloody hell...'

Charlie's chuckle curled its edges sordidly.

'Told you,' he said. 'Someone's having a good night up there, aren't they?'

Now that he could hear it, Bob could hear nothing else. The moaning. The groaning. The faint and altogether more disturbing sound of flesh slapping against flesh.

'You're wrong in the head,' Bob said. 'That's not for our ears, is it? Just a couple having fun, as is their want. And good on them, I say, like.'

Charlie leaned in.

'Then why's that window open then, hey?'

'Well, it's not because they wanted two old men to stand outside and listen in, that's for sure!' Bob replied, but Charlie wasn't listening. 'I'm going,' he said. 'Been a good night, Charlie, but I'm too old for this kind of buggering about.'

'Got room up there for another?' Charlie called out, ignoring Bob.

The sounds from the window stopped and a moment later, the large silhouette of a man filled it.

'Who's out there? Who said that?'

To Bob's horror, Charlie stepped out into full view, and waved.

'What the hell are you doing?'

Bob tried to pull Charlie back into the shadows, but Charlie was having none of it and shrugged him off.

That was enough for Bob. He was going home, and whatever Charlie wanted to do, that was his business. He was eighty years old, he was pissed, he was tired, and he didn't fancy having his nose ripped off by a naked, sweaty man stopped mid-coitus.

Turning on his heel, Bob walked off. By the time Charlie realised he was gone, it was too late, and Bob could hear his old friend shouting his name into the dark.

A while later, and seemingly no closer to home, Bob paused to get his bearings. His retreat from where Charlie had led him had been hasty, and with his poor eyesight, plus all the booze, he hadn't taken much notice of where he'd been wandering. His only aim had been to get away from Charlie as quickly as possible, and that he'd managed, but now was probably a good time to work out exactly how to get home from where he was. If only he knew...

The fact he could still get lost in a town he'd lived in his whole life never ceased to amaze Bob. Arguably, his sense of direction had diminished with his advancing years, and his memory wasn't what it was, but still, Leyburn was home, always had been, so how the hell could he not know where he'd ended up? To make matters worse, his phone was dead, so he couldn't even satnav his way back to his front door, or as was more often the case, stare at the blurry screen in his hands while trying to use it as some kind of home-seeking device.

Weariness came at Bob like a wave on a stormy sea, and he decided that perhaps the best thing to do was to sit down somewhere and have a little rest before going any further.

Somehow, he'd wound up walking through a collection of small industrial buildings and units, and the only way that could've happened was to have taken a left instead of a right at the main road. Or was it a right instead of a left? Bob hadn't a clue.

He needed to sit down and think, and as luck would have it, as that thought entered his mind, he spotted a picnic bench outside of one of the warehouses. He stumbled over to it, lowered himself down, burped loudly enough to scatter a few sleepy pigeons from a tree, and again tried to locate the footpath in his mind that would take him home.

Bob had just about managed to untangle his memory enough to know not only where he was, but how to get to where he wanted to be, when he heard voices. They came from the building he was sitting outside, a building that, as far as he could tell, was lifeless. No light spilled out into the night from any window or door.

The voices had been soft, distant, and on a night so dark, had caused the hairs on the back of Bob's neck to stand to attention.

Maybe I'm hearing things, he thought, but then the voices came again, louder this time. Then across those came the muffled shouting of a man, which was cut off so sharply that to Bob it sounded as though someone had just switched off a radio.

With the shouting gone as suddenly as it had appeared, the silence of the night seemed to pulse around Bob. He froze, listened for those other voices, heard a murmur, or was it laughter? Then panic took him and, without really thinking why, Bob was on his feet and running. He may not have known where his home was right at that moment, but he was sure as hell that it wasn't here, and for some reason, that voice, and the way it had so abruptly stopped, had given him the heebie-jeebies.

Turning a corner in the road, Bob chanced a look back at where he'd just bolted from like a spooked rabbit, laughing at himself at what he easily convinced himself was nothing more than his over-active imagination.

Scared of the dark at my age, he thought. God, he was relieved that Charlie wasn't there to witness it, or he'd never hear the end of it. And it was right then, as he briefly imagined Charlie's raucous laugh and mocking face, that Bob saw a large shadow roll out of the building, chased seconds later by thin orange tongues of flame licking hungrily at the night.

TWO

Police Constable Jadyn Okri was standing in Leyburn marketplace wondering why he was spending the last moments of a damp, Monday evening listening to Dave Calvert, the team's newest member and fledgling Police Community Support Officer, wax lyrical about the many joys of goat husbandry.

'They're proper characters, all of them,' Dave said, clapping his large, meaty hands together to warm them up in the cold of the night. 'There's not one that's like another, that's for sure. And they've a sense of humour, too. Cheeky buggers, the lot of them.'

'A goat has a sense of humour,' Jadyn said, unable to hide the disbelief in his voice.

'Sounds daft, I know, but it's true,' Dave said.

'How do you know, though?' Jadyn asked. 'It's not like they can tell jokes, is it?'

'I wouldn't put it past them.'

'I would.'

'I'm serious,' Dave said. 'Goats, they're funny, like; hang around with them long enough and you'll see.'

'See what, exactly?' Jadyn asked, utterly unable to imagine what Dave was getting at. 'They're goats, not stand-up comedians appearing on yet another panel show on TV.'

'They gang up on me.'

The laugh burst from Jadyn before he was able to do anything to stop it.

'Goats gang up on you?' he said, shaking his head. 'Come on, Dave, give it a break!'

'Trust me,' said Dave, his eyes widening as he spoke, and tapping his temple, 'they're cunning little buggers, all of them. And when they're in a group? You're in trouble, you mark my words.'

Jadyn looked at the larger-than-life man in front of him, whose broad back and thick neck had more in common with the game of rugby than it did with the finer points of goat husbandry.

'Have you seen you?' he asked. 'How can anything, never mind a goat, gang up on you?'

'The worst of the lot are Dorothy and Rose,' Dave said, clearly not listening. 'They're right mischievous, those two.'

'You've named your goats?'

'Why wouldn't I?'

'And you went with Dorothy and Rose because?'

'They're characters from one of my favourite TV shows,' said Dave.

'There's no one on TV called Dorothy or Rose,' said Jadyn.

Dave did a very good impression of someone genuinely shocked by what they'd just heard.

'Then you've never seen The Golden Girls, have you?' he said, held up his fingers in front of his face, and started to count. 'I've got Dorothy, Rose, Blanche, and Sophia; they're my golden girls. Then I've got Cagney and Lacey, Barbara and Margo—'

'You really aren't joking, are you?' said Jadyn.

'I never joke about my goats,' said Dave. 'It's a very serious business, is goat husbandry.'

'Except for when they're ganging up on you to play practical jokes,' Jadyn laughed.

'If you don't believe me, then come round and see for yourself,' suggested Dave.

Jadyn was frantically trying to think of a way of politely

declining Dave's offer when he spotted someone making their way towards them from the bottom end of the marketplace. And judging by the way they were weaving about, they'd had a few.

'Who's this, then?' Dave asked, seeing where Jadyn had been drawn.

'Not a clue,' said Jadyn. 'Looks like he's had a skinful, though, doesn't he?'

The man, who was now close enough for Jadyn to see that he was in his senior years, was waving frantically as he approached.

'Reckon we should meet him halfway,' Jadyn suggested. 'Get there before he trips up and next thing we know, we're calling an ambulance and escorting him to hospital.'

Jogging over, and with Dave just a few steps behind, Jadyn got to the man just in time to witness his feet get in a tangle and send him flying. Instinct took over and Jadyn threw himself forward, catching the man barely a second before he faceplanted, and in the process, sending himself down onto the Tarmac to act as an impromptu crash mat.

'Fire!' the man shouted, wrestling with Jadyn on the ground. 'There's a fire! Fire! And a voice! Fire!'

Jadyn's only thought right then was about the pain in his legs from landing hard with a hefty old man in his arms.

'You need to get up,' he said. 'Please? Then we can have a chat about—'

'Fire!' the man said again, and started pointing back down the way he'd just come, jabbing his finger hard behind him. 'Fire! Down there, like! Fire! I saw it! Heard voices, too. Fire!'

With the ease of a parent lifting a small child, Dave heaved the man off of Jadyn and placed him carefully back on his feet.

'There you go,' he said.

The man wobbled a little but managed to stay upright.

Jadyn rolled onto all fours and, with a groan, pushed himself up to his feet. Then he caught a whiff of the man's breath and was nearly back on the ground again, so laced it was with booze. Behind it, Jadyn caught the acrid tang of cheese and onion crisps. Then the man burped, and the cocktail was further disturbed by the reek of pickled eggs.

'Sir,' Jadyn said, managing to not gag too obviously at the foul stink leaking from his mouth, 'perhaps it would be better if we headed over there for a chat?'

He pointed to his patrol car.

'I don't give a monkey's where we chat,' the man said. 'All I know is there's a fire and you have to stop it! Fire!'

'We're the police,' Dave said.

'Exactly,' the man said.

'Exactly, what?' Jadyn asked.

'You're the police, so you can call them, can't you, the Fire Brigade? Get them down here, for the fire, I mean. They'll need to put it out. Those voices, too, I heard them.'

Carefully, and very aware that the man wasn't all that steady on his feet, Jadyn led him over to the car, opened it, then guided him to sit down in the back seat.

'You're not arresting me, are you?' the man complained, panic in his voice. 'It wasn't me! I didn't start it!'

Jadyn tried to reassure him.

'Please,' he said, 'if you can just give us your name, and tell us exactly what—'

'You can't arrest me, I'm innocent!' the man yelled, and tried to push himself out of the car, and instead managed to fall backwards and flounder for a moment like an overturned turtle. 'That fire, it's nowt to do with me, is it? I don't even smoke!'

That last comment caught Jadyn off guard, so to get things under control, he pulled out his notebook and took down the man's name and contact details.

'Thumbs?' he said, not entirely sure he'd heard right. 'That's not your name, is it?'

'My name's Bob, but Thumbs is what everyone calls me, so I guess it is, yes,' the man said, then held up his hands. 'See?'

And indeed, Jadyn could, because where Bob should've had

thumbs, he instead had two stumps, one a little longer than the other.

'This one, chainsaw accident,' Bob said, somehow managing to wiggle the longest of the stumps on his left hand. 'And this one?' Instead of wiggling it, he pinched the stub on his right hand and gave it a shake. 'Got infected after a squirrel bit it.'

Jadyn decided not to put this extra information down in his notebook, though the squirrel attack did intrigue him.

'So, this fire, then,' he said. 'And you mentioned voices?'

Bob was out of the car like he'd just had an electric shock.

'It's down there!' he said, his voice urgent, once again jabbing a pointy finger into the night. 'Warehouses. Can't remember where they are exactly, but they're there, aren't they? You know the ones, don't you? Out that way a bit, near the railway, I think. Yes, that's where they are. But that's where I saw it, the fire, I mean, heard those voices. There was a shout, just before I ran off. And I wouldn't have seen it if I'd not given up on Charlie and him listening to people having sex through a window, so that's something, isn't it?'

Wherever this conversation was coming from or indeed going to, Jadyn had no idea, and he was growing very confused very quickly.

'Listening to people having sex?' he said. 'Not sure I understand.'

'I wasn't!'

'But you just said—'

'That was Charlie!'

'Who's Charlie?' Dave asked.

'He's my oldest friend,' Bob explained, 'and a bit of a bastard, too, like, but in a nice way, if you know what I mean?'

Jadyn wasn't sure that he did.

'He wouldn't mind me saying so. No, maybe he would...

'We were out having a few drinks to celebrate my eightieth, you see,' Bob continued, 'and we were walking home, like, and that's why we ended up listening to the sex, except I wasn't. Listening to it, I mean. The sex. Not on purpose, anyway. It was hard not too, really, what with the window open.'

Jadyn could feel a headache coming on.

'Can we get back to this fire?' he asked. 'You know where it is, yes? Can you take us there?'

Bob hesitated before replying.

'I think so,' he said eventually.

'Then that'll have to do, won't it?' Jadyn said, and with a look at Dave, had the PCSO in the passenger seat as he clipped Bob in, then headed around to the driver's door, jumped in, and started the engine. 'Which way?' he asked.

Bob didn't answer.

'Bob,' Jadyn said. 'I need to know where I'm going. If there's a fire, if you heard voices, then—'

A tap-tap-tap on his shoulder silenced Jadyn, and he turned to see that Dave was staring past him through the windscreen.

'Not sure we'll need Bob's directions,' Dave said, pointing a meaty hand across Jadyn's chest.

Jadyn turned and there, flickering in the distant darkness, he saw orange flames dancing.

THREE

Harry was very close to concluding that the best way to pack everything up for a house move was to pile it all up and set it on fire. Half of what he'd packed so far, he'd not actually looked at since moving to the Dales, and the rest of it he had little interest in keeping. He wasn't big on possessions, and packing to move house was only strengthening that viewpoint. And yet here he was, kneeling on the floor of his bedroom, and stuffing it all into a range of different-sized boxes to take with him to the new house.

The new house...

It wasn't all that long ago that Harry had moved into the first house he'd ever owned, a lovely little cottage in Gayle, overlooking the beck. He'd seen that ancient waterway dry to nothing but a trickle over the summer, turn into a raging torrent in autumn, and even freeze over in winter. That he was already preparing himself to say goodbye to it seemed a little ridiculous, but then, he'd learned since arriving in Wensleydale that life had a habit of throwing him curve balls.

A soft huff caused Harry to pause the packing as a wet, black nose appeared next to his face and pushed gently against his cheek.

'You bored, then, Smudge?' Harry asked, giving his dog a scratch on her head.

Smudge wagged her tail, then leaned in for a cuddle.

'You're a soft idiot, you know that, don't you?' Harry said, stroking the thick, black hair on Smudge's back.

'Talking to yourself again, then?'

The voice had come from the bedroom door.

Harry turned to see Grace smiling down at him.

'What time is it?' he asked.

'Just gone midnight,' Grace said. 'Dad's asleep on the sofa, and Ben's just about finished in the kitchen.'

'How is he?' Harry asked.

'Ben? Quiet,' said Grace. 'Something up?'

Harry wasn't sure.

'Liz is away,' he said.

'Probably just missing her, then,' Grace suggested. 'When is she back?'

'Not till Saturday,' said Harry. 'She's away at a hen do I believe, though how a hen do can last a full week I don't know. What's wrong with just going out for the night?'

'Where is she, then?' Grace asked.

'Some spa hotel somewhere,' said Harry. 'Abroad, I think.'

'Ooh, posh!' said Grace. 'Never been to a spa. Would love to go, though.'

'I bloody well wouldn't,' Harry grumbled, shuddering at the thought of someone giving him a massage.

'Not a fan?'

'Never been,' Harry said. 'Aim to keep it that way, too. Can't see myself enjoying it.'

'You never know.'

'Oh, I think I do.'

Harry could imagine few things worse than spending time in a hotel dedicated to walking around in dressing gowns, massages, and weirdly exotic aromas, all under the guise of health and well-being.

'I'd best cancel, then,' said Grace.

Harry narrowed his eyes.

'Not funny.'

'How are you doing up here?' Grace asked, laughing at Harry's response.

Harry stood up and glanced around the room. The bed was in pieces and stacked in a corner, the mattress leaning up against a wall. A collection of boxes stood to the side, and Harry couldn't really remember what some of them contained. The chest of drawers was where it always had been, except that it was now empty, the drawers tied in securely so that they wouldn't fall out when it came to carrying it downstairs and out of the house.

'Just about done,' Harry said.

'That's the whole house packed, then,' said Grace. 'Hasn't taken long, has it?'

'I travel light,' Harry said. 'And it's not exactly a huge, rambling property, with dozens of rooms to sort. Even so, for the life of me, I've no idea how I've managed to accumulate even half of what we've packed up.'

Grace came over and slipped an arm around Harry's waist and gave it a squeeze.

'Still looking forward to it? The move, I mean.'

'The move, no,' said Harry. 'Getting into the house? Very much so.'

'Same,' said Grace, squeezing Harry a little. 'You'll miss this place, though.'

Harry thought about that for a moment. On the one hand, he would, because it was the first place he'd ever owned. But on the other, it was just a house, and it was who was in it that made it a home. Smudge had, quite to Harry's surprise, been an essential ingredient. Then Grace had come along, and he knew that together was better because it just was. Not that he had a problem with being on his own, quite the opposite, really, but he knew that there was only so much of himself he could bear. Smudge and Grace, they brought out the best in him, and had somehow managed to help him realise that life wasn't all darkness and shadows and shades of grey, but a wonderful thing bursting with colour, even if some of that colour was his own occasionally very bad language.

'It's been fun,' Harry said. 'Love this little place. But it'll be nice to be somewhere a little bigger, won't it? Getting a little weary of banging into things all the time.'

'And by things you mean the walls, the doors, the cupboards ...'

'Everything,' Harry smiled.

Pulling himself free of Grace, Harry sealed the box he had just finished packing, then carried it over to the others.

'Guarantee, I'll unpack this lot in the new place and want to get rid of most of it.'

'There's really not that much,' said Grace, looking at the boxes.

'And what there is, I'm not sure's worth the keeping,' added Harry.

A couple of minutes later, and now downstairs, Harry popped his head around the lounge door to see Grace's dad, Arthur, happily snoring away. Smudge padded into the room and lay herself down beside Grace's dog, Jess. They both wagged their tails and shuffled in close to share their warmth.

'He didn't have to come over, you know,' Harry said.

'There was no stopping him,' said Grace. 'He insisted. And you know what my dad's like.'

'I do,' said Harry. 'Stubborn, like his daughter.'

'Says the pot to the kettle!' said Grace. 'Anyway, you say stubborn, I say strong-willed.'

'Wouldn't have you any other way,' smiled Harry.

Leaving Arthur and the dogs, Harry then led Grace through to the kitchen. Ben was doing a wipe down with a spray bottle of cleaner and a cloth. Against the far wall was a pile of boxes containing everything from salt and pepper and pasta to knives, plates, and a toaster.

'Nearly done?' Harry asked. 'You didn't have to clean the place, though, you know that, right?'

Ben smiled.

'I've worked with Mike too long now to not do a proper job.'

That comment made Harry grin. Considering the life his brother had been living before joining him in the Dales, the turnaround was nothing short of miraculous. Ben's prison days seemed little more than a distant memory, and he had changed so much since, in no small thanks to his boss, Mike the mechanic, who ran the local garage, and of course Liz Coates, one of Harry's PCSOs and Ben's girlfriend. They'd moved in together a good while ago now, and they seemed to be very happy together. But even as Harry nodded his approval at the work his brother had done, he could see a shadow in the younger man's eyes.

'And how are you doing yourself?' Harry asked, his tone relaxed, so as to not sound like he was prying.

Ben gave a yawn.

'Tired,' he said.

'Heard from Liz?'

'Not much,' said Ben. 'She's too busy being pampered.'

'Can't think of anything worse.'

'Same.'

Harry glanced over to Grace at this.

'See?' he said. 'It's not just me.'

'Must be a family thing, then,' said Grace.

Ben leaned over and gave the kitchen sink another wipe.

'I think we're done, don't you?' Harry asked.

Both Grace and Ben agreed.

'Then let's head off,' said Harry. 'We've a couple of days yet before we move in, so plenty of time to do whatever's left. Which isn't much, looking at things.'

'I'll go wake my dad,' said Grace, and left Harry with Ben.

Alone with his brother now, Harry turned to Ben.

'You're sure you're alright, though?' he asked.

Ben smiled, but Harry wasn't so sure his brother's eyes were joining in.

'I'm fine, Harry,' Ben said. 'I'm missing Liz, obviously, but she's back at the weekend.'

Harry narrowed his eyes.

'What?' said Ben, noticing Harry wasn't satisfied with his answer.

'There's nothing else bothering you?' Harry asked. 'And don't go telling me to mind my own business; you are my own business.'

The smile on Ben's face faded.

'Can't hide anything from you, can I?'

'No, you can't,' said Harry, concern for his brother now twisting his gut. 'What is it, then?'

'It's nothing, really,' said Ben, folding his arms, shrugging his shoulders. 'It's just...'

'Just what?'

'I'm not sleeping,' Ben said at last, giving his head a scratch.

'Any reason?'

Ben fell quiet, but Harry just waited, knowing his brother would speak, once he knew what it was that he wanted to say.

'I keep dreaming about it,' said Ben at last. 'About what happened to Mum, what Dad did ...'

Harry remembered it all too well himself, would never forget it, though he wished he could; the open door, the blood, their mother on the floor...

'Sometimes, I wake up, and I can smell it ... the blood...'

'How long's this been going on?' Harry asked.

Ben shook his head.

'I don't know, a few weeks, maybe?' he said. 'It happens now and again, always has. Bound to, I suppose, isn't it? But it's got worse this last while.'

'Do you think some counselling might help?'

'Maybe, but not sure I'm ready to trust someone again with what's in my head, not after last time.'

'Last time?' Harry said, then remembered; Ben had been receiving counselling from someone who they'd eventually found out was playing the long game of revenge, and had killed their father. Not that the man's death was any great loss, Harry thought. 'Well, it's worth thinking about,' he suggested, not wanting to press too hard. 'Trauma has a habit of rearing its ugly head when we least expect it.'

If there was one thing Harry knew about, it was that; his own nights were still broken, not only by the awful death of their mother, but by the violence and horror he had lived through as a soldier, and so many of the crimes he'd dealt with over the years.

'I know,' Ben said. 'Maybe I will. I'll think about it, anyway.'

'No good bottling it all up,' Harry added. 'That way madness lies, and worse. Trust me on that, I've seen where it can end up, lost friends to it.'

'I know,' said Ben, 'I know, and I should've said. Just didn't want to bother you with it, that's all.'

'Yes, you should've,' said Harry. 'And you're not bothering me, either; you're my brother. We look after each other. It's what we do, remember? Does Liz know?'

At this, Ben fell silent.

Harry folded his arms.

'I'll take that as a no, then.'

'Wasn't really sure what to say,' said Ben. 'I don't want her thinking I'm mad or losing it or something.'

Harry took a slow, deep breath, then exhaled and stared at Ben from beneath a heavy brow.

'What's mad is living with someone and not telling them,' said Harry. 'You can't keep secrets, not if you're serious about where you two are going. And you are serious, aren't you, about Liz?'

'Wouldn't be living with her if I wasn't,' said Ben.

'Then you promise me, as soon as she's home, you talk to her, understood? It's the only way, Ben, believe me. You start hiding things, bottling it up, and sooner or later, you'll explode. And the trouble with explosions is that they don't give a damn who gets in their way.'

'It's not that easy though,' Ben began, but Harry cut him off.

'I never said it was, but you can't go on planning a future with someone if you're keeping secrets from them, can you?'

'We're not planning a future.'

'Of course you are,' said Harry. 'You've only just now said as much yourself. I'm not saying you're about to walk Liz up the aisle, but neither of you are in it just for the sheer hell of it, are you? So, treat yourself and her with the respect you both deserve: tell her.'

After a moment of hesitation, Ben said, 'I will, Harry.'

'Good.'

Then, before Harry knew what he was doing, he was hugging his brother.

'You alright?' Ben asked, his voice muffled by Harry's thick shoulder and tight embrace.

Harry released Ben, more than a little shocked by what had just happened.

'On the subject of talking about things,' Ben said, 'how are you with everything now?'

'How do you mean?'

Ben gave Harry a look that Harry himself would've been proud of.

'You mean Gordy.'

'How is she?' Ben asked. 'Have you heard from her?'

It was just over two months ago since Gordy had left the Dales to take up her new role in Somerset, and three months since the funeral of Anna, Gordy's partner, and the local vicar.

'She's okay, I think,' Harry said. 'Settling in.'

'What you said, at the funeral I mean...'

'Gordy will be fine, eventually,' Harry said. 'She's a survivor. She'll come through it and wear the scars proudly, I'm sure. Anna was very special. There's no just getting over something like that, so we'll all be keeping an eye on her, even from afar.'

'And what about you?' Ben asked. 'What about the rest of the team? Is there a replacement?'

'Gordy's irreplaceable,' said Harry, his voice firm, as though to suggest otherwise was patently ridiculous.

'You know what I mean.'

'I do,' Harry said, 'but so far, all I'm being told is that things are under review.'

'Sounds ominous.'

'Doesn't it?'

Harry's phone buzzed, and he almost welcomed the distraction, reeling a little as he was from finding himself in the odd position of being the one the other brother was concerned about.

'Who the hell would be calling you at this time of the night?' Ben asked.

Harry looked at the number.

'It's not just who,' he said, 'it's why ...' and answered.

FOUR

Matt woke with a start, to a house dark and cold and silent. Beside him, his wife Joan was out for the count, her faint snuffling snore little more than a soft purr. In the room opposite, their daughter, Mary-Anne, was also asleep, and Matt was sorely tempted to get up just to go and look in on her. Goodness, she's beautiful, he thought, as he tried to work out what had disturbed him. And the smell of her, when he rested his face against her head, kissed her, made raspberry sounds on her stomach ... it was intoxicating.

Then he heard it; his phone, which was next to him on the bedside cabinet he'd found in a junk shop a few years ago, along with its twin on the other side of the bed next to Joan, was buzzing and flashing.

Matt rubbed his eyes, yawned, then reached for it.

'Morning, Harry,' he said.

'Don't remind me,' Harry replied. 'Sorry to wake you.'

'Not to be helped,' said Matt. 'Aren't you on leave?'

'I am,' said Harry. 'Jadyn just called.'

'He did? Sorry about that. He knew to call me, they all do.'

'Doesn't matter,' said Harry. 'I think he just did it out of habit rather than on purpose.'

'So, what's happened, then?' Matt asked. 'I'm assuming this

isn't just you giving me a call to ask for a bit of advice on ... actually, I'm not sure what advice you'd be coming to me for.'

'Pies, probably,' said Harry.

'I'm a leading authority,' Matt replied, and heard Harry laugh at that.

'There's a fire over in Leyburn,' Harry said. 'A warehouse, I think.'

'Why's Jadyn called you, then?' Matt asked.

'There's a witness,' Harry explained. 'An eighty-year-old out for a few beers on his birthday heard voices at the scene shortly before the fire started.'

'You mean it was deliberate?'

'I mean,' said Harry, 'that I need you to head over there and manage things. Jadyn and Dave will do a fine job, I'm sure, but I think I'd prefer your guiding hand over there as well. Little bit more experience and all that. And as Gordy's no longer around...'

'Oh, so that's it, is it?' Matt said, feigning hurt at Harry's words. 'The only reason you've called is because your favourite Detective Inspector is no longer available? That hurts, Harry, that really hurts...'

'She's not just no longer available, she's moved,' Harry said, clearly missing his attempt at humour by a wide margin.

Hearing the weariness in his boss's voice, Matt decided to hurry the conversation on. 'Where is it, this fire, then?'

'Leyburn,' Harry said. 'Fire Brigade were on their way when Jadyn called. I've asked him to send you the exact location, though I doubt it'll be difficult to find; fires at night are pretty easy to spot.'

'I'd best get going, then,' said Matt. 'Anything else to tell me?'

'Only that the witness doesn't have thumbs,' said Harry. 'You didn't need to know that, and neither did I, but Jadyn told me anyway, regardless, so I thought I'd share.'

'No thumbs? How's that even possible?'

'Be sure to let me know,' said Harry. 'By which I mean—'

'You really don't care.'

'Not in the slightest.'

'How's the packing going?' Matt asked.

'Pretty much done,' said Harry. 'Keep me posted on the fire.'

'I will.'

Conversation over, and now wide awake, Matt slipped his feet out of bed, stretched, then stood up. Tip-toeing out of the bedroom, he nipped into the bathroom, splashed cold water on his face, brushed his teeth, then popped back into the bedroom to get dressed. When he re-entered, Joan was sitting up in bed.

'Something up?' she asked.

Matt quickly explained what he'd learned from Harry, though kept back the information about the thumbs.

'You weren't going to just sneak out, though, were you?'

Matt sat down next to her.

'And miss out on this?' he said, and leaned over to plant a soft kiss against her even softer cheek.

Kiss done, Joan gave him a gentle but playful shove.

'Get away with you and your monkey business, you daft sod,' she said, leaning lazily back into her pillow. 'Any idea when you'll be back?'

Matt stood up to pull on his clothes. 'Not a clue,' he said. 'I'll let you know how we're getting on, though.'

A few minutes later, fully dressed, Matt walked over to the bedroom door, then turned around to smile at Joan. He gave himself just enough time to take in the view and marvelled. She was so beautiful, so bloody wonderful, so funny and loving and clever and just downright startling, that he still pinched himself daily that she'd agreed to be a part of his life.

'Want me to grab something from Leyburn for dinner?' he asked. 'Anything you'd like?'

Joan snuggled herself back down into bed.

'See if you can come back with something that isn't a pie,' she said. 'There are other places to go to other than Andy's bakery, you know.'

'Challenge accepted,' Matt laughed. 'Chinese? I'll grab a bottle of red from Campbell's as well.'

Joan's eyes were closed now, but she managed a nod and a smile.

'Whatever takes your fancy.'

Leaving the comfort of home, Matt climbed into the old Police Land Rover and headed off towards Leyburn. Bainbridge was a quiet place to live, and at this hour it was little more than a ghost town, the village green adding to the strange stillness, which itself was accentuated by the eerie shape of the old stocks still sitting where they had done for so many years. As far as Matt knew, they'd been there since the seventeenth century, an uncomfortable stone provided for the poor unfortunate locked into them for whatever misdemeanour it was that had ended them there in the first place.

Above the village, though not really visible until you were driving past it, the old Roman fort stared down. Matt often wondered how the place would have looked back then, a series of remote wooden palisades dotting the Dales, connected by the thin thread of a road that stretched across the fells. He'd walked that road too many times to mention, and been called out on occasion with the Mountain Rescue Team to bring home stranded walkers with twisted or broken ankles, or bikers who'd come a cropper thanks to a misjudged corner or a wayward stone.

The journey down the dale was almost magical, Matt thought, as the Land Rover rolled on, the drone of the tyres almost mournful as the miles flew by, the road empty of all traffic bar his own vehicle, and distant lights of remote farmhouses twinkling like boats bobbing on the waves in a thick, black sea.

Arriving in Leyburn, Matt followed the satnav on his phone, but quickly realised that even if he didn't have an address, like Harry had said himself, the location of the fire would've been easy to find.

On the other side of town, an orange glow bubbled over the rooftops, and as he drew near, his window down, Matt was able to smell the fire as well as see it. Turning a corner, he saw embers like fireflies dancing and spiralling into the air, catching thermals caused by the fire that had created them. If it wasn't so terrifying, it would've been enchanting, he thought.

Around another corner, the fire came into view. Flames were licking the darkness hungrily, and the sound of the inferno filled the night with the snap, crackle, and pop of wood splintering, metal twisting, glass shattering. As he drew closer, the red glow of the fire mixed with the flashing blue lights of the fire engine in attendance, and Jadyn's patrol car.

Matt parked up, then made his way over to where he could see Jadyn and Dave standing.

Jadyn came over to meet him, leaving Dave with the patrol car.

'So, what have we got, then, beyond the obvious?' Matt asked.

He could see that the fire was under control, but the damage was extensive, the warehouse barely more than a steel frame. The panelled walls had in many places collapsed inwards, though here and there some panels still held on, and to Matt looked like bedsheets hanging on a washing line. The inside of the warehouse was thick with smoke and stubborn knots of fire refusing to be extinguished. He could smell charred wood in the air, melted plastic, and something else, too, something strangely familiar but that he couldn't quite place.

'What did Harry tell you?' Jadyn asked.

'That your witness has no thumbs,' said Matt.

'We've already taken Mr Ackroyd home,' said Jadyn. 'Figured it was best to let him sleep it off.'

'Sleep what off?'

'The booze. He'd been out for his birthday and by the smell of him, drunk half the beer in town, and then moved onto whisky. Had breath on him that could cut through lead. I'll head round in the morning for a more detailed chat.'

'He saw someone leaving the scene, though, yes?' Matt asked.

'Not exactly sure what he saw, really,' said Jadyn. 'Said he heard muffled voices, a shout, and saw something leave the warehouse before the fire took.'

'Something? A person, a vehicle, what?'

'He wasn't sure. I've called for an ambulance, though, seeing he said he heard voices. Just in case.'

Matt looked again at the fire and shuddered, momentarily horrified at the thought of being trapped inside it.

'They've not found anyone yet, though?'

'The fire was raging when they arrived,' said Jadyn. 'Took a while to get it under control before they were able to send anyone in.'

'It's not just the fire that's the issue,' said Matt. 'The structural integrity of the building will be shot to pieces by the heat, and there'll be the danger of walls and whatever was stored in there collapsing. Not a safe place to be.'

'There's a couple of CCTV cameras,' said Jadyn. 'Hopefully, they've caught something.'

'You've been in touch already with whoever's running security, then?'

'I have, but there was no answer. I'll keep trying, then just head over to the address tomorrow.'

Matt looked around where they were standing.

'No houses close by,' he said.

'It's not really overlooked at all, is it?' said Jadyn, then pointed through the darkness, back up into Leyburn itself. 'There's a street just over there, but you'd not see anything going on. I think that might be where our witness, Bob, was before he ended up here.'

'Really? Why's that, then?' said Matt, then added, 'Come to think of it, it is odd that he was here at all, isn't it? Just how drunk was he?'

'Drunk enough to end up at the other end of town to where he was supposed to be,' said Jadyn. 'And if someone started this deliberately, then we're already coming up short with ways to try and find them. I'd like to think those security cameras will be of use, but that's about it.'

'What about the owner?' Matt asked.

'You mean you've not guessed already?' Jadyn asked.

'And how am I supposed to do that?'

'The smell,' Jadyn said. 'You must've noticed it, Matt, surely!'

Matt remembered then that he had noticed something odd in the air, as familiar as it was out of keeping with what was happening, which was probably why he couldn't quite place it.

'I did, actually,' said Matt, and sniffed again, noting a deep earthy note behind the burning, a faint hint of chocolate even. 'What is it, though?' he asked.

Jadyn laughed.

'You really don't know?'

'Nope,' said Matt, really concentrating now, trying to decipher the scents overwhelming him.

'It's the smell of a morning when you get up, the air fresh enough to freeze your breath as soon as you're out of bed, and you need a pick-me-up to help you face it,' said Jadyn.

'Very poetic.'

'I'll have you know that I did very well in English at school,' said Jadyn. 'Won a poetry competition, too.'

'You didn't!'

'Why would I ever lie about that?'

Matt then realised what the thick, rich, bittersweet smell was, mixing in with the tang of a burning building.

'Is that coffee?'

Jadyn showed Matt the screen of his phone. 'I did a quick search of the business name and found this...'

Matt read the website's header.

'Bean and Gone,' he said.

'Clever, right?' said Jadyn.

Matt wasn't so sure it was, but kept quiet.

'I've had a look through the website,' continued Jadyn. 'It's an independent coffee company. They import the beans, roast them on-site, that kind of thing. Looks like they're big on ethics, farmers getting fair pay, the environment, that kind of thing. Or at least that's what it says. They've a subscription service, too. Probably manned entirely by hipsters.'

'Hipsters?' said Matt. He'd heard the word bandied about for years, never really taken much notice.

'Beards, topknots, turn-ups on their jeans, that kind of thing,' said Jadyn.

'You mean man buns, don't you?'

'As far as the eye can see.'

'And people subscribe to coffee?' Matt asked, baffled as to why anyone would, when it was readily available, well, everywhere. 'Why? I mean, can't they just buy it from a shop, like normal people?'

'Coffee is a real hobby for some,' Jadyn explained.

'By some, you mean hipsters and man-bun types again, don't you?'

'Yes and no,' Jadyn said, laughing. 'Some people just get really into their beans, the grinders, all kinds of crazy.'

'Have they not got anything better to do with their time?' Matt asked, somewhat baffled.

'It's not my thing either, if I'm honest,' said Jadyn. 'I mean, I love coffee, but I don't want to have to bother with all the knobs and dials and steam wands.'

'Coffee subscription,' Matt said, shaking his head, then an idea struck him. 'Now, a pie subscription? That's something I could get behind.'

'You'll have to see if you can find one, then.'

Matt asked, 'Do we have contact details for the owner? We need to speak to them as a matter of urgency.'

'Contact details on the site just go through to an answer machine,' said Jadyn. 'The address is a PO Box number.'

'Do we have a name?'

'According to the website, Bean and Gone is owned by a Mr Adam Heath,' said Jadyn. 'No address though, other than the PO Box I just mentioned, obviously. That's all we have so far, though, which isn't much.'

'It never is at the start of any investigation,' said Matt. 'However, I'd prefer to find him before he turns up to find his business like this.'

'Yeah, this is going to be devastating,' Jadyn agreed.

With little else to say, and quietly concerned about the report from the witness, Matt fell into silence, and watched as the firefighters gradually brought the blaze under control. The heat of the fire eventually eased, and by the early hours of the morning, the building was little more than a smouldering wreck, blackened by the flames, and steaming still from the water used to douse them.

Dawn was close to breaking when one of the firefighters, a woman with long brown hair pulled back in a tight ponytail, her eyes weary from the long night, approached. Matt and Jadyn were with Dave, who was talking about his goats. Matt had never given much thought to how big a part of Dave's life his goats were. He certainly knew now, though, and more besides, and if he ever considered buying a few goats for himself, what Dave had so enthusiastically talked about would surely be enough to put him off the idea immediately. Though he was pleased to have the interruption, Matt saw worry in the woman's eyes.

'What's wrong?' he asked. Then he answered his own question. 'You've found something, haven't you?'

'Yes,' the woman said, but before she was able to finish what she was saying, Matt already had his phone in his hand.

'It's a body, isn't it?' he asked.

'I'm afraid so,' the woman replied. 'How did you know?'

'Gut feeling, and it's rarely wrong, though I wish it was sometimes, you know?'

'I do,' the woman said. 'We've a fire investigator on the way.'

'I'll call in forensics and an ambulance,' said Matt, gesturing to his phone.

'Weather forecast isn't good,' the woman then added, glancing skyward. 'Sooner we can have people on-site, the better.'

'Risk of damage?'

'Exactly. With anything like this, we're always up against it with the weather. Any evidence as to what caused the fire in the first place can easily be washed away by even the lightest of showers.'

'Any thoughts on how the fire was started?' asked Jadyn.

'The origin was in the centre of the warehouse,' said the woman. 'Sacks of coffee beans. And they don't exactly just burst into flames, do they?'

'You think an accelerant was used, then?' said Matt.

'Not for me to say,' said the woman, but the look in her eyes was confirmation enough.

'Let me know when the investigator's arrived,' Matt said, and lifted his phone to his ear.

'Want me to call Harry?' Jadyn asked.

'Not really, no,' lied Matt.

Jadyn was already on the phone.

FIVE

When Harry arrived at the scene of the fire, it was already a hive of activity. The air still carried the sharp tang of burning and smoke, and he could see thin wisps of white curling up from the ruins of the warehouse.

It wasn't just the smell of the scene, though, but the sound of it that assaulted Harry. Water from the hoses still dripped from broken beams and ruined walls, hissing and spitting on still-hot ash and ember, like fat sputtering in a pan. Voices jostled to be heard above the din of activity, of vehicle engines ticking over, equipment being put into use or stowed away.

An ambulance was on the scene, parked near the fire engine. He also saw the old Police Land Rover, Jadyn's patrol car, and two large white transit vans. He pulled his own vehicle to a stop behind a Range Rover he recognised immediately, and saw that the driver was sitting inside it. He also noted the aroma of coffee perfuming the air with notes of burned chocolate, caramel, and dry earth, and remembered what Jadyn had said about the business that used the warehouse.

'Now then, Margaret,' Harry said, coming up alongside the driver's door.

The window was down and Margaret Shaw, the district

surgeon, reached out a small, pale hand and in it Harry saw an open packet of biscuits, half of them already gone.

'HobNobs?' Margaret asked. 'They're the chocolatey ones. Decided to treat myself.'

'Bit early for me,' said Harry.

'It's never too early for a biscuit.'

'You've been in, then?' Harry asked.

'I have,' said Margaret. 'Waited for you though before heading off.'

Harry was immediately concerned.

'Really? Why?'

Margaret turned to face Harry, her bright eyes looking not just at him, but into him, like she was probing him, trying to find out a deeply kept secret.

'Not seen you since the funeral,' she said, and nibbled a biscuit.

'Life's busy,' Harry replied.

He and Margaret had first met at a crime scene during his first few months in the Dales. Since then, in addition to various other similar meetings, they'd bumped into each other in Hawes, sometimes in Leyburn, waved as they passed each other on the roads, and sometimes in a pub here and there.

'How's the move going?' Margaret asked.

'It's going,' said Harry. 'All packed up except the last few bits and bobs. Should be in at the weekend.' He gestured at the burned shell of a building a short walk away from where he was standing, the skeletal remains curled with smoke like black lace caught in a tree. 'What about all this, then?'

'I've ticked the box to say they're dead,' said Margaret. 'Hardly a taxing task, really, all things considered. Unlike what Rebecca's going to be dealing with.'

Rebecca Sowerby, Margaret's daughter, was the pathologist and it was her Scene of Crime team's vans that Harry had spotted when he'd arrived, the team themselves rushing around in their white paper suits like worker ants dressed for a '90s rave.

'Fire investigations are a tough call,' Harry said, and looked to the sky, which was grey and low and foreboding.

'On that, the fire investigator's here as well,' said Margaret. 'He's pushing hard to gather all the evidence he can before the weather breaks. That's why everyone's rushing about, trying not to bump into each other, and failing miserably by the looks of things. The only thing riper than the stink in the air from the fire has been the language.'

No sooner had Margaret mentioned the weather, than Harry saw the first few drops start to land around him, bursting into tiny watery crowns as they slammed into the ground.

'You spoke too soon, Margaret,' he said, watching as the air filled with the sound of more hissing and popping as the rain grew harder and dashed itself into the fading warmth of the fire.

'Not sure you can blame me for that,' Margaret replied. 'You spoke well, you know.'

Harry was watching the SOC team. The urgency in their work had immediately increased with the first spots of rain, and with it growing heavier by the second, the urgency was becoming desperation. That they were still managing to give the impression of measured control in what they were doing was nothing short of miraculous, he thought. Then Margaret's words came to him again.

'What was that?' he asked, having not quite understood what she had just said.

'Anna's funeral,' Margaret explained. 'What you said, it was ... well, it was quite unexpected.'

'That a compliment?'

'Very much so. Did you write it yourself?'

'I did,' said Harry, not really wanting to talk about it and hoping they could just move the conversation along. 'Gordy asked me to say something. Not really sure why. I think she just needed the support of having someone else involved.'

'Anna was a wonderful vicar, you know,' said Margaret. 'She gave a lot to the community. It'll be a tough job to replace her. I don't envy whoever it is the church ends up appointing.'

Harry thought back to the service, how full the church in Askrigg had been.

'The choir sang well,' he said, as if the simple statement would disguise the memory of the event, not just how raw it was still, but how honoured he'd felt to be a part of it. He'd spoken at funerals before, fallen comrades who needed a respectful send-off. But this had been different. But then, he was different, and losing Anna, the impact of that on Gordy, on the team, on the community, was something that had affected him deeply.

'Of course we did!' said Margaret. 'Pulled out all the stops. Really went for it. It's what Anna would've wanted.'

Harry laughed.

'Can't say I was expecting that last one that you sang, though.'

Margaret's laugh joined in with Harry's so loudly that it pinned his to the ground.

'Always Look On The Bright Side Of Life? That was Anna's personal request, you know? Very organised woman, to have her funeral all planned out. But then I guess that comes with the profession, doesn't it? Be a bit of a poor show for a vicar to have not had something sketched out for their own big send-off.'

'Gordy told me that afterwards,' said Harry, smiling, not just at the memory of the song, but at the looks on some of the faces of those in attendance. 'Pretty sure I could hear her laughing from beyond the grave.'

'You have to, though, don't you?' Margaret said. 'Look on the bright side, I mean? Otherwise, what's the point?'

'Sometimes, I've not faintest idea,' said Harry, his eyes back on the fire, his thoughts on the body found in the centre of it. 'But I suppose you're right.'

'Right? Of course I'm right!' said Margaret. 'Why the hell do you think Anna requested it?'

A fist thrust itself out of the open window of the Range Rover and Margaret thumped Harry on the arm hard enough to make him flinch.

'What the hell was that for?' Harry asked, rubbing his arm, a little surprised at the power behind the punch.

'Of all the people to be looking on the bright side, you bloody well should be,' said Margaret. 'And don't you go forgetting that, either.'

'I am!' said Harry, but found himself caught in the fierce glare of Margaret's eyes as they narrowed at him. 'I mean, I'm not forgetting it. I'm definitely looking on the bright side! Of course I am!'

'Really?'

'I wouldn't've bought a house with Grace if I wasn't.'

'Do a better impression of it, then,' Margaret said, then she gestured at Harry with a wave of her hand. 'I know this is who you are, this rough, gruff exterior, this tough, ex-soldier stuff, because you wear it like thick armour, but look at what you've got; if you don't start celebrating it a bit more, it'll be more than a thump you'll be getting, you mark my words!'

'Is that a threat?' Harry asked.

'Does it need to be?' Margaret replied. 'Because believe you me, I've no problem at all in coming round to your house to plant a boot firmly up your arse!'

Harry roared at that, and more so because of the determined stare Margaret was giving him.

'Point taken,' he said.

'Good,' Margaret said. 'Have you heard from Gordy?'

'I have,' said Harry. 'She's okay. I said we'd go and visit soon, once she's settled in. Don't want her to think we're checking up on her, but at the same time...'

'You want to check up on her,' said Margaret. 'Got to admire her, though; moving down there on her own, when really the only reason she was going in the first place was because of Anna.'

'That's just who Gordy is though, isn't it?' said Harry.

'Strong and determined?'

'Bloody-minded more like.' Harry stifled a yawn. 'Anyway, I'd best get on. I'm sure Rebecca has plenty to tell me.'

'No doubt,' agreed Margaret. 'But before you go, just one more question ...'

'What's that, then?'

Margaret once again reached out with the packet of biscuits.

'Are you sure you don't want one?'

'Very,' said Harry, and leaving Margaret to finish off the biscuit she'd just pulled out of the packet before she headed home herself, he marched off to where Matt was standing with Jadyn and Dave.

As Harry approached, Matt lifted a hand in a wave and Harry returned it, then spotted someone in full PPE jogging over to meet him halfway. Behind them, the warehouse was cordoned off with plenty of police tape, so much so that Harry wondered if Jadyn had just got a little bit carried away. It now looked like it was there to stop something escaping, rather than to just warn people to stay away.

Harry stopped and waited for the individual to arrive.

Coming to a stop in front of him, they lifted up the facemask that was covering their mouth and nose.

'Hello, Rebecca,' Harry said.

'Harry,' Sowerby replied, tired eyes set in a soot and dirt-covered face, though where her facemask had been resting, the skin was clean.

'Anything to tell me?'

'Well, we're nearly done,' Sowerby said. 'The fire investigator's just finishing collecting what evidence he can before everything gets washed away by this rain.'

'Anything from them yet?'

Harry wasn't expecting much, but thought he'd ask anyway.

'Actually, yes,' said Sowerby.

'Really? What?'

'They've confirmed that they think the fire was started maliciously.'

'How?'

'Glass from the windows.'

'I'll need a wee bit more than that,' said Harry.

'A wee bit?' said Sowerby, attempting to put a faint Scottish lilt into her voice. 'Gordy's still here in spirit, then, even though she's actually no longer around?'

'Seems that way, yes,' said Harry. 'Now, about this glass...'

'When glass is damaged by fire, it cracks from the frame edges,' Sowerby said.

'Thermal stress, you mean?'

Harry was impressed he'd remembered that detail, something that must've been lodged in his brain from a previous case.

'Exactly that,' said Sowerby. 'If it blows out, you'll still find soot damage on the bits of glass scattered around.' She pointed over towards the building, to a wall that was still fairly intact, considering the damage the fire had caused. 'You see that window over there, or what's left of it, anyway? No soot damage, and the breaks have circular fractures.'

'Meaning?'

'Someone smashed that one before the fire started, or at least before it took hold enough to blow out the windows.'

'Any marks in the frame?'

'You mean from where someone might have forced it? No, just the broken glass.'

'Looks like someone could've broken in, though. But why? It's a coffee business. Who would want to steal coffee?'

'Someone who was very, very tired?' Sowerby suggested. 'The investigator found multiple origins of fire, so put those two things together and it's looking increasingly likely this was deliberate.'

'Any accelerants used?' Harry asked.

'I'm a pathologist, remember? You'll have to wait for the FDR.'

'The fire damage report?' said Harry. 'I'm not very good at waiting. Question is, though, was the fire set to kill whoever that is, to disguise whatever actually happened, or was it just a case of bad luck that they were there in the first place? And at risk of repeating myself, why a sodding coffee warehouse?'

'Maybe the victim was the one who set the fire, and they just didn't get out in time,' suggested Sowerby. 'Though again, that does leave you with the whole, *why a sodding coffee warehouse* question, doesn't it? I'll have a better chance at answering that once I've had a look at the body, and read the FDR myself.'

'Think you'll get much from the body?' Harry asked.

Sowerby shook her head.

'I'll do my best,' she said, 'but it's going to be a tough one. Whoever it is, they're a charred mess. Looks like they were right in the middle of where the fire was started.'

'Bloody hell,' said Harry.

'Thought you might say that.'

Harry thought back to what he'd learned from Jadyn.

'The witness says he heard voices and maybe saw someone leaving the scene.'

'Well, as I said, the fire investigator is fairly convinced an accelerant was used,' said Sowerby. 'The body was found where the fire originated, next to a store of coffee beans.'

'Yeah, I've never attended a crime scene that smelled like this one,' said Harry and saw Sowerby's nose wrinkle a little.

'Can't see me having a flat white for a while after this; the smell of it,' she said.

Harry had to agree on that.

'Bit odd though, isn't it?' he said. 'And I know I'm coming back to it again, about why a coffee warehouse. I mean, with this kind of thing, it's usually either arson for the sake of seeing something burn, or deliberate, because whoever did it is after insurance, or it's some kind of business rivalry.'

'It could still be any one of those,' said Sowerby.

'I've dealt with arson before,' said Harry. 'But never has it ever been a warehouse storing coffee. And why bother to break in first to set it and get it going? Most times, it's been a fire built by a wall from a stack of pallets or something, or a Molotov thrown through a window. Nice and easy; set the fire, run like hell, watch it burn from afar.'

'You're trying to rationalise why someone who just likes to burn things would just like to burn something,' said Sowerby.

'Of course I am,' said Harry, and looked around where they were standing. 'Why this building? Why here? Why now? They're the questions.'

'And I'll be leaving you to answer them, seeing as I'm the pathologist and you're the detective,' said Sowerby.

'Thanks for reminding me.'

'Happy to help. I saw you talking to Mum, by the way. Figured it was best to catch you now, tell you there's not much to go on yet. And to rescue you from her.'

'I didn't need rescuing.'

'Harry, everyone needs rescuing from my mum, especially those she has a bit of a soft spot for.'

'She does not have a soft spot for me.'

Sowerby's answer was a raised eyebrow.

The rain grew heavier, and Harry zipped up his jacket.

'I'll not keep you,' he said.

'You're not,' said Sowerby, and covered her mouth and nose once again with the mask. 'I'll be in touch.'

'I'll look forward to it.'

'Liar.'

'Fair,' said Harry, and watched Sowerby jog back over to join the rest of her team, who were now milling about in the rain like festival goers looking for somewhere to shelter.

With the pathologist gone, Harry hurried over to Matt, Jadyn, and Dave, cursing the weather under his breath.

'You lot must be knackered,' he said.

'These two are for sure,' said Matt, jutting a thumb at Jadyn and Dave.

Jadyn yawned, and Dave quickly followed.

'Jen's back today, isn't she?' Harry said. 'And Jim's on duty as well.'

'Jen's shift starts this afternoon,' said Jadyn, fighting back another yawn, then giving up halfway and just letting it rip.

'Do that again, and you'll suck in half the oxygen in Leyburn,' said Matt.

Harry turned to face Jadyn and Dave.

'When we're done here, I want you two back home and in your respective beds,' he said. 'Get yourselves some rest, and we'll have you in for the shift after that.'

'No, we're fine, really,' said Dave, but his words were quickly caught up in a yawn of his own. Harry was reminded of a television programme from his childhood, of a cat called Bagpuss who yawned like no other.

Harry waited for Dave's yawn to finish. There was a flicker to the man's eyelids that told Harry Dave could, at any moment, drop like liquid and fall asleep in the dirt.

'I don't want fine,' he said. 'I want wide awake and alert. You're no use to me or this investigation otherwise. Is that understood?'

Jadyn and Dave gave a nod.

'Do we have anything else on the business owner?' Harry asked.

'Adam Heath, imports coffee,' said Jadyn. 'That's all we know so far, and the smell made that pretty obvious, without even looking at the website.'

'I had a quick look at that before I drove over,' said Harry. 'Not cheap, is it?'

'It's not like what you get in the supermarkets, no,' said Jadyn.

'I gathered that from the liberal use of the word artisan all over the place.'

'What's wrong with the word artisan?' Matt asked, his brow creasing with confusion.

'It's everywhere, isn't it?' said Harry. 'Artisan this, artisan that; artisan gin, artisan bread, artisan jewellery, and now artisan bloody coffee! There was even an artisan pub back where I used to live in Somerset! How can a pub be artisan? How? What does it actually mean, anyway?'

'Made by hand, I think,' said Matt.

'But you could say that about anything, couldn't you?' Harry replied, wondering why he was suddenly so worked up. 'And with everyone using it, well, it kind of detracts a little from those who can genuinely say that's what they are, doesn't it?'

'Fair point, actually,' said Dave. 'It's like with cheese, isn't it?'

'Is it?' Harry asked, concerned Dave was about to try to persuade him again to try the stuff he made. So far Harry had managed to dodge that bullet, but it wasn't easy, given Dave's boundless enthusiasm for his small flock of goats.

Dave gave a nod.

'Used to be everything was handmade, if it was done by a small producer, but now everything's artisan.'

Harry noticed that Jadyn was staring at him, bemusement in his eyes.

'What is it, Constable?'

'Nothing,' said Jadyn. 'I just think we've maybe gone off on a bit of a tangent.'

He has a point, thought Harry, though sometimes a tangent was needed just to give the brain a quick reset.

'We've no other contact details, then, other than the website, for this Mr Heath?'

'Actually, we have,' said Matt.

Harry was impressed.

'That was quick.'

'I did a search on Companies House and we've an address over in Richmond. I was waiting to speak with you before heading over. Also, I think his name rings a bell, though for the life of me I can't work out why.'

'Does it do any more than that?' asked Harry, looking at the DS.

'Not yet, no,' said Matt. 'Just a bell at the moment, but I'll let you know.'

Harry saw then that Sowerby was again making her way over towards him.

'Surely you've not solved the case already,' Harry said, as she came to stand with him and the others.

'No,' she said, 'but there is something odd. Thought it'd be best to mention it now, help you get ahead of things if you can.'

'You mean odder than a body being found in a burned down coffee warehouse?' said Harry.

'Books,' said Sowerby.

'What about them?' asked Harry.

'We found a pile of them in what we think was the office.'

'How did you find books in that?' Jadyn asked. 'Don't books burn? I mean, they're made of paper, aren't they, and paper burns? It's what my dad uses instead of firelighters back home. Refuses to buy actual firelighters for some reason, like the very act of doing so is to question his fire-making skills, as though, deep down, he's this hardcore survivalist who knows all about bushcraft and lighting fires and building shelters when, in fact, he lives in Bradford, and the closest he'd ever get to an actual survival situation is what to do if the nearest supermarket ran out of red wine. I mean, what would we have with the cheese?'

Harry hoped that Jadyn was just rambling because he was tired, not that he was following in his own footsteps and developing a skill to rant on about even the tiniest thing should the urge take him.

'They do indeed burn,' said Sowerby, glancing at Harry quizzically after Jadyn's random outburst. 'But if you've a great stack of them, there's a chance those in the middle will be protected from the heat and fire by those around them.'

'Like insulation, you mean?' said Dave.

'Exactly like that,' said Sowerby. 'The fire didn't destroy everything, rarely does. The office was burned, but not as badly as the rest of the warehouse. Some parts of the building were barely touched, others were an inferno. Fire's a strange thing.'

'Books, though,' said Harry. 'I'm still not sure why you're telling us this?'

Sowerby lifted up an evidence bag. Inside the bag he saw a book.

'That's not really making it any clearer,' said Harry, and

gestured at Dave and Jadyn. 'Any chance of getting to the point before these two here fall asleep in front of us?'

'It's a Folio edition of The Adventures of Tom Sawyer,' Sowerby explained. 'People collect them.'

'So, Adam Heath collects books,' said Harry. 'There's no crime in that, is there?'

'There were boxes of them, though,' said Sowerby. 'And why keep them here in the first place?'

Harry reached for the evidence bag and had a closer look at the book. None the wiser, he handed it back to Sowerby.

'You're right,' he said. 'That is a bit odd. Anything else?'

'Only that we're done,' said Sowerby. 'And good job, too, with this rain, which is, unsurprisingly, going to get worse before it gets better.'

'You'll be in touch?' Harry asked.

'As soon as I have anything and just as soon, even if I don't,' said Sowerby, then she turned on her heel, and headed back towards the vans.

Harry instructed Jadyn and Dave to head off, and after a very short-lived attempt at rebellion, they both agreed. Once they were on their way, he turned to Matt.

'Richmond,' he said, and walked over to the Police Land Rover.

'I'm driving, then?' said Matt, following on behind.

'Looks that way, yes,' said Harry, and he yanked open the passenger door and climbed in.

SIX

'Visited the castle yet?' Matt asked, as he drove Harry to Richmond through rain thick enough to force him to go considerably slower than Harry would've liked.

Tuesday was already well on its way, and lunchtime had already zipped past, and Harry was keen to push on, even though investigations had a habit of resisting all calls for urgency. He was hungry, though, so regardless of where they found themselves in Richmond itself, he'd be making sure they found something to eat; his stomach had already moved on from a general grumbling to an out-and-out assault, and it was making him grumpy. There was enough going on in his head as it was, what with the house move, Gordy's move down south and the local impact of Anna's death still being felt up and down the Dales, and now this fire; the last thing he needed was to deal with any of it on an empty stomach.

'No,' said Harry, for a moment wondering which castle Matt was talking about.

He'd visited the castle at Middleham, not as a tourist, but as a detective, while investigating a case that had started very strangely indeed, with someone seeing ghosts, but ended up taking a darker turn into abduction and murder. The castle at Bolton he'd seen often enough, but so far not ventured inside its walls. Richmond castle, to which Matt was obviously alluding, was considerably more off his radar than the other two, and Richmond wasn't a place he'd visited more than a handful of times, if that. In fact, he wasn't entirely sure he'd been there at all, just convinced himself he had been because he'd heard it mentioned so much.

'That's a pity,' said Matt, slowing down for someone driving even more cautiously than he was. 'It's definitely worth a visit.'

'I'm sure,' said Harry.

'You won't know about the legend of the drummer boy, then?'

'You're right, I won't,' Harry agreed. 'But something tells me you're about to enlighten me.'

'I am,' said Matt. 'Are you sitting comfortably?'

'I'm in the passenger seat of an old Land Rover,' said Harry.

'That'll be a no, then.'

'Exactly.'

Matt coughed dramatically to clear his throat.

'So, there's a legend about a tunnel,' he began, his voice lowering so much it was almost a whisper, in an obvious attempt to try and sound mysterious. 'Stretches all the way from Richmond Castle to Easby Abbey. That's another place you should make a point of visiting as well, but anyway ...' Matt paused for dramatic effect. 'Back in the eighteen century, and worried that people might be able to use this legendary tunnel to get inside the castle and get up to mischief, they started to look for it.'

'They?' said Harry, interrupting. 'Who are they, exactly?'

'Soldiers, I think,' said Matt. 'Anyway, the entrance to a tunnel was found, but because the soldiers were all too big to fit in it, they grabbed one of the regimental drummer boys and had him go inside instead.'

'That sounds just like the Army,' said Harry. 'Passing the shite jobs down the line. And my guess here is that this story doesn't have a happy ending.'

'They order the lad to walk along the tunnel, rapping out a steady beat on his drum,' Matt said. 'They would then follow the sound along aboveground.'

'Well, that wouldn't work, would it?' said Harry, but Matt shushed him with a raised finger and a sideways glare.

'Finish your story,' said Harry.

'So, this lad, he's sent down this tunnel, and the soldiers, they can hear him leave the castle, right? They follow the sound of that drum across the marketplace, and then all the way to the banks of the River Swale. Then, about half a mile from Easby Wood, the drumming ... just ... stopped!'

Harry waited for Matt to say more, but when nothing was forthcoming, he said, 'Is that it?'

Matt feigned a look of shock.

'What do you mean, is that it? No one knows what happened to the drummer boy!'

'Or if there even was one in the first place,' said Harry.

Matt asked, 'Do you want to know the possible explanations for what happened?'

'Is one of them that the tunnel collapsed?'

'Yes, but that's not very interesting, is it?'

'Believable, though,' said Harry, but Matt ignored him.

'One is that the lad ended up in some chasm in Hell or something, but the one I like the most is that he found King Arthur and his knights asleep in a chamber and lay down to join them until they're all needed again. There's even a stone in the spot where his drumbeats were reportedly last heard. Oh, and some say, if you listen carefully, you can still hear the drumbeats today, especially at night in the marketplace.'

Harry could see why Matt liked the tale of the drummer boy. There was a certain romance to it, and the mystery certainly sat well in a place like the Dales, where history and legend seemed to tumble into each other around every corner, like the rolling plumes of early morning fog.

With Matt's words still in his mind, Harry thought back to his chat with Margaret. Whether she'd meant it to or not, her words had struck a note with him, and like or not, he knew she had a point. His life, and Ben's, had changed dramatically since heading north, to the point where everything before seemed like the life of someone else.

And perhaps it was, Harry thought, because he had changed, more than he sometimes realised. Maybe he should celebrate things a bit more, like Margaret had suggested. How, though, that was the issue. Celebrating didn't come so naturally to Harry as a grumble or a rant, but even he knew his rough edges had been smoothed a little by the Dales and the folk he now classed as friends. So, change was possible.

'We're here,' Matt said, interrupting Harry's thoughts.

Harry yanked himself back into the moment, happy for an excuse to not be analysing himself.

Matt had pulled them up outside a three-storey stone terrace, with impressive bay windows on both the ground and the first floor. The road the house was on rose gently on cobbles worn by centuries of traffic, which shone in the sun that was working hard to break through the cloud. The rain was still falling, and the cobbles glistened like gemstones.

'By the looks of things, importing coffee certainly pays well,' he said.

'Doesn't it just?' agreed Matt, leaning over the steering wheel to stare at the house through the smear of rain on the windscreen. 'This is Frenchgate Street, the kind of place I can only ever dream of being able to afford. Not that I'd live here even if I could. Too busy for me, Richmond. It's lovely, like, a proper old market town, but I just can't see myself in a place like this. Or Joan, for that matter.'

'You're not actually thinking of moving, are you?' Harry asked, sensing that Matt had certainly pondered it enough at some point in his life to bring it up.

'Not a chance of it,' Matt said. 'Not now, anyway. Happy where we are, thank you, and that'll do me just fine.'

Harry really didn't want to get out in the rain and, almost as though the weather could read his thoughts, the rain somehow grew heavier.

'Come on, then,' he said, opening his door. 'Let's get this over and done with.'

The rain drove into Harry, not because the wind was behind it, but simply because there was so much of it, the weight of it pressing down on his shoulders, drilling into his head.

Stepping down onto the cobbles, he was very aware of just how slippery they were, so made certain that each and every step he then took was firm.

From the cobbles and across the equally perilous flagstone pavement, Harry stepped up to the front door of the house and huddled beneath a stone lintel, Matt stepping in beside him. He then reached for the large brass knocker and rapped it hard against the door.

'Do that again, and I might have to arrest you for breaking and entering.' Matt smiled.

'It wasn't that hard,' said Harry. 'Anyway, we want him to hear it, don't we?'

A couple of minutes passed, but no one came to the door.

Harry reached for the knocker again, and Matt clasped his hands over his ears and leaned away.

'Quite the comedian sometimes, aren't you?' Harry said, and crashed the knocker into the door.

Still nothing.

'One last try,' said Harry, and as he did so, he heard the rattle of a window opening above.

Looking up, he saw a man's face staring down at them, his pale, naked torso taking a battering from the rain.

'Mr Heath?' Harry said, calling up, the rain stinging his eyes and blinding him as he did so.

The man continued to stare.

Harry reached for his Police ID and lifted it, fully aware that there was little chance the man would be able to see it, never mind read what it said.

'Police,' he said. 'Detective Chief Inspector Grimm, and Detective Sergeant Dinsdale. Can we come in?'

The man stared for a moment longer, then disappeared back inside the house, swishing the window shut behind him.

'Well,' said Matt, 'that wasn't mysterious at all, was it? He'll be needing a quick towel down after that.'

Harry leaned into the door, resting his ear against the wood. He closed his eyes and tried to tune out the sound of the rain. Then, from far off inside the house, he heard footsteps.

Harry pulled himself away from the door as the clatter of latches and locks being opened jittered into the moment.

The door opened.

The man was a few inches shorter than Harry, wider around the middle than his shoulders were broad, completely bald, and wearing a white dressing gown.

'Mr Heath?' Harry asked.

'Who's asking?'

Harry again revealed his ID.

'Can we come in?'

The man shook his head.

'I'm busy,' he said. 'Can you come back later?'

'Not really, no,' said Harry. 'That's not how this works, not generally, anyway. It's about your warehouse.'

'I'm not Mr Heath, you see,' the man said, and Harry noticed then that the accent wasn't a local one, and seemed to have more in common with private education than the Pennines. 'And there's really very little point in asking me anything about him.'

'This is his house, though, isn't it?' Matt asked.

'It is,' said the man.

'And you're in it,' said Harry.

'Yes.'

Harry could feel his frustration building. Either this man was being deliberately obstructive or he was astonishingly oblivious to the fact that he was talking to two detectives.

'Can I ask you name, please?'

'Yes.'

Silence.

'That was me asking,' said Harry.

'Was it? Oh, sorry, it's Henry Dodd,' the man replied. 'But like I've just said, I know nothing of Mr Heath, only that he has a rather splendid house, and we were very lucky to be able to book it at such short notice.'

'Book it?' said Harry.

'Airbnb,' said Henry. 'Don't think it's been listed for long. My wife and I, we fancied a break, what with it being our wedding anniversary, saw this, booked it, and here we are. Rather jolly it is, too.'

'You don't know where Mr Heath is, then?' Harry asked.

'Sorry, no,' said Henry. 'Wish I could be more help.'

A woman's voice called out from somewhere in the house.

'Will there be anything else?' Henry asked, and Harry heard a hint of urgency in the question.

'Don't suppose you have any contact details for Mr Heath, do you?' Matt asked.

'No,' Henry replied. 'Well, not for him personally, but we do have a contact number and address, just in case of any problems. Shall I get it for you?'

'If you would be so kind,' said Harry, unable to hide his irritation, not least because he and Matt were now thoroughly drenched from standing outside the house.

Henry turned from the door to disappear back into the house, and reappeared a moment or two later with an address and telephone number jotted down on a piece of notepaper.

'There you go,' Henry said.

'Thank you,' said Harry, as the woman's voice called again from inside the house, this time louder and with a note of annoyance.

'I'm supposed to be fetching the champagne,' Henry said with a wink. Then before Harry and Matt could say goodbye, he'd shut the door in their faces.

'He was in a bit of a hurry,' Harry said, and looked at the piece of paper Henry had handed them, which was already going soggy in his hands.

'Where are we heading, then?' Matt asked.

'Caldbergh,' said Harry, struggling to read the handwriting, and saw Matt frown. 'Something the matter?'

Matt scratched his chin, then his nose, then shook his head.

'Yes and no,' he said. 'There's something familiar, I'm sure there is, but I just can't remember what.'

'How about you keep trying to remember as we drive, instead of while we stand here getting even more drenched?' Harry suggested.

'It's nowt but a bit of rain,' said Matt, following Harry back to the Land Rover.

'Sometimes, though,' said Harry, 'I wouldn't mind a bit of something else that wasn't.'

Once inside the vehicle, Harry's stomach reminded him of just how empty it was.

'Though I hesitate to ask this,' he said, clipping in as Matt climbed in behind the steering wheel, 'but do you know anywhere good we can grab a quick bite to eat? My stomach's just about ready to eat itself.'

'Funny you should ask,' said Matt, a little too knowingly.

'Why?'

Matt held up a hand as though to still Harry's questioning.

'Trust me,' he said, and a couple of minutes later, had them parked up in the centre of Richmond.

Harry stared through the Land Rover windows at the market-place and knew then for sure that he'd never visited Richmond. The view before him was postcard perfect, or it would've been if it weren't for all the parked cars and vans and the occasional truck. But regardless, the grand sweep of the place was still something to behold.

Built on a slope, with a church in the centre of the cobbles under the glare of the numerous historic buildings that lined its boundary, Harry was sure that if he listened carefully enough, he would hear an echo of the horses and carts that had once traversed the ancient space long ago.

'Over there,' Matt said, pointing through the window before unclipping his seatbelt and opening his door. 'Come on.'

Harry followed Matt from the Land Rover and across to a small establishment on a corner. From its open door, a rich aroma was slipping joyfully into the wet day, one so enticing that it was all he could do to not just rush in and eat everything, regardless of what it actually was.

'That smells good,' he said, stepping inside the shop.

In front of Harry was a glass counter behind which all manner of pies were on offer.

'Very popular with squaddies,' said Matt, as they both stared at the wares on offer. 'What're you going to have?'

'What do you suggest?' Harry asked.

'All of them,' Matt answered. 'But I'm going for the chicken curry.'

Harry raised an eyebrow at that answer.

'Not a pork pie, then?'

'Had that last time,' Matt smiled.

Harry focused on the pies. His stomach grumbled even louder.

'Meat and potato,' he said.

Pies purchased, Harry soon found himself walking back through the rain to the Land Rover, with a hot pie warming his hands.

Climbing into the vehicle, he didn't wait on decorum and took a bite. Then another. He noticed that Matt, having climbed in beside him, was looking at him.

'Good, isn't it?' Matt said.

'It's a proper pie,' said Harry.

'Thus the name of the shop, I suspect,' said Matt.

And for the next few minutes, before they drove off to their next destination, Harry simply sat with Matt in almost reverent silence, savouring every bite of one of the best pies he'd ever tasted.

Yorkshire, he thought, really was quite something.

SEVEN

Detective Constable Jen Blades was, in pretty much every way possible, broken. She'd done races before, plenty actually, but this one? Dear God in Heaven...

It had seemed like a sensible idea at the time, but then every decision made in the warm afterglow that runners experience on finishing a race seemed like that, didn't they? That heady sensation of invincibility and elation, a belief that anything and everything was possible, and would also be fun, so why not do more, only harder and longer, and over more extreme terrain?

And, so far, those decisions had been sensible.

This time, though? Not so much.

At over a hundred miles, the distance had been more than she'd ever attempted before, all of it covered in three days, the route taking in mountains, valleys, and terrain as likely to kill you as inspire. The weather had been on the verge of psychotic, a mean-spirited thing of anger and violence that had chased the runners from start to finish, seemingly intent on ruining them utterly. And yet, so many of them had persevered and triumphed.

Race over, the journey back had been by train and taxi, the mere notion that she would've been able to drive so soon after such an undertaking so sublimely ridiculous that even now Jen shuddered at the thought of it. And despite giving herself a couple of days to recover in a dark hotel room somewhere close to the race itself, she still felt as though what she needed more than anything right now was every single part of her to be replaced.

Everything ached. Everything hurt. So much so that for a good few hours after the race, all she'd done was flit between crying and being unconscious. The massage after the race had been necessary but agonising. She'd done her best to keep stretching, to stop herself from seizing up, but after something so arduous, it all seemed futile. The only difference now was that she was awake more than she was asleep, which meant more time to experience the pain. And there was just so much of it.

Phone in sick, she'd thought, that was the answer. Just call Harry, be honest, recover. But then she'd received the text from Jadyn, something about a fire, then later, about a body, and all thought of making that call had evaporated.

That didn't make any of this easier, though. How was it that a car could be so agonising to get into? Actually, forget the car. What about clothes? It was as though all of her skin had become hyper-sensitive, but not in a good way, and even the softest garments she could find was sensation overload, causing her to squeeze her eyes shut as she got dressed. Her body had screamed at her to stop, to just lie down, die even, but she'd gritted her teeth, pushed through the agony, taken painkillers, and somehow managed to end up fully clothed.

The thing was, Jen knew that the pain was temporary. Nothing was actually broken. She was bruised, her body was healing, and in a few days she'd be looking back at the race with a strange and somewhat misplaced fondness, one that recalled the agony of it with affection, the moments where she'd wanted to just give up, lie down, and wait to be picked up by whatever rescue team was on call for the race, as events that were simply adventure in its purest form.

Jen laughed, and the bright lights of agony that ripped through her only made her laugh more, as though the pain was simply encouraging itself.

Having arrived home early evening, she'd been welcomed at the door by Steve, the monitor lizard she shared her house with. He'd been, as usual, magnificently indifferent to her arrival, perhaps even a little irritated that she'd insisted on him getting out of the way so that she could get in the front door with her bags. And off he'd plodded, back through to the lounge to take up the whole sofa, which Jen was sure he considered his.

She'd left Jadyn in charge of checking in on Steve, to make sure that he had enough water and food. When she'd asked Jadyn if he'd be happy enough to do it, the stark horror in his eyes at the request had worried her, but he'd agreed, nonetheless.

It wasn't that Steve didn't like Jadyn, more that he viewed him with the distrusting eye of a monarch wary of any prospective suitor interested in his daughter. Obviously, Steve was no replacement father figure, but just try telling Steve that, Jen thought with a smile, as she slipped her key into the ignition.

With a deep breath, she eased her vehicle away from the kerb and headed out of Middleham and up the dale to Hawes. She would take care of things at the office, and act as a point of contact should anything come in about what had happened in Leyburn. And if she was needed, she was only a short drive away.

She drove cautiously, trying to ensure that every corner was smooth, that the fewest gear changes possible were taken, and that any potholes in the road were avoided. The journey was still agony, but she gritted her teeth and focused on arriving in Hawes marketplace, parking up, and slumping down in a chair in the office. What she hadn't expected was to turn up and find Jim having an argument with a middle-aged couple carrying day-sized rucksacks new enough to still be wearing their price tags.

'Jim?'

Jen's voice cut Jim off mid-rant. Though, what he was so worked up about, she had no idea as yet. Whatever it was, it had certainly got him riled, which was odd in itself; Jen couldn't recall a single moment in all the time she'd known him that Jim had shown himself to have enough of a temper to be able to lose it.

The couple turned as one to stare at Jen.

'Oh, another one,' the man said, looking down at Jen from behind a rough, grey beard and eyebrows Gandalf the Grey would've been proud of, a comparison Jen was almost embarrassed she was able to make. She'd read the Lord of the Rings, but it was the films she loved the most, especially the first half an hour or so of the first one, which was little more than Hobbits and Hobbiton, of growing vegetables, having friends, and popping to the pub; a kind of idyll she hoped to one day have. This was a dream she'd yet to share with anyone, and especially not Jadyn.

'Detective Constable Blades,' Jen said, introducing herself, her voice pinched by the pain stabbing every part of her body with pins. 'Maybe it would be best if we sat down for a chat? Tea always helps.'

She looked at Jim, but all she saw in his eyes was a wildness that was not only uncharacteristic, but clearly feeding on the exhaustion she recognised in them because she was feeling it herself. What on earth was going on?

'Well, I can tell you for nothing, that tea will not help, not by a long shot,' the man said. 'Never in my life have I been spoken to like—'

'Well, there's a first time for everything, isn't there?' Jim said, butting in.

'Jim,' Jen said, her voice firm and calm as she tried to get him to focus on her for a moment. 'Tea, yes?'

'We don't want tea,' the man said. 'We want an apology.'

'Well, you won't be getting one, not by a long shot,' Jim said. 'How can you even ask that? I mean ... I...'

Jim's voice caught in his throat and with a shake of his head, he turned and walked away.

'Don't you go walking away from me, young man,' the man said, and made to follow him.

Jen held up a hand and stepped in front of the man, making it absolutely clear he was to go no further.

'Don't you go assaulting my husband,' the woman said, joining in at last.

'Please,' said Jen, 'if we could all just take a breather for a moment, calm down, then perhaps I can get to the bottom of what's happened, see if there's a way to resolve it?'

'Sheep, that's what happened,' the man said. 'There we were, happily minding our own business, driving along, enjoying the scenery, and the next thing we know, there's a flock of them in front of us.'

'They've damaged our car,' said the woman.

At this, Jen saw Jim bristle, but was pleased that he kept his mouth shut, and his distance.

'Perhaps it would be best if you told me exactly what happened, from the beginning,' she said.

'There's nothing to tell, is there?' said the man. 'We're up here to explore the Dales, see what all the fuss is about, and already I've lost a headlight and have a dented wing.'

'And how did this actually happen?' Jen asked. 'Your dented wing, I mean. Did you swerve when you saw the sheep and go into a wall?'

'Sheep, that's what happened! I've already said that!' the man said. 'Are you not listening? They just jumped out at us and next thing I know one of them has hit my car!' He clapped his hands to emphasise the sound of the impact. 'Unbelievable! I mean, who lets animals like that just wander around in the road, anyway? It's not safe. Fields have walls and gates, don't they? Aren't they for keeping sheep and cows contained?'

'You hit a sheep, then, is that what you're saying?' Jen asked, now ignoring everything else that the man had said.

'No, we're not saying that at all,' said the woman. 'We did not hit a sheep; the sheep attacked us, that's what happened. Just flew at the car, nothing we could do about it.'

Jim marched over.

'Go on,' he said, staring at the couple. 'Tell Jen why you're here. Tell her *exactly* why.'

Jen waited.

'Well, it's quite simple, really,' said the man. 'We want to know whose sheep it was that caused the damage so that we can get them to pay for it.'

Jen did a double take.

'What was that now?'

'Well, it'll mess with my no-claims bonus, won't it?' the man said. 'So, it seems only right that the owner of the sheep pays for what it did to our car.'

'And what about the sheep?' Jen asked. 'The one that you hit?'

'What about it?' said the woman. 'We didn't hit it, did we? It hit us! Those animals were mad. What kind of person just lets them wander all over the place, anyway?'

Jen saw Jim's face turn red, his jaw clench.

'Can I ask if you checked on the sheep?'

'What?'

'The sheep,' Jen said. 'The one you hit; did you check on it, after you collided with it, make sure it was okay, not injured, or if it needed help?'

'Of course we didn't!' the man snapped back. 'It limped off with the others. And they all look the same anyway, don't they? Not like we'd have been able to find it.'

'You just said that it limped.'

'I did.'

Jen was now beginning to understand exactly why Jim was so angry.

'So, you saw that it was injured, but did nothing about it? And you didn't think to find the farmer yourself?'

'That's why we're here,' the woman said. 'You need to find them so that we can sort this out!'

'You're right,' Jen said. 'We do need to sort this out. Immediately. Jim?' Jim turned his attention to Jen. 'Do we know where the incident happened?'

'We do,' Jim said. 'Out the back of Burtersett, on the lane heading over to Semerwater, at the crossroads with the Roman road. That's why I can't believe they didn't think to stop by the farm. Not like it's far away, is it? And they could've tried any one of the houses in the village; everyone knows everyone else. Someone would've been able to get a hold of us, I'm sure of it. And the last thing Dad needs is to have one of the sheep wandering around injured. It'll be a bugger to find, and something else for him to worry about. He doesn't need it, Jen.'

'But you think you can find it, yes?'

Jim gave a firm nod.

'Fly will, I'm sure. He's at the farm with Mum and Dad. He's a dab hand at splitting a flock. And he's just getting better and better now; best sheepdog we've ever had.'

Jen rested a hand on Jim's arm.

'Then off you go,' she said. 'Head home, grab Fly, and find that sheep. I'll head up to the auction mart and get a message to the vets. Let them know there's a chance you might be needing their assistance.'

Jim glanced at the couple standing in the room, and Jen saw confusion in their eyes.

'What about these two, though?' Jim asked.

'They're going to pay for whatever needs doing,' Jen said, and turned her eyes on the couple. 'Aren't you?'

The man baulked.

'Pardon?'

Jen waited for Jim to leave before she responded.

'My understanding is this,' she began. 'You hit a sheep while driving. Accidents do happen, of course they do, and in this case, I think it's both admirable and commendable that you've not only gone out of your way to contact the police about what happened, but offered to cover the costs.'

'That's not what—'

'In fact,' Jen continued, pushing on with her attempt to turn this to Jim's advantage, and somehow persuade the couple to do the right thing, 'I wish more tourists were as caring and thoughtful as you. Sheep are the livelihood of so many in the Dales and the loss of even one is keenly felt. If we can find the animal in question, and save it, then I think we can all be proud of how we have joined forces to ensure the best outcome, can't we?'

By this point, Jen wasn't entirely sure what she was saying, but her focus was more on bamboozling the couple with politeness than going by the book, while at the same time seeing that what she was offering them was a way out. Warranted, she could do little, if anything, about what had happened, but that didn't mean she wasn't going to at least try. She knew that Jim and his parents were having a tough time of it since his dad's accident on the farm a while back, so a little help wouldn't go amiss right now.

'Oh,' the man said, 'well, if you think ... I mean...'

'If I can just take your details,' said Jen. 'Then what we can do is head up to the vets and have a word; what do you think?'

The man glanced at his wife.

'That ... yes, well, it sounds...'

'Excellent,' said Jen, and walked over to the office door and opened it. Then, with a wide smile, she gestured for the couple to step outside. 'After you.'

EIGHT

As Matt drove them into Caldbergh, the Land Rover having bounced them along needle-thin lanes littered with puddles, which they wore along their verges like costume jewellery, the rain started to ease.

Harry's fingers were still greasy from the meat and potato pie. The thought of it made him want to turn around and grab another.

'This is the second place today that I've never been to,' he said, as Matt brought them to a stop.

The hamlet—because that's really all Caldbergh is, thought Harry—comprised a collection of farmhouses and buildings, a small number of cottages, and a road that ended at a gate leading into a field. And yet it still held enough rugged beauty to have him wonder, as he did so often, not only what good fortune had sent him north to live in such a place, but why. He wasn't going to question it though, or analyse it too much; best to just accept it and smile.

'Of course!' Matt suddenly exclaimed, turning to look at Harry with some kind of realisation in his eyes.

'Of course, what?' asked Harry, unclipping his seatbelt, and opening his door, happy that as he did so he wasn't hammered by rain.

'I remember now,' said Matt. 'That thing that's been scratching at the back of my mind.'

'And?' asked Harry, staring up at the sky warily, relieved to find that the rain was all but spent, but also fully expecting it to open up on him any second and give him another drenching.

'Remember when Jen was hit by a car?' Matt asked, opening his door and slipping out of his seat. 'We searched for the wing mirror at the bottom of Temple Bank?'

'Not something I'm likely to forget,' said Harry, remembering how Jen had been more than a little bit lucky to survive what had happened that day.

'It was a Mr Heath who reported the car she was hit by, because after knocking into Jen, it nearly crashed into him a few minutes later just outside Wensley,' said Matt. 'He'd noticed that the wing mirror was missing as well.' He laughed then.

'Why's that so funny?'

'No, it's not that,' said Matt. 'It's Mr Dodd, the man we just spoke with at Heath's place in Richmond.'

'What about him?'

'If I'd remembered earlier, then I'd have known, wouldn't I, that he wasn't Adam Heath?'

'Not necessarily,' said Harry. 'That's a good while ago now, isn't it? You can't be expected to remember every face of every person you deal with in every case you investigate.'

Though saying that, Harry had a feeling he probably could, some more clearly than others for lots of reasons, none of them good.

'The hair though,' said Matt. 'That's the giveaway, isn't it?'

'You do remember that I never actually met Mr Heath, don't you?' Harry said. 'So I can't actually comment on anything about him, never mind his hair. And anyway, Dodd didn't have any, did he?' he added, noting to his surprise that not only was the threat of rain easing, but that the cloud was breaking, and sunshine was cutting through, causing the wet roads and houses to shimmer.

Matt got out and came around to join Harry.

'Exactly,' he said. 'And from what I recall, Adam Heath very much did, on his head, on his face, and all of it ginger. No grey either, the lucky sod.'

Harry stared at the houses in front of them.

'Which one is it, then?' he asked.

'If memory serves, it'll be that one,' said Matt, pointing across from where they were standing to an impressive house very much out of Harry's price range.

'Lights are on,' he said. 'Someone's home, then. Nice place to live as well, isn't it?'

'Name me somewhere in the Dales that isn't.'

Harry remembered one right away.

'Capstick's place, over in Oughtershaw,' he said. 'That farm was a mess.'

'That's a while back, isn't it?' said Matt.

'My first few months here,' nodded Harry, remembering finding Capstick's body crushed under his own trailer. 'Seems like an age ago.'

Matt smiled and rested a hand on Harry's shoulder.

'And look at you now,' he said. 'You're almost as much of a local as I am myself!'

Harry couldn't help but laugh at that.

'Kind of you to say so,' he said, 'but if there's one thing I've learned, it's that you could have lived here for years and never be that.'

Matt dropped his hand back to his side.

'Oh, I wouldn't be so sure,' he said. 'Take The Fountain as an example; there's plenty of folk who I see in there regularly who don't even live in the area, who travel up every weekend or as often as they can. And there's others who've moved to the area and are more involved in what's going on at that pub, and in Hawes itself, than folk who've lived here their whole lives.'

'I suppose so,' said Harry, 'but I still don't think I qualify quite yet.'

'You'd be surprised.'

'You're right, I would.'

Matt led Harry across the road to the house. 'I know where I live isn't exactly a place bouncing with life, but I think I'd find living here a little too quiet. It's lovely, like, but there's something missing.'

Harry smiled.

'You mean a pub, don't you?'

'Yes.'

Harry walked up to the door and gave it a sharp knock, then stood back to see if he could spot movement in any of the windows. A few moments later, the door opened.

Standing in front of them was a woman with shoulder-length red hair and bright eyes. Age-wise, Harry guessed she was in her mid- to late-seventies. She was dressed in denims and wrapped in a fleece jacket. On her head, she was wearing what to Harry looked like an army surplus winter hat with fleece earflaps hanging down.

'Hello,' she said, smiling brightly, her voice clear and strong. 'Can I help?'

Harry pulled out his police ID.

'DCI Grimm,' he said. 'And this is Detective Sergeant Dinsdale. We're looking for a Mr Adam Heath.'

'Adam's my son,' said the woman. Her smile faded a little as she glanced again at Harry's ID. 'Is something wrong? Has something happened?'

'We were given this address by someone staying at his house in Richmond,' Harry explained. 'And we do need to get in touch with your son rather urgently, Mrs Heath, so if you could help, that would be hugely appreciated.'

'He rents that house out quite a lot,' Mrs Heath said. 'Travels a lot with work, you see. And less of the Mrs Heath; my name's Peggy.'

'Can we come in?' Harry asked. 'This shouldn't take long. But always better to talk inside rather than on a doorstep.'

Peggy frowned, looked Harry and Matt up and down, then stepped back into the house.

'Yes, of course,' she said. 'Come in.'

Stepping inside, Harry expected to be shown through to a lounge or kitchen and no doubt offered the usual mug of tea, but instead, Peggy pointed across the hallway to a pile of boxes at the bottom of an impressive staircase. The house was cold, which explained the hat that Peggy was wearing, and the fleece jacket.

'If you could grab a couple of those each and follow me upstairs, that would be a huge help,' Peggy said, and without waiting for an answer, she swept up the stairs, taking two at a time with ease.

Harry glanced at Matt and saw his own bemusement reflected back at him. With a shrug, he walked over to the boxes and took hold of two, only to find that they were considerably heavier than they looked.

Matt did the same, groaning as he lifted them.

'Funny old job this, isn't it?' he said, then followed Peggy up the stairs.

At the top of the stairs, Peggy called from the other side of an open door.

'In here, if you could, thank you.'

Harry followed Matt into the room and found himself standing in a room more reminiscent of a library than a bedroom. The walls were lined with bookshelves, and sitting at a desk in front of a computer was Peggy. A small fire was lit in a grate, but as yet, was doing little to affect the temperature of the room.

'Over there if you could,' said Peggy, pointing to a corner of the room.

Harry and Matt obliged, and with nowhere to actually sit in the room, turned around to find Mrs Heath staring up at them from her office chair.

'You're looking for Adam, then.'

'Yes,' said Harry. 'And as I said, we were given this address as a contact by the people renting your son's house for their holiday.'

'I can give you his telephone number,' said Peggy. 'He used to live here, you know? Moved back to Richmond, into his own house, a while back now. Can't think of exactly when it was. I think he got a little weary of all these books. They keep me busy though, and I actually make a nice bit of money from them, too, you know, which is even better!'

'He helped us with an investigation a while back,' said Matt.

'He did? I can't remember that at all,' said Mrs Heath, then added, 'Actually, it might be a good idea to have a chat with Shane and Jack as well; they're bound to know where he is.'

Harry glanced at Matt, thinking about the body in the burned-out warehouse.

'Shane and Jack?'

'They work for him. Shane for a few years now, and Jack came on board just a few months ago, I believe. Don't ask me what they do. I drink coffee, but I'm more of a tea person. Mind you, I have just bought myself one of those posh little coffee machines that makes lattes; I'm quite the barista, even if I do say so myself! But I can't get all excited about it like some folk can; all that nonsense about different beans and roasts, and what grind is best for this, that, and the other. Can't say I can ever tell the difference.'

'So, you don't know where your son is, then?' Matt asked.

Peggy shook her head.

'No, I don't,' she said. 'Well, not exactly, no.'

'How do you mean, not exactly?' asked Harry.

Peggy reached across her desk, grabbed something, and handed it to Harry.

'I know he's in Scotland, but that's all,' she said. 'He's always loved the place, ever since he went to the Highlands with the Scouts when he was a boy. Sometimes, I think he loves it more than the Dales.'

Harry looked at what Peggy had given him; half a dozen post-cards of various scenic views, clearly of the Highlands. He flipped them over, saw spidery handwriting passing comment on the usual postcard fayre of what the weather was like, places Adam had eaten, and a few mentions of haggis, mostly battered.

'Been there for a couple of weeks now,' Peggy continued. 'Likes to get away. Oh, and here's the number...'

She pulled a Post-it Note off the top of the desk and handed it to Harry.

'But you don't know where he's actually staying?' asked Matt. 'Like the address of the house or cottage or hotel or wherever it is?'

'No, I'm afraid that I don't,' said Peggy. 'But then there's really no need, is there? He's hardly a teenager anymore, getting into scrapes and worrying me and his father sick! I'm pretty sure he can do what he wants at his age.' She tapped her hand on Harry's knee and gave him a wink. 'I bought him condoms for his eighteenth, you know. I thought that was very forward-thinking of me. Not sure he ever really forgave me for it.'

'Why?' asked Harry.

'Probably because he opened them in front of his friends,' said Peggy, though Harry detected the slyest of smiles.

Yeah, Harry thought, you meant for that to happen, didn't you? A lesson inside a lesson, perhaps.

Harry punched the number into his phone and let it ring.

'No answer?' asked Matt when Harry eventually gave up and killed the call.

'Nope.' Harry looked at Peggy. 'Do you have contact details for Shane and Jack?'

'I do,' said Peggy. 'Their phone numbers, anyway. But the easiest thing to do would be to pop into Adam's warehouse in Leyburn; they're bound to be there.'

'It's because of what's happened at the warehouse that we need to speak with Adam,' said Harry.

Then he explained just enough about what had happened to make sure Peggy understood how urgent it was that they got in touch with her son, while keeping the details about the discovery of the body to himself for now. He wouldn't say anything about that until they had a positive ID, not least because when they'd arrived, he'd thought Adam was most likely their victim, but now they had two more possibilities and he wanted to be certain.

Peggy sunk back in her chair with the weight of the news.

'But that warehouse ... the business ... that's Adam's life!' she said. 'He's spent years building it up. Destroyed? What, the whole place, just gone? How's that possible?'

'I'm afraid so, yes,' said Harry.

'You really mean it's been burned to the ground? How? It's a warehouse! Why would it even be on fire? That doesn't make any sense at all!'

'Which is why, as I'm sure you can understand,' said Harry, 'it's vital we speak with your son. And you're sure you have no idea where he is?'

'Not a clue,' said Peggy with a shrug. 'Shane and Jack, it's them you need to speak to. They'll know; I'm sure they will.'

'Those contact details, then, Peggy, if you have them to hand?'

Peggy turned her chair around to check through her drawers, and pulled out a small black address book.

'Here,' she said, flicking through the pages, her actions frantic now, her hands shaking, thanks to the news Harry had shared. 'I was planning on having them all round here in a couple of months for a bit of a do; tea and cake, that kind of thing.'

'Thank you,' said Harry, jotting down the details. 'I think that's all for now.'

Peggy went to get out of her chair, but Harry shook his head.

'It's fine, honestly; we'll see ourselves out,' he said.

'Are you sure?' said Peggy. 'But I've not even offered you any tea. And that's what I always do with visitors. Don't get many, you see, not out here; bit of a dead end, isn't it? Pretty, but there's nowhere to go after, other than back. I'm rambling, sorry. But you're sure you won't stay for tea?'

Harry could see in Peggy's eyes how much she wanted them to stay. But they needed to get on.

'Very kind,' he said, 'but we really need to head off.'

'Only if you're sure.'

'We are,' Harry said. 'But thank you. And we'll be in touch.'

Leaving Peggy upstairs in her office, Harry led Matt back

downstairs and out into the day. The afternoon was already growing late, but the sun was brighter than ever now, burning through enough cloud to show streaks of blue beyond it. Then, as he went to speak, a thunderous sound crashed into the moment, and two fighter jets blasted overhead, and up the Dale.

Matt joined Harry in staring at them as they flew off.

'Always amazes me,' he said, 'how when I'm on the top of somewhere like Penhill, I'm looking down on those pilots. Sometimes they're so close I can actually see them in their cockpits.'

'It's a great place to practise flying low,' said Harry, as he took out his phone and once again tried Adam's number.

With no answer, he shoved the phone back in his pocket, and as they climbed back into the Land Rover, Matt asked, 'What do you think about all that, then?'

Harry didn't answer. Instead, he was staring into the middle distance. On the one hand, he was bothered because Adam was unreachable, and on the other, because something was bothering him, and it wasn't just the two new names they'd been given, or the distant rumbling of the fighter jets.

'Something up?' Matt asked.

'The books,' Harry said.

'What about them?'

'Last night, at the fire; Sowerby came over with something in an evidence bag, didn't she? It was a book.'

'Folio edition,' said Matt, remembering. 'You think it's important?'

'Well, I know what it's not,' he said.

'A coincidence?' said Matt.

'Exactly.'

'So, what next?'

Harry wasn't sure. The day would soon be done, and although investigations took little notice of the passing hours, he knew a tired team was no use to anyone. Jen would be in the office, having returned from her time away at a running event, and they'd had no contact from her, so he could only assume things were fine up the dale, or at least in hand. Liz was on leave, and Jadyn and Dave would be around tomorrow, and considerably fresher than they had been that morning.

They had two new names to chase up, Adam Heath to find, and he didn't expect anything from Sowerby for a while, so they wouldn't have a positive ID of the body in the warehouse until then. He knew that the obvious possibilities were Adam, Shane, and Jack, but he couldn't know for certain, and he needed to keep an open mind.

Glancing at the contact details Peggy had given them for both Shane and Jack, he said, 'Let's head back to the office, check in with Jen and arrange a team meeting for the morning. I'll give Shane and Jack here a call on our way back and either arrange to meet them or leave messages. But I think that's all we can do for now.'

'Agreed,' said Matt. 'Anyway, you'll still have a few things to pack, won't you?'

Harry shook his head.

'If it's not packed by now, I don't need it,' he said.

Matt started the engine, and they were soon bouncing back down the lanes to head up the dale to Hawes. As his bed was now in pieces, Harry would be staying over at Grace's, and the realisation, that in a few days, he would never be staying there again, but instead heading back to their very own shared home, one they'd bought together, made him beam. If this was what happiness was, then he was more than happy to take a big, fat slice of it.

NINE

Jadyn woke up with a start, the harsh rasp of his alarm so loud he was sure someone was taking to his skull with a drill.

Sitting up, he prised his eyes apart, and took a moment to bring himself online. He knew he was in his house in Reeth, but what he couldn't understand is why he reeked of bonfires and coffee. Then he remembered, and as he swung his legs over the side of his bed, the evening before flashed through his mind in fast forward.

He must've just collapsed into bed he realised, stumbling over his clothes piled on the floor at the foot of his bed. The smell of smoke and coffee was even stronger there, with an added note of damp. Unpleasant.

Jadyn scooped up the clothes, shuffled his way out onto the landing, then downstairs, where he shoved them in the washing machine.

Checking his phone, he saw that the day was already half done, had a moment of stark panic that he was so late for work that Harry would demand blood, then remembered Harry had sent both him and Dave home to rest. Relief flooded through him as he checked his messages and opened one from Dave, which said he would see him in Leyburn at two. To Jadyn's horror, he realised that gave him less than an hour to sort himself out and make it there in time.

Deciding to wake himself up with some coffee, Jadyn only got so far as putting on the kettle, before the smell of the grounds turned his stomach. Instead, he grabbed a glass of milk, necked it, then headed back upstairs to wake himself up with a shower. That done, he was dressed and back downstairs for a breakfast of cereal, toast, and a protein shake, then out the door.

Reeth greeted him with a chill breeze cutting its way across the village green as he made his way to his vehicle. He loved the place, though found himself wanting to spend more and more time with Jen.

Heading down the hill out of Reeth, he swept over the bridge, sending a smile to the vehicle parked on the corner on the other side, a military troop carrier which had, for reasons unknown to him at least, been painted in Police livery.

The road followed the direction of the River Swale, before cutting back over it, and it was there that it and Jadyn parted ways, as he sped on up into the moors above. Rattling over a cattle grid, he wound his way along a thin road booby-trapped with numerous bends and hidden dips. It was no wonder so many bikers would travel to the Dales at the weekend, he thought, though doubted he would ever trust himself enough to ride one.

After the military ranges on his left, above which were flying red flags to indicate live firing would be taking place at some point that day, he was onto a wider, straighter road, then coasting down into Leyburn, to stop in a parking area opposite the old Police station. Dave was there waiting for him and waved.

'In you jump,' said Jadyn, pulling up beside him, window down, and Dave climbed in, leaving his own vehicle snuggled up between an old pickup with straw bales in the back, and a van which Jadyn noticed sported a chimney.

'Anyone sleeping in that, you think?' he asked, as they drove off.

'More fool them if they are,' said Dave.

A few minutes later, they pulled up outside a small terrace house with neat window boxes and a very clean, bright yellow front door. A sharp knock had it opening a moment later, and Bob was standing in front of them wearing hair that gave the distinct impression of him having just been electrocuted in a somewhat comical fashion. He was wearing a long, dark blue dressing gown, and stared out at them through bleary eyes.

'Thought it might be you,' he said. 'I've avoided answering the door most of the day. Head's a bit, well, you know...'

Remembering the night before, and the state Bob had been in when he'd stumbled over to tell them about the fire, Jadyn wasn't at all surprised.

'Best cure for a hangover is a Virgin Bloody Mary,' said Dave.

Jadyn was surprised to hear that Dave even knew what that was.

'Can't see you drinking something like that,' he said.

'Oh, I don't,' said Dave. 'Because I don't drink enough to get hangovers. But if I did, that's what I'd have. Probably with an egg in it.'

'An egg?' Jadyn exclaimed. 'Why? I mean, an egg! That makes no sense.'

'Trust me,' said Dave.

'Not sure that I do on that,' said Jadyn, then he looked at Bob. 'Can we come in?'

Bob stepped back and gestured inside.

Jadyn led the way into Bob's house and found himself in a cosy room with a fire crackling in the wood-burning stove, and a black and white movie playing on the small television in the corner.

'High Noon,' said Dave.

Bob laughed.

'Well done,' he said. 'Classic. One of those movies I always put on when I just need to relax and recover. Makes every day feel like a Sunday afternoon, if that makes sense.'

'Oh, it does,' said Dave.

Bob guided Jadyn and Dave to sit down on a sofa, then perched himself in an armchair by the fire.

'Sorry,' he said, getting up again. 'Should've offered tea.'

'No need,' said Jadyn.

'No need for tea?' Bob replied. 'Are you alright, lad? What about coffee?'

Jadyn shook his head.

'We'll just ask you a few questions, have a chat about last night, then be on our way, if that's okay.'

Bob leaned back in his chair and rubbed his head.

'I've taken paracetamol,' he said, 'but it's done bugger all. I tell you, that's the last time I go out for a beer with Charlie. He's a terrible influence. You'd think we'd have grown up by now, wouldn't you, learned our lesson? Turns out not, doesn't it? Old and stupid, both of us.'

Jadyn took out his notebook and saw Dave do the same.

'If it's okay,' he said, 'we just want to go over last night again.'

'No bother at all,' said Bob. 'But if I have to leave you suddenly to pay a visit to my porcelain friend, I hope that's okay.'

Jadyn ran through the initial details of what he knew, then said, 'The main thing we're interested in really is what happened right before the fire.'

'The voices, you mean?'

'Yes, and if there's anything else that you've remembered since.'

Bob sunk deeper into his chair, closed his eyes.

'Don't worry, I'm not falling asleep, like, just thinking...'

'Do you know how many voices?' Jadyn asked. 'Were they male, female?'

'I don't know how many,' Bob said. 'I just know there was a few of them. It wasn't like a crowd, more like the sound you get when you walk past a few people muttering to each other at a table in a pub. That make sense?'

Dave said, 'There was another voice as well. Someone shouted I think is what you said.'

At that, Bob's eyes pinged open.

'The shout? Yeah, I remember that alright. It's kept me awake most of the night it has.'

'Can you describe it?'

'Angry,' said Bob. 'Very, very angry. Then it was cut off real sharp, like, and I never heard it again.'

'Did you hear what it said?'

'Words, you mean?' Bob shook his head. 'No, I don't think so.'

'You're sure about that?' Jadyn asked. 'If you can remember anything at all, it could be really important to finding out what happened.'

Bob closed his eyes again, rubbed his forehead.

'They sounded surprised and angry,' he said. 'Like whoever it was, they'd just walked in on something they shouldn't have.'

'Did you see anyone outside the building?'

'No,' said Bob. 'There was nowt going on that I could see, no one outside. I thought the place was dead, to be honest, middle of the night and all that. That's why I was so spooked by the voices, just wasn't expecting to hear them. And then my imagination started to play silly buggers, didn't it? So I ran.'

'And you're sure you couldn't make out anything that was being said or shouted?'

Jadyn knew he was pushing the point, but he wanted to make sure.

'Fairly sure,' said Bob, but then he leaned forward and added, 'No, wait, there was something...'

'What?'

Bob held up a hand and Jadyn got the hint, giving him space to think, to remember.

'That was it,' he said at last. 'Yes ... something like ... no, give me a moment ... it was...'

Jadyn watched Bob squeeze his eyes shut as though to force what he could remember to come clear in his mind.

'... I think that the person shouting first sounded surprised at whatever it was that was going on ... something like, *What the hell are you doing* I think, but with more swearing, and something else ... *Where are you taking it all?* maybe. Can't be completely sure on that.'

'And then the shout was cut off, yes?' said Dave.

'There was more swearing,' said Bob, suddenly looking more alert, as though the memory of the previous night was growing clearer by the second. 'Something about how they'd never trusted them, then there was laughter, more shouting, then that was it, silence. That voice, it just stopped dead, right after ... yes, that was it; sounded like someone hit them with something, like a hard tap-tap, or something. It was fast. Maybe they hit whoever it was with something to shut him up. That doesn't make much sense, does it?'

Jadyn checked his notes from the previous night.

'You said you saw something as well, before you saw the fire?'

'I did? Oh ... now, what was that? A shape, wasn't it? Big thing, coming out of the warehouse.'

'Can you give us a bit more than that?' Dave asked.

'It was just this shadow coming out of the building,' said Bob. 'Really slowly, like, as well. And no sound either. Bit spooky all of it, that's for sure.'

Jadyn turned to Dave.

'Can you think of anything else?'

Dave frowned, suddenly deep in thought.

'Your friend, Charlie, do you know if he saw anything?' he asked.

Bob shook his head.

'No, he wasn't with me then. I left him outside that house where that couple were going at it like—'

Jadyn stood up, as much to stop Bob from talking as it was to draw things to a close.

'Well, thanks for this, Mr Ackroyd,' he said. 'Very useful, I think. If we have any further questions, or need something clarified, we'll be in touch.'

'Well, just pop round whenever you want,' Bob said. 'Not like I'm busy these days.'

Leaving Bob with a number to call if he remembered anything else, Jadyn and Dave slumped back into his vehicle. The day was all but spent and a message on his phone from Harry informed him of a team meeting in the morning.

'What do you make of all that, then?' Dave asked as Jadyn started the engine.

'Nothing good,' said Jadyn, pulling away from the kerb. 'Nothing good at all.'

TEN

Come Wednesday morning, Jim was up early enough that when he stepped outside into the backyard, everything was still wrapped in darkness. He had jobs to get on with, because there was still no way his dad could manage everything that needed to be done, and there was no way he could leave it all to his mum. So, with his own job as a PCSO to go to later on, being up with the lark wasn't so much a choice as a necessity. Fly was happy to join him, cheerfully trotting alongside as he headed out to check on the sheep.

As Spring was getting on now, lambing was all but finished. There were still a few ewes to give birth, and they were in pens close to the farm, to make it easier to keep an eye on them, and to deal with the births once they started. The rest of the flock were out in the lower fields. They wouldn't be out on the higher pastures till summer had started, and they'd had their fleeces sheered.

After checking the half dozen or so ewes in the pens, and seeing no sign of any of the remaining lambs looking like they wanted to make an appearance, Jim made his way to one of the farm's quad bikes, and climbed on. Fly jumped on behind, where his dad had crafted a simple box of wooden slats. It served as a place to put feed, bales of hay, and a dog in need of a lift.

His main job that morning was to check the sheep. Keeping an eye on them was vital to ensure that as many survived as possible. Sheep had a habit of dying for no reason, and like many farmers, Jim half wondered if they did it on purpose out of sheer bloody-mindedness. Lambs, though, were especially vulnerable.

Thankfully, with only a small number left to be born, trauma at birth wasn't something that was worrying Jim as much. Neither was the issue of the ewes not bonding with their lambs. It happened often enough for it to cause them a few headaches, but this year it hadn't been too bad.

They'd been able to persuade many of the sheep who had lost lambs during birth, to take on the lambs that were either a triplet, and therefore at risk of being underfed and dying from malnutrition or had been rejected by their mother. A quick rub down in the afterbirth was usually enough of a disguise. They'd had a few lambs going spare, and they'd been sold for a few quid as pet lambs at the auction mart, no doubt to folk looking to have a go at rearing one or two in their garden.

The only two risks he now had to worry about were disease and predation, and there was only so much you could do about either. The vets were especially busy at this time of year, and calling them out was never cheap, but it was necessary. As for predators, well, both Jim and his dad kept an eye on crows, making sure the fields the sheep were in were away from where they were nesting.

To make doubly sure that the birds weren't an issue, they'd both done their rounds with a gun, either shotgun or air rifle, to keep the numbers down as much as they could. His dad had suggested a bit of crow pie, having had it often enough as a child, or at least that's what he would have Jim believe.

Jim, though, was neither sure about the veracity of that story, nor convinced about the taste of a crow meat pie. The ones he'd shot always seemed to be little more than feather and bone, and there was just nothing appetising about them at all. He'd eaten plenty of other things they'd caught on the farm, especially rabbit and squirrel, but as yet, nothing had persuaded him to pop a few crow kebabs on a barbeque.

Foxes were another issue, and that was one of the things Jim was keeping an eye out for. They knew where the foxes were and kept an eye on them, because the damage even just one could do to a flock was shocking, not just in the number of losses, but the violence of it. Neither he nor his father could patrol the fields day and night, but if they spotted new activity, then they'd be out with a rifle and a thermal scope that night.

Jim didn't have a problem with the harsh realities of farming. He'd grown up with it, knew that no matter how fluffy and cute lambs looked, their value was in either their meat or as mothers, or for the occasional lucky male lamb, a tup. There was certainly no value at all in the fleece, which struck him as criminal.

A while later, and with just a couple of fields left to check, Jim was feeling a little better than he had when he'd risen. The idiocy of his altercation the day before was now all but forgotten, the injured sheep had been found and dealt with, and amazingly at the couple's expense, thanks to Jen. Dawn was breaking, the forecast was good, and the rich scent of the earth, the sweet tang of grass, all served to present him with a day he would, if he could, have happily just continued to spend on the farm.

Jim rolled the quad bike through another gate, shutting it behind him. Thick, golden rays of sunlight cut through the fading cloud, and warmed him. Then, far off, he caught the liquid burble of a curlew. He turned to see if he could spot it, staring up the fells to where it had probably flown in from, his guess being it had caught a thermal and glided up from the nature reserve below Marsett at the far end of Semerwater. He lifted a hand to shield his eyes from the sun, saw the distant dot of a bird in flight, heard the call again, and then it was gone.

God, it's beautiful out here, Jim thought, reaching behind him to give Fly a scratch under his chin. Fly wagged his tail and nuzzled into his hand, but as Jim reached over to give the dog a rub on his back, he growled. Then his hair bristled down his spine.

Jim turned to see where Fly was staring. At first, he couldn't see what was bothering him. Then a flash of brown grabbed his attention, and he saw it, a large fox happily trotting across the field carrying something in its mouth.

'Bastard ...'

Jim yanked the throttle and raced off after the animal. The fox was, for a moment, unaware that he'd been spotted, and just kept on with its happy jaunt. Then it heard Jim's quad bike, and ran.

'Hold on, Fly,' Jim shouted, knowing that Fly would be hunkering down behind him, and if the going got too rough, he'd jump off anyway. Not that they were able to make much speed across the field, but the distance closed quicker than the fox expected and as it came to the walled boundary, it leapt with just enough panic to drop what it had been carrying in its jaw.

Jim came to a dead stop where the fox had jumped the wall. There was no way he could catch it, or anything he could do to try and stop it, but standing up on the quad bike gave him a good view of the field on the other side. He watched the fox race away, then saw it stop, turn to stare at him for a moment, then continue on its way.

Jumping off the quad bike, Jim knelt next to what the fox had been carrying; a lamb, with the most perfect black face he'd ever seen, its glistening eyes staring up at him in terror.

Fly leaned over and gave its nose a lick.

To Jim's surprise, the lamb gave the weakest of bleats.

'Bloody hell, Fly, it's alive!'

Jim ripped off his jacket and wrapped it around the lamb, lifting it off the ground with a gentleness only a farmer who loved and respected the animals in their care could ever display. Its mother would be missing it for sure, but right now, he needed to get it back to the farm and checked over.

Jumping back up onto the quad bike, and with Fly up behind him, Jim lay the wrapped-up lamb in his lap and headed home, but as he did so, he spotted a ewe standing between him and the rest of the flock, a single lamb at its side. The ewe let out a loud and desperate baa. And the lamb in his lap replied.

Jim watched as the ewe edged closer, its lamb following along behind, bouncing in the air and kicking its legs out.

'Come on, then,' Jim said to the ewe. 'Best you follow on, like, okay?'

Back at the farm, Jim had no trouble in persuading the ewe and its lamb into a spare pen. Then he went inside the farmhouse to the kitchen, where his mum and dad stared up at him from the kitchen table and their breakfast.

'Bloody hell, lad,' said his dad. 'What've you got there?'

'Just chased a fox,' Jim explained. 'It was carrying this poor little bugger with it. Dropped it to get over a wall and away from me and Fly. I know where it's headed, so we can go lamping tonight, see if we can't get it.'

'And it's alive?' asked Jim's mum, nodding toward the bundle in his arms.

Jim showed them the lamb's head and it let out another bleat.

'That's a bonny-looking one, isn't it?' said his dad.

'It's one of the ones we're keeping on as a tup,' Jim said. 'Looks like we made a good choice, too; it's got some fight in it. I brought it back here because I thought we might need to get the vet out, but I'm not so sure now.'

Jim's dad stood up, and Jim saw pain in the man's face, but said nothing about it, as he came over to check on the lamb himself. He gave it a scratch behind the ears, and it bleated once more.

'I'll call them anyway,' he said. 'I'd rather be sure.'

Then Jim's mum was standing next to him.

'You'd best give that little chap to me,' she said.

Jim was confused.

'What? Why?' he said, holding the lamb a little tighter, like he didn't want to give it up.

'You've seen the time...?'

'No,' said Jim. 'I've been a little bit busy, what with—' And then he saw the clock on the wall. 'Bollocks.'

'You're already late,' his mum said. 'But you still need to shower. You can't go to work like that.'

Jim handed the lamb to his mum.

'I was just about to come out looking for you,' said his dad.

'Harry's going to kill me,' said Jim. 'I won't be there till half nine at least!'

'It's my fault,' said his dad, and he slapped his leg. 'Me and this stupid limb of mine. Why won't the bloody thing heal?'

Jim heard the anger and despair in his father's voice.

'Dad, it's not your fault. I lost track of time, that's all.'

'Either way, you tell Harry this is on me. He can even give me a call if he wants; I'll explain.'

'Okay, Dad,' said Jim, turning on his heels and raced through the house and upstairs to shower, change, and see if he could still do a good impression of a PCSO. His worry was, he was finding it increasingly hard to make it altogether convincing.

ELEVEN

Having given Jim enough extra time to be late for the meeting and still get away with it, Harry had had no choice but to get things underway.

Jen had already taken him to one side for a quick chat beforehand, and explained what had happened the day before with Jim, the sheep, and the couple who had hit one of them. Jim's response was a worry and Harry wanted to know more, but he'd been impressed with how Jen had sorted the situation out; very diplomatic. Until Jim arrived, there was nothing he could do about it all, though.

So, with Matt, Jadyn, Dave, and Jen currently in attendance, they'd quickly got through everything in the Action Book—little more than a follow-up on a car theft and a brawl outside a pub in Askrigg—before getting on with the investigation into what had happened over in Leyburn. Jen had already been updated on it all by Jadyn, which pleased Harry. So, really, all that had remained was to divvy up tasks for the day ahead. Jadyn was, as ever, standing to attention at the board, ready to jot down notes.

'I've had nothing back yet from Sowerby,' Harry said, 'and I don't expect to either. Can't say I'm all that confident about her finding anything, if you consider the damage caused to the victim's body by the fire, but you never know.'

'We're talking about the same pathologist here, aren't we?' said Matt.

Harry ignored him and carried on.

So, that leaves us with the chat you had with our one witness to what might or might not have happened, Mr Bob...' Harry glanced over at Jadyn. 'What was his name again?'

'Thumbs,' said Jadyn. 'Sorry, I mean Ackroyd, Bob Ackroyd.'

'And how did it go?' said Harry.

'He was fairly hungover,' said Dave, jumping in, 'but I think it was pretty useful, though Jadyn would be a better judge of that than I am.'

Jadyn said, 'The night of the fire, he wasn't exactly clear about what he had or hadn't seen and heard, but we managed to get a little bit more out of him.'

'Like what?' asked Jen.

Jadyn put down his pen and pulled out his notebook, flicking through to the page with the notes from their chat with Bob.

'What I've got here is that the voice he heard shout said something like *What are you doing, where are you taking it all*, and *I never did trust you*, or words to that effect. Plus, he's certain he saw something large leave the building, though he was also sure it was quiet as it did so. Oh, and whoever it was who was shouting, Bob said they were cut off, like they just suddenly stopped shouting. He said there was shouting, some laughter, then he described the voice as stopping dead, but after someone hit him with something.'

'They hit him?'

'Bob heard what he described as a hard tap-tap. Maybe it was nothing.'

'There's no such thing as maybe it was nothing,' Harry said. 'Certainly sounds like someone stumbled onto something they shouldn't have, doesn't it? Bit of an argument, someone decides someone else should shut up, then things maybe got violent.'

'That last bit, though,' said Jen, 'about never trusting or whatever it was; sounds like they not only stumbled into something they shouldn't have, but knew whoever it was doing whatever it was they shouldn't have been doing. And I know just how complicated that sounded, but I think it makes sense. Sort of.'

'It does,' said Harry. 'Just. And that thing leaving the ware-house could be a van.'

'Dave and I are going to head over for another look around,' said Jadyn. 'And I need to find out about the CCTV, see if there's anything there as well; I've tried, but still not got through to anyone.'

'Not sure we'll learn anything from it,' said Harry, 'but always best to be thorough.' He looked over to Jen, and handed her an evidence bag containing the postcards Peggy had given them.

'I'm going to be having a chat with Shane and Jack,' he said. 'Assuming, of course, that I can get in touch with either of them.'

'They've not returned your calls, then?' asked Matt.

Harry shook his head, wondering which of the three Bob Ackroyd had heard.

The office phone rang, and Jadyn picked it up.

Everyone stared at the constable as he said very little and listened a lot.

'Who was that, then?' Harry asked when he'd hung up.

'Jim,' said Jadyn. 'Well, not Jim, his mum, actually. There's been some trouble with a fox and a lamb or something.'

'What's that got to do with him being late?' Harry asked.

'I don't know,' said Jadyn. 'She spoke very fast, said it was her and Jim's dad's fault, said you should call them if you need an explanation, then hung up.'

'Well, hopefully, we'll see him sooner rather than later,' said Harry. 'Now, where were we?'

'Shane and Jack,' said Matt.

'That was it,' said Harry. 'Like I said, I've left numerous messages for both of them and Adam, but I've heard nothing back yet. And that's a worry, what with the body and what our friend Bob over-heard. However, at least we have their addresses, so that's something;

I'm going to head over and give them a knock as soon as we're done here.' He looked back at Jen. 'Now, those postcards ... I've been thinking, and worrying, I hasten to add, that even if we are able to have a chat with either Shane or Jack, hopefully both, there's probably even less chance of them knowing where Adam is than Peggy, isn't there?'

Jen frowned.

'Why?'

Harry said, 'If you go away on holiday, do you give your friends the address of where you'll be staying?'

Jen shook her head.

'Why would I?'

'And when you went away this weekend for the run, what then?'

'Actually, that's different,' said Jen. 'Jadyn had to know where I was, what I was doing, race times, everything; he was my emergency contact in case anything happened.'

'So, you've proved my point, haven't you?' said Harry. 'There's no reason really for Adam to have told his two staff the address of where he's staying. Frankly, I can't think of anyone who manages staff who would.'

'You've very suspicious, aren't you?' said Matt. 'What do think they'll do; turn up at your door with all their work problems and ask you to solve them?'

'Exactly that,' said Harry, as though all Matt had done was state the bleeding obvious. 'You go away on holiday to get away from work, don't you? That's the whole bloody point! You don't want the people you work contacting you about why the photocopier isn't working or whatever.' He paused, took a breather. 'Now, being the natural pessimist that I am,' he continued, 'I'm going to assume that both Shane and Jack won't know where Adam is either, especially if you consider that his mum's no wiser. Which means, Jen, that those postcards could well be all we have to go on.'

Jen screwed up her face in disbelief.

'These?' she said, lifting them.

'Exactly those.'

'You're asking me to find someone based on half a dozen post-cards that seem to talk about haggis a little too much?'

'Yes, I am,' said Harry, and smiled. 'I know how much you love a challenge.'

'Do I, though? Really?'

'It'll be a walk in the park compared to what you were doing over the weekend,' said Harry, doing his best to sound encouraging. 'I know it's not much, but what do you think?'

'Well, I'll give it a damned good try,' Jen said.

'Peggy said that Adam's a big fan of Scotland, has been since he was in the Scouts, visits quite often, too. That doesn't mean, though, that he stays in the same place every time, or that there's anything suspicious going on. But we do need to find him. I'm worried we haven't.'

Harry stood up.

'Matt, I want you to go and have another chat with Peggy. Those books are bothering me. See if you can find out more about them, where she buys them, that kind of thing.'

'You really think they're important?' Matt asked.

'I want to be sure either way,' said Harry. 'See if she knows why her son was keeping books in his warehouse.'

'Maybe it was just extra storage,' said Jen.

Harry shook his head.

'I don't think so. Peggy's house is large, she lives on her own, and it was easy to see that she's organised.'

'She's also good at persuading two coppers to do her heavy lift-ing,' said Matt with a laugh.

'Well, at least you'll be useful while you're there, won't you?' said Harry. 'Now, any questions?'

With no one, not even Jadyn raising a hand, Harry turned for the door, only for it to open in front of him and for Jim to step inside.

'You made it,' said Harry, but his words fell on deaf ears,

mainly because Jim started to babble as soon as he closed the door behind him.

'I'm so sorry,' he said. 'I lost track of time. I was out with the sheep, checking for my dad, like, because he's still not quite right, is he? And it was a beautiful morning, and then there was this fox, and it had a lamb, and we chased it, the fox I mean, not the lamb, and the lamb, it was alive, would you believe it? Alive! So, I had to take it back to the house, like, and then its mother followed, so that slowed us down, and—'

Harry held up a hand.

'Jim,' he said. 'Slow down a bit, will you?'

'What?'

'You're talking too fast,' said Matt. 'Anyway, your mum rang. We know what happened. Sort of.'

'I'm really sorry I'm late,' Jim said, his eyes wide and on Harry. 'I didn't mean to be. I ... it's just that ... I mean ... shit...'

Harry frowned, gave the scars on his chin a scratch, then said, 'Let's you and I have a chat, Jim, what do you say?'

He saw Jim's eyes widen at the suggestion.

'What? Why? Am I in trouble? I didn't mean to be late. I'm really sorry, Harry, it's just...'

'It's just that you and I are going through to the interview room to have a brew and a chinwag, that's all,' said Harry. 'Matt?'

'On it,' said Matt, and walked over to the kitchen area in the corner of the office.

'Come on,' said Harry, and gently guided Jim out of the office, down the corridor, and into the interview room.

TWELVE

With tea and biscuits brought in by Matt, Harry poured Jim and himself a mug each, and sat back in his chair. It creaked unnervingly.

'Really need to get new chairs,' he said. 'There's going to come a day where I'm in here in the middle of an interview, and I'm going to wind up on my arse.'

Jim laughed, but Harry noticed the lad's eyes weren't in on it. They were distant, scared almost.

'So, from the beginning,' said Harry, taking a biscuit.

'I'm sorry,' said Jim. 'I really didn't mean to—'

'I know,' said Harry. 'But what I need right now is a bit of background, isn't it? Like an investigation, really; I need to know all the facts, find out what's actually going on.'

'Why?'

'Because I'm your boss, that's why,' said Harry, annoyed that a sharp edge had crept into his words a little too easily, so he eased back immediately, and hoped Jim hadn't noticed too much. 'And because I care,' he added. 'We're a close team, we're friends, so why don't you tell me what's been going on?'

Jim gave Harry a confused look, clearly taken aback.

Harry thought back to what Jen had filled him in on earlier. He was fully aware of how Jim was taking up the slack at home, filling in for his dad, whose injury was taking longer to heal than would've been liked. But then, that was the human body; as miraculous as it was, an injury like that in someone the age of Jim's dad, who had lived a hard life anyway, could take a while to come good. He also wondered if the man was acerbating things by insisting on trying to do things he shouldn't, thereby prolonging the time it would take to heal.

Jim held onto his mug a little longer than usual.

'I just lost track of time, that's all,' he said. 'It won't happen again.'

'I'm going to need a little more than that,' said Harry. 'Details, Jim, details ...'

'I don't know what else to say.'

'How's your dad doing?' Harry prompted.

Jim gave a shrug, but Harry saw worry in his eyes.

'Bad, then?'

'No, not bad,' said Jim, 'not really. I mean, he's fine, isn't he? The injury, it's healing ...'

'Just not fast enough, right?'

'I guess.'

'What hours are you working on the farm?'

'No idea,' said Jim, shaking his head. 'Dad can't get out and about as well as he did, and he gets tired more easily, like, and his fitness isn't what it was because, like I just said, he's not out and about, so it's kind of just snowballing, I think.'

'What about your mum?'

'She's working hard, too,' Jim said. 'We all are, but I'm the youngest, aren't I? I have to do more. I can't not, if that makes sense. They need me to do more, otherwise Dad's never going to get better, is he? And then what?'

Harry said nothing, just gave Jim the floor.

'If he doesn't get better, who's going to look after the farm? Mum can't do it, can she? Not on her own. My brother, he was supposed to be the one who'd take it on, or at least run things in

Dad's place, and then I'd join in, and we'd run it together. That was the plan. But after we lost him, everything changed, and now it's just me. But I didn't want to just go into farming because it was expected, did I? I wanted to do something else, be something else first, and that's what I've done, isn't it?'

'You have, that,' said Harry. 'And you've done it well.'

'And I'll keep doing it well,' said Jim. 'I'll just have to be more organised on the farm, that's all. I've maybe let things get a bit out of hand, if you know what I mean. I can sort that, I'm sure I can.'

'Jim...'

But Jim wasn't listening, he was talking, and his words were throwing themselves out of him with the wild abandon of a runaway train.

'And then Dad'll be better, won't he? He'll be up and at them proper, like, probably fitter and stronger than ever! He's indestructible, I'm sure of it.'

'Jim...'

'You should see him when he's firing on all cylinders! He's up earlier than everyone; carries a bale in each hand like they don't even exist. And his knowledge of sheep farming, the care he has for his animals, it's amazing, Harry, it really is!'

'Jim!'

Jim's mouth fell open, clearly expecting to continue throwing words across the table, but none came out.

'That's better,' said Harry.

'What is?'

'A bit of silence.'

'Oh, I'm sorry, I didn't mean to...'

'Don't start again,' said Harry, a smile creasing his lips as he held a finger up to stop Jim from rambling again.

Jim gave a short nod, grabbed his tea, took a sip, then reached for a biscuit.

Harry gave him a few seconds to calm down a little.

'I'm going to ask you a few questions,' he said, once he'd seen Jim's shoulders relax a little. 'And I want you to answer them honestly. Don't think about the answers. Don't overanalyse what you're going to say. Just answer. Understood?'

'You're going to ask me some questions? Yes, I think so,' said Jim.

'I'm serious, here,' said Harry. 'I want you to answer them from your gut, not your head.'

Jim frowned.

'My gut? Actually, no, I don't understand.'

Harry tapped the side of his own head.

'We think too much sometimes,' he said. 'All of us. We depend on this to the point of ignoring everything else, all the other things that matter. Everyone's guilty of it. We try and pick things apart, take in all the variables, analyse every outcome, then every outcome of every outcome, and before we know it, we're dangerously close to doing the wrong thing because it makes the most sense and has the least amount of risk, instead of the right thing, which doesn't make as much sense, and may end up coming back to bite you on your arse.'

'Okay ...' said Jim.

'Do you see what I'm saying?'

'No.'

'Let me put it another way,' said Harry, wondering how tactful he could be. 'You need to grab life by the balls and give them a damned good squeeze.'

Turns out, not very, he thought.

Jim, who had been taking another mouthful of tea, spluttered at Harry's words.

'What?'

'We waste so much time trying to second guess every possibility,' Harry said, 'that all we really end up doing is freezing up, getting stuck in a rut, and not actually moving on to where we want to be, doing what we want to do, being who we want to be.'

'But I am doing what I want to do,' said Jim. 'Really. If that's what this is about, if you're worried that I'm losing interest in my work, I'm not!'

'No,' said Harry, 'I'm not worried about that in the slightest. You're a bloody good PCSO, one of the best I've ever worked with actually, but let's not get sidetracked, hey? Now, back to the questions...'

'The ones you want me to answer from the gut.'

'Exactly that.'

'I'll try. Sounds a bit philosophical.'

'You won't try, you'll do,' said Harry. 'They're different things entirely. And as for this being philosophical, this is me you're talking to! So, no it isn't. It's just life, that's all, and I'm trying to help you think about what you do with it. Got it?'

'Yes,' said Jim.

Harry placed his elbows on the table, his hands clamped together.

'Are you going to be a PCSO for the rest of your life?'

'What? No, I mean I—'

Harry jumped straight back in.

'What about becoming a constable?'

'We've talked about that before; you know it's not for me.'

'What else do you want to do?'

'I don't know, I mean—'

'Can your parents run the farm alone?'

'No, of course they ca—'

'Would you ever leave Wensleydale?'

'Why the hell would I ever do that?'

'Do you want to take on the farm?'

'I can't.'

'That's not an answer,' said Harry. 'Do you want to take on the farm?'

'I said I can't!'

'That's your head talking, Jim! Come on, from the gut!'

Harry knew he was pushing hard now, but he needed to because he knew that Jim probably needed to face up to a few things.

'But I can't!'

'Why?'

'Because...'

'Because what?'

'Because it was supposed to be my brother, not me, that's why! Bloody hell, Harry! What is this?'

Harry stood up, then leaned forward, his hands on the table, and towered over Jim.

'So, you're going to spend the rest of your life being held back by the ghost of your brother, is that it?'

'No.'

'Is that what he would want?'

'No.'

'Is that what your parents would want?'

'No!'

'So, answer the damned question!' Harry roared. 'Do you want to run the farm or not? From the gut, Jim! The gut!'

'Yes!' Jim said, now on his feet as well, his voice cracking as he shouted back at Harry. 'Yes, of course I want to run the bloody farm! I've always wanted to run it! I grew up there, Harry, it's in my blood! But it was for my brother to do, not me, Harry, not me!'

Harry allowed them both a moment of silence, then sat back down.

Jim hesitated, glanced at the door like he was about to bolt, then sat back down himself.

Harry folded his arms and stared at Jim.

'I'm not telling you to stop being a PCSO,' he said.

'Well, it kind of felt like that,' mutter Jim.

'What I am telling you, though, is that you need to start being honest with yourself.'

'I am being honest with myself.'

'No, you're not,' said Harry. 'I pushed you hard, then, because I needed you to hear your own thoughts out loud. And it sounds to me like you're holding yourself back from the one thing you want to do more than anything else.'

'I love being a PCSO,' said Jim, his voice quieter now.

'Well, believe you me, the whole team loves you being one,' said Harry. 'And I'm not saying you can't be one, either. What I am saying is that maybe we need to look at things differently.'

Jim frowned.

'How do you mean?'

'We've Dave on board now, haven't we?' said Harry. 'None of us expected that, and yet here we are. My advice? Head home this evening and chat with your parents, have a serious discussion about how much you're really needed on the farm, and be honest with them, because you can't do both jobs like you are, or all you'll end up doing is each of them badly. Balance, Jim, that's what we're looking for.'

'I don't know how to make it work, though,' said Jim. 'I've tried, I really have.'

'You've tried on your own, yes,' said Harry, 'so what say we try together? You, me, your parents, the team? What do you think?'

'I don't know...'

'Jim...'

'Okay, sorry, I mean that would be great.'

Harry stood up again.

'Of course, it'll be great, it was my idea,' he said. 'Now, how's about we crack on with the rest of the day?'

THIRTEEN

Having delivered tea and biscuits to Harry and Jim, Matt had jumped into the Land Rover and headed back down the dale to pay a visit to Peggy, over in Caldbergh. The drive was considerably more pleasant than any of the journeys the day before. With the sun fully out, and the roads now burned dry, he wound down the window and rested his arm out in the open to enjoy the cool breeze over his skin. The air was cold enough to sting a little, but he didn't care, and spent a good while just leaning back and letting the Land Rover pull him forward, the sonorous drone of the tyres ever present beneath him.

When at last he came to Caldbergh, he expected the small huddle of dwellings and farm buildings to be as quiet as they had been the day before. And they were, except, that was, for Peggy's house, thanks to who was currently standing at the front door.

Where Matt had parked the day before, two vehicles were now sitting, neither of which looked entirely at home in their surroundings. He drove past, turned around, then did his best to squeeze in after them while also allowing enough space for farm traffic to trundle by if it needed to. He didn't want to annoy any farmers. Matt then climbed out to have a look at the vehicles.

The first was a grubby grey saloon that may have, at some point in its early years, been black. It was hard to tell so pitted and faded was the paintwork, and so unclean. The interior was leather, but worn through to the threadbare cloth beneath. The rear seat was covered in various jackets and bags, the front seat barely visible beneath empty crisp and snack packets. The footwell was home to an almost admirably large collection of drinks cans. Matt didn't want to guess at the smell inside should he be unlucky enough to venture in there.

The other vehicle was the polar opposite of the first. It was small, clean, and new. The kind of car suited to zipping around the streets of a town or a city, and its metallic blue paint reflected the sky. Inside, the car was utterly spotless.

Raised voices caught Matt's attention, and he turned from the two cars to stare over the narrow road and up the path to Peggy's house. He could see that the door was open, but he couldn't see Peggy, bar a tuft of red hair just visible between the front door and the two people he'd spotted standing in front of it, their backs to him.

Matt walked over the road, up the path, and having not had his approach noticed by either Peggy or two individuals standing between her and him, announced his arrival with a cheery, 'Good morning!' and a violent clap of his hands that cut the air like the crack of a whip.

The two figures, who were seemingly caught up in a very important conversation with Peggy, stopped talking and turned to stare at Matt.

Matt smiled, then pointed to the figure on his left.

'Well, you I know,' he said, narrowing his eyes. He then pointed at the other and added, 'But you? Never seen you before in my life. My guess is, though, that the small car is yours, correct?'

The figure on his left, a woman with blonde hair, huge tortoiseshell glasses, tight-fitting denim trousers, and a light blue, close-fitting down jacket, gave Matt a smile.

'It is,' she said. 'And you are?'

Matt ignored the question and turned his attention to the other figure, a tall, thin man with a nose like the beak of a crow, and eyes as warm as a dentist's welcome.

'Hello there, Askew,' he said. 'So, that other vehicle must be yours, right? And I don't think we need to over-analyse how I'm able to be so sure, do you?'

Matt, like the rest of the team, had bumped into Richard Askew enough times to know that when it came to being the kind of journalist no one liked, the man was an expert.

'You know each other?' asked the woman, as Peggy now stepped into view.

'Thank goodness you're here,' Peggy said, looking at Matt. 'These two, they just turned up on my door half an hour ago, and they're both refusing to leave.'

'That's not quite accurate,' said Askew. 'We're happy to leave, once you've answered a few questions.'

'But I don't want to answer your questions,' said Peggy.

Askew responded with, 'Is that because you have something to hide?'

'Of course I don't have anything to hide! You're twisting what I'm saying!'

'Then a few questions won't harm anyone, will they?'

Matt could see a look of exasperation in Peggy's eyes.

'But I don't even understand why you've asked the ones you already have,' said Peggy, 'or why you think you should come into my house!'

Matt pushed between Askew and the woman and stood next to Peggy.

'Right then,' he said. 'Let's all start from the beginning, shall we?'

'Not a problem,' said Askew. 'I'm here about the fire at the warehouse.'

'And we're not together,' said the woman, and Matt saw such a look of disgust flicker across her face that he believed her without question. 'I'm Bryony White.'

'And I'm Detective Sergeant Dinsdale,' said Matt. 'Askew's a journalist, which explains why he's here, poking around in things like a starved rat in a bin bag...' He let that hang for a moment, enjoying the way Askew's eyes narrowed at him. 'So, what about yourself, then, Bryony? What brings you to Caldbergh?'

'I'm a freelance journalist,' Bryony said. 'I provide features for magazines mainly, newspapers occasionally, and news and other websites more often than both put together.'

'Fascinating,' said Matt unconvincingly and not even trying to hide the fact that he was lying. 'But I think it's best if you both leave now, don't you? I'm sure Peggy here has plenty to be getting on with, and that none of it involves you.'

'I'm writing a feature for a coffee magazine,' said Bryony, almost cutting Matt's last word in half. 'I was trying to get in touch with Adam, you see, because his brand is really getting noticed.'

'Did you have a meeting planned with him, then?' Matt asked.

Bryony shook her head.

'This job came in at the last minute, so I dashed over to see if I could grab a few minutes with the man behind it all, but when I saw the warehouse...'

'You somehow ended up here,' said Matt. 'And how did that happen, exactly?'

'She followed me,' said Askew. 'I remembered then that Adam was a witness in a case a while ago. Not sure I actually reported on it, but I like to keep a detailed file on anything important.'

'I bumped into him at the warehouse,' said Bryony. 'Never ignore a good lead, right?'

'I've told you I don't know anything,' said Peggy. 'Please go.'

'But you must know where he is,' said Askew. 'Surely, I mean, he's your son.'

'He's in Scotland, I've told you that!' Peggy replied, the words blurting out of her in frustration.

'But where in Scotland exactly?' Askew pressed. 'Surely you must see how important it is that your son knows about what's happened. What if the fire had spread? People are asking questions. Other businesses on the industrial estate are worried. If it was an accident, what caused it? If it wasn't an accident, then why did it happen at all? What if they're next?'

'And why would they be next?' Peggy exclaimed. 'You're not making any sense!'

'Just asking questions, that's all,' said Askew. 'The public have a —'

'Don't say it,' said Matt. 'Don't you dare...'

Askew turned his eyes to the DS.

'Say what exactly? That they have a right to know?'

'Couldn't help yourself, could you?' said Matt, bristling now. 'And the public doesn't have a right to know. At all. Because it's not about rights, is it? It's about you and ... and...'

Matt took a breath, exhaled, did his best to calm down.

'Ms White, Mr Askew?' he said, his voice measured again. 'I think you've bothered Mrs Heath enough, don't you?'

'You can't arrest us,' said Askew. 'We're not breaking the law.'

Matt rubbed his chin, then looked past Askew to his car.

'You know, I had a little nosy round your vehicle,' he said. 'It looks very similar to one we're trying to trace in relation to another investigation.'

Matt saw Askew's eyes flicker at that, a flash of concern lighting up the deep, cold darkness they sat within.

'What investigation? What do you mean?'

The concern quickly twisted itself with confusion, and if Matt wasn't too mistaken, he saw a faint smile now on the faces of both Peggy and Bryony.

He pulled out his phone.

'Yes, well, I can't disclose that, can I? But that car of yours is very similar indeed. The way I see it, I think I might have to call this in and have it picked up, just to make sure.'

'But it's my car! It lives on my drive!'

'I also noticed that those front tyres are looking dangerous close to the legal limit,' continued Matt, enjoying how wound up Askew was getting, and hoping that he might at any point just pop off like a broken Jack-in-the-box. 'Wouldn't be too surprised either if it's not taxed.'

'Of course it's taxed! You can't do any of this! You're making this all up, every bit of it!'

'Officer Okri?' Matt said into his phone, ignoring Askew and walking back towards the two vehicles. 'I need you to run some plates for me. Got a pen to hand?'

Askew pushed past and was across the road before Matt was even at the end of the path.

'This is harassment!' he called back to Matt, as he yanked open the driver's door.

'Yes, it is, isn't it?' Matt replied. 'In fact, that's exactly what I thought when I turned up here and saw you pestering Mrs Heath. Which is why it's probably a good idea for you to get shifting. By which I mean bugger off.'

Matt watched as Askew jumped into his car, wrestled for a moment with his seatbelt, which refused to clip in, started the engine, and drove off in a deeply unimpressive cloud of dust and scattered grit. Matt turned back up the path and stuffed his phone back into his pocket.

'You weren't talking to anyone on your phone at all just then, were you?' said Bryony.

Matt just smiled.

'Best you get on your way as well, I think, miss,' he said. 'Give Peggy her day back, if you would be so kind.'

Bryony gave an understanding nod, and headed up the path, back to her own vehicle.

Matt turned back to Peggy.

'Right then,' he said, 'how's about we go inside and have a little chat about those books of yours? What do you say?'

FOURTEEN

Arriving at Shane's address, a small, modern house in the village of Spennithorne, Harry knew immediately that no one was home. Spennithorne was yet another place he'd never been to, or at least never stopped in, anyway. It lay just a few minutes away from Leyburn and seemed very content indeed on maintaining its distance.

Harry guessed that the house was a simple two-bedroom, with one of those being barely large enough to fit a single bed. The garden out front was small and neat, a patch of grass kept well. On closer inspection, surprise that it required so little effort, seeing as it was fake. Realistic, yes, but Harry couldn't see the attraction. The curtains were open on both the ground and first floor, and there were no lights on anywhere in the house. Seeing as it wasn't a huge, rambling property with numerous nooks and crannies to hide in, he knew Shane wasn't home.

Walking up to the house, Harry knocked on the door, not because he expected an answer, but more for something to do. Also, there was always a chance that knocking on a door would arouse the suspicion of a neighbour, and thereby act as a nice and very sharp hook to reel them in on, especially if you did it a few times and with enough volume to irritate.

By the fourth knock at the door, Harry was about to give up and head back to his Rav, when a voice called from over to his right. He turned to see a large man with beefy arms folded across his chest staring at him from behind a very well-kept rose bush. The roses weren't in bloom as yet, but the bush itself was so neat, so perfectly kept, that Harry knew it would be a sight to behold once the buds burst. The rest of the garden was much the same, with shrubs and bushes and pot plants all placed as though at any point a photographer for Country Life magazine might just turn up unannounced for a few snaps. The man had the look about him of someone who spent a little too much time keeping an eye on things.

'He's not in,' the man said.

'No, he's not,' said Harry.

'Then what are you doing still knocking? You're disturbing the peace. It's not on.'

Harry left Shane's house and headed over to speak to the man. His approach did nothing to shift the man's glare or his forearms, which he could see, as he drew closer, were covered in tattoos, none of them good. He'd seen similar, usually on lads who'd been behind bars.

'Any idea where he is?' Harry asked.

'Not sure why I would tell you even if I did,' the man said.

Harry decided to play his trump card early and pulled out his ID. He saw the man's eyes widen, then narrow almost immediately, his jaw clenching in the process.

'He in trouble, then?' the man asked.

Harry shook his head.

'I just need to speak to him, that's all.'

'I've heard that before,' the man said.

That response was enough to make Harry wonder if he'd guessed right about those tattoos and where they'd come from.

'When did you last see him?' he asked.

'Yesterday,' said the man. 'He works in Leyburn, something to do with coffee.'

'Rough time?'

'In the morning, eightish.'

'He didn't come home?'

'I don't spy on my neighbours.'

'Does he have a car?'

'Blue Ford Fiesta,' said the man. 'New thing. Very shiny.'

Well, that's something, thought Harry. If they could find that, maybe they'd find Shane, assuming of course, that they hadn't done so already and were simply waiting for the confirmation from Sowerby.

Harry handed the man a card.

'If he does come back, call me,' he said, pointing at the card to make it absolutely clear his number was on it.

The man took the card, but didn't even look at it.

Harry turned around and headed over to his Rav.

'You know what, I've just remembered. There was someone there yesterday,' the man called out as Harry opened the driver's door.

Harry paused, turned round.

'It was early evening,' the man said.

Leaving the car door ajar, Harry jogged back over, and took out his notebook.

'Description?'

'Can't say I got a good look,' said the man. 'Short, black hair, I remember that, but nowt else, really. Couldn't even tell you if it was a man or a woman. They were slim, though. Not like you and I.'

Harry ignored that last comment and asked, 'Do you know what they were doing, why they were here?'

'I didn't go over and ask them, if that's what you mean,' the man said. 'But they kept checking their phone; my guess is that whoever it was, they were trying to call Shane, but he wasn't answering. Maybe they were expecting him to be there or something?'

'Thanks,' said Harry. 'Much appreciated.'

The man's only reply was a grunt as he turned on his heel and headed into his house, shutting the door firmly behind him.

Back in the Rav, Harry headed off to the next address. He called ahead, just in case, but as with Shane, there was still no answer.

The address Peggy had given him for Jack was over in Bedale. The road was the main one through the dale, so leaving Spennithorne, Harry headed east and was soon picking up speed. Here, the countryside was considerably gentler, with rolling fields left and right, and pretty villages with grand houses staring at passersby.

Arriving in Bedale, Harry followed the traffic through the town centre, spotting a chip shop getting itself ready to open for lunch. If he had time, he'd pop in there after he visited Jack's place. No, it wasn't healthy, but he wasn't really in the mood for either a cold, limp salad in a plastic bowl from the supermarket, or a packet of sad, and disturbingly cold sandwiches which had somehow had all the taste removed. Food from a chippy was honest, it was tasty, and it was usually good value.

With that thought fixed firmly in his mind, Harry left the town centre and, a few minutes later, was on a small street of terrace houses, all of them of different shapes and styles. It was obvious to Harry that they were all more than a century old, and he guessed much older still.

Squeezing the Rav between the rear end of a transit van, the bumper of which was hidden behind stickers confusing humour with abuse, and a VW Golf that had been lowered so much Harry suspected it would have trouble driving over a white line, never mind a speed bump, he locked the vehicle and walked along to the second address Peggy had given them.

Arriving at the correct front door, he was as disappointed, if not more so, as when he had arrived at Shane's place in Spennithorne. At least Shane's house looked as though the man lived there some of the time. Jack's house, though, was the exact opposite; the curtains were worn and pulled shut, the door was so battered that it looked like the general way to open it was to give it a swift kick, and the white paint covering the rendered brickwork was peeling badly. This, he thought, was not a property loved by those who lived in it.

Harry walked up to the door and gave it a knock. He wasn't expecting anyone to answer, and no one did. So, he knocked again, harder this time, and was surprised when the door popped open in front of him.

Harry pushed the door open a little further, then leaned his head inside.

'Jack?'

The room was all in shadow and he could make out little beyond the expected rough outline of a sofa, and perhaps a television against a wall.

No one answered.

'Jack? My name's Detective Chief Inspector Grimm. Just wondered if we could have a chat?'

Still nothing.

Pulling a small torch from his jacket pocket, Harry flicked it on and stepped inside. He reached out for the closest light switch, but no sooner had light flooded the room, Harry was tempted to kill it. Yes, there was a sofa, and yes, there was a television, but the room was hardly one that he could ever imagine someone relaxing in. Well, not now, anyway, seeing as the sofa was upside down, and the television had been hit hard enough to smash the screen into jagged shards. The rest of the room was in no better shape, with takeaway cartons of food kicked across the floor and an open bottle of wine on its side, its contents having puddled artistically on the grubby carpet.

Harry looked at the damage, allowed himself a moment to take it all in, from the door to the sofa to another door in the wall opposite, the line of food spilled from the cartons, the bottle of wine ... and he realised something; this wasn't just a burglary, someone had been chased.

Harry was through the other door in a heartbeat, crashing through it with little regard for what was on the other side.

'Jack? Jack! This is the police! Jack!'

The room beyond the ruined lounge was a small dining room. It, too, was in a topsy-turvy state, with chairs on their side, and the table pushed at an odd angle. Another door led to a small galley kitchen, and it looked relatively untouched.

Though, perhaps that has more to do with the mountain of unwashed dishes in the sink, he thought. From the dining room, a narrow set of stairs led up to the bedrooms. Harry took them two at a time.

'Jack? It's the police. Can you hear me, Jack? Jack!'

Something bad happened here, Harry thought. He had no idea what or why, or if it was connected to what had happened at Adam Heath's coffee warehouse, but if Jack was still here, then judging by what he'd seen so far, he had a horrible feeling that Jack might be dead or dying.

Three doors led off of the small hallway at the top of the stairs. The first was for the bathroom, and the smell from it was enough to have Harry stay well clear. The next room was a bedroom, and it was tidy, but only because there was no furniture inside it. It was completely empty and smelled a little of damp. The third door led to another bedroom. Harry found the light switch and blasted the room with brightness.

A clothes rack tossed across the floor.

A small television lying on its side.

Blood splattered on the walls.

A bed, the duvet on the floor.

And there, lying on top of the duvet, was a man in a black hoodie and jeans, face hidden.

Harry dropped to the floor.

'Jack?'

He reached up to the man's neck, checked for a pulse.

'Bloody hell, you're alive, lad...'

Harry pulled out his phone and called an ambulance. That done, his medical training kicked in, not just what he'd learned as a police officer, but the deeper skills of when he'd been in combat. Everything was instinct, like he wasn't even thinking, as he checked the man for broken bones, for injuries, for bleeding. Then, satisfied that there was little he could do until the paramedics arrived, he did his best to make sure the man—he had no idea yet if it was Jack or not—was comfortable, and called Matt. The conversation was short: Matt was on his way.

FIFTEEN

'What an absolute bloody mess,' said Matt, arriving just after the paramedics and joining Harry outside. The place was cordoned off with tape, and the street was lined with goose-necking neighbours trying to see what was going on.

Harry was making a point of keeping out of the way as they dealt with whoever he'd found in the bedroom. He'd done his best to communicate to them that the house was now a crime scene, but understandably, their only concern was the welfare of the person they were there to stabilise and take to hospital, not to preserve possible evidence of what had or hadn't happened. And really, there was only so much they could do about that, as they worked to get him onto a stretcher, down the stairs, and back outside into the waiting ambulance.

'It is that,' said Harry. 'How was Mrs Heath?'

'She needs hired help,' said Matt.

'How many boxes this time?'

'Six. And books are heavy, Harry. No light reading at all.'

'Did she have anything to say about the books found at the warehouse?'

'She thinks they're ones that Adam must've picked up for her from the Post Office and just not got round to dropping them over.'

'Why would they be at the Post Office?' Harry asked.

'If they try and deliver when she's not in, they go back to the sorting office,' said Matt. 'Peggy then has to go and pick them up herself. Adam must've offered to do it for her.'

It was a fair enough explanation, thought Harry. 'Anything else?'

'Journalists,' said Matt. 'Richard Askew, and someone new, called Bryony White.'

'Never heard of her.'

'Same,' Matt said. 'Very much the polar opposite of him, though. She was well dressed, neat, blonde hair, fancy glasses.'

'And Askew looked like he'd just been dragged out of bed by an angry bear?'

'Exactly like that. And I think the bear had chewed on him a little, too.'

'Anyway, back to this place,' said Harry.

'Could be a burglary gone wrong,' Matt suggested.

'That's what it looks like,' Harry agreed. 'Maybe the burglar was disturbed by whoever that is we've just seen carted off to hospital.'

'No ID yet, then?'

'I didn't find anything and neither did the paramedics. I've knocked on a few doors, though. Neighbours said they keep away from the place, mentioned drugs, that the place is always a mess. They've only ever seen one person living there this past year. Their description matches who I found, which isn't saying much.'

'Why's that?'

'Everyone I've spoken to has given me the same description; a man wearing a black hoodie and jeans. That's all anyone could tell me.'

'A little suspicious,' said Matt. 'A hoodie is a great way to stay hidden, it's a good disguise.'

'It is rather,' Harry agreed. 'Anyway, my guess is that it's Jack. None of them have spoken to him, though, said he kept himself to himself.'

'Have you had a good look around the house yet?' Matt asked.

'No,' said Harry. 'Can't say I want to, either. I was waiting for you. Two pairs of eyes, right?'

'Could do with those overalls that Sowerby and her pals are always modelling so well for us,' Matt said.

Harry pulled out some disposable gloves from a pocket, handing Matt a pair.

'These'll have to do, I'm afraid. Sowerby's sending a couple from her team out. Should be here in about an hour or so. As there's no body, she's not needed. And she's still busy with everything from yesterday.'

'Don't envy her that job.'

Gloves on, Harry led Matt around the house, first to take photos of everything they could in each room, then to have another look around, to see if anything jumped out at them to give them some idea of what had happened, all the time making sure they'd didn't disturb anything; neither of them fancied a falling out with the SOC team. He noticed flies this time as well. Probably feasting on the takeaway leftovers, he thought, and had been disturbed by all the comings and goings.

By the time they'd finished a circuit of the house, Harry was still none the wiser. And that bothered him.

'Something just doesn't smell right,' he said, standing outside again with Matt.

'There's nothing in that house that is even close to smelling right,' said Matt. 'And it's not like Jack, assuming that was him, wasn't at least trying.'

'How do you mean?'

'There's cleaning stuff in the bathroom,' said Matt. 'Plenty of it, too. It just hasn't made any difference. Means the pipe work is probably shot, the whole suite needs replacing, the stink is in the floorboards, the brickwork...'

'What I said about you getting distracted...'

'Yeah, sorry,' said Matt. 'Kitchen is the same, though. Yeah, there's a pile of stuff in the sink to be washed up, but it's only a couple of days' worth. I had a proper look, and there's stuff on the draining board clean and dry. And those takeaways in the lounge? I think they were piled up neatly before they were kicked over during whatever happened in there.'

'All very interesting, but not really what I mean,' said Harry, but he logged what Matt had said just in case it was important later on. 'This is wrong, but I don't know why, not yet anyway.'

'Explain,' said Matt. 'Verbalise it. Might help.'

Harry laughed.

'How's that funny?'

'That's pretty much what I had Jim do back in Hawes before coming here,' Harry said. 'He was over-thinking everything, so I decided to push a few buttons, if you know what I mean, see if I could get it out of him, what the problem really is.'

'And did you?'

'I think so.'

'He wants to be on the farm, doesn't he?'

'He does, but he also wants to be a PCSO, part of the team. It's a tough call.'

'It is, but fair enough, like,' said Matt. 'That lad's an excellent PCSO, but farming, that's where he belongs, really, isn't it? Can't escape the fact, not that he wants to. We can all see it. And it's always been just a matter of time before he admitted it to himself.'

'Don't think he's quite there yet,' said Harry. 'Not far off, though. I said for him to have a day just out and about, being a visible PCSO presence around the villages, popping into shops, talking to people, that kind of thing. It'll do him good, keep his mind busy. Then, when he's done, I've asked that he chat with his parents tonight about it all. I said that we, as a team, need to see what we can do to come up with something that'll work.'

'Part-time, you mean?'

'Possibly,' said Harry. 'But we'll discuss that later. Focus, Matt...'

'Me? You're the one who mentioned Jim.'

'What do you think, then?' Harry asked. 'About what happened here? Any ideas?'

'There's a good chance it's exactly what it looks like,' said Matt. 'But I know what you mean about something seeming wrong somehow.'

'Why?'

'Well, just look at the place!' said Matt. 'Why would anyone want to break in, in the first place? What's there to nick?'

'That's exactly what I've been thinking,' said Harry. 'So, my first thought is drugs, obviously. We'll have to wait for the SOC folk to see if they can find anything, though.'

'There's no smell of it in the air,' said Matt. 'Not sure we'd notice, mind.'

'Cannabis? There is on the street though,' said Harry. 'But that doesn't mean anything. I'd be more inclined to think whoever broke in would've been after product with a higher street value, maybe even cash.'

'We need to talk with Jack, then, don't we?' said Matt.

'We do,' said Harry. 'He wasn't conscious when I found him and still wasn't when the paramedics managed to get him out of there.'

'Must've been a hell of a beating.'

'Judging by the state of the house, I think that's a safe assumption.'

Harry had seen plenty of beatings in his time, and this one was definitely up there with the most serious. Someone had really gone to town on Jack, and Harry guessed he was lucky to be alive. And that thought raised a question; why had they stopped short? Why go so far, then stop? That was hard to do when the rage took over and the red mist came down.

'So, what now?' Matt asked.

Harry went to answer Matt's question, but was interrupted by his phone buzzing in his pocket. He pulled it out.

'It's Jen,' he said, glancing over at Matt as he answered the call, putting the detective constable on-screen so that he could actually see her, rather than just hear her voice.

'So, Jen, what have you got? Anything useful? I could do with some good news right now.'

'Well, I've got those postcards in front of me and if I'm right, a lead, I think,' said Jen.

'Really?'

'Don't sound so surprised!'

'I'm not surprised at all,' said Harry. 'I knew you'd come up with something. Well done.'

Jen laughed.

'What is it you always say? Detective, remember?'

That made Harry laugh as well.

'Well, get to it, then,' he said. 'What is it you've called to tell me?'

'So, those postcards, I'm going to assume you noticed that they're all scenery ones, yes?'

'Are they? Can't say I took much notice.'

'Well, they are,' said Jen, lifting the postcards up to show Harry what was on them. 'And the location of each of the photos is written on the individual cards themselves. We've got the Three Sisters, Loch Atriochtan, Buachaille Etive Mor, Loch Leven...'

'All very interesting,' said Harry, already wondering where this was going, his impatience kicking in a little too keenly. 'But how's any of that helped? You said you had a lead. Cut to the chase, Jen ...'

'The photos on the postcards are all from famous scenes in the Highlands,' Jen said. 'More specifically, we're talking mainly in and around the valley of Glen Coe.'

'Has she got something?' Matt asked, and came around to stand next to Harry. Wafting a hand in front of his face, he muttered, 'Bloody flies ...' He turned the wafting into a wave at Jen; Jen waved back.

'Well, she's just given me the whistle-stop tour of the sights of

Glen Coe,' said Harry, thinking of Gordy, who'd always spoken fondly about the area.

'Lovely place, that,' said Matt. 'Joan and I travelled up there years back, like, before she was in the wheelchair. Only seems like yesterday, really. Funny that, isn't it, how time just buggers off? Had a great time. The mountains are stunning. Got plenty of walks in, lots of camping out in the hills. And the Clachaig Inn; what a place! We ended up dancing a few nights away there, I can tell you. So much whisky...'

Harry held up a hand to stop Matt from talking.

'So, you've narrowed it down to Glen Coe,' he said, talking again to Jen. 'That's a fairly huge area, you know.'

'That's just from the photographs on the postcards, though,' Jen said. 'There's more detail in what Adam's written on them.'

'You've an address?'

'No, but I've got plenty of other clues.'

Harry laughed at that.

'What's so funny?'

'That word,' he said. 'Just makes it sound like you've gone all Agatha Christie on me. But go on, what are they, these clues?'

'There's mention of a bridge,' said Jen, 'a hotel by the loch, a chippy that serves battered haggis—'

'This is Scotland we're talking about,' Harry sighed. 'My guess is there's not a chip shop in the whole country that doesn't serve battered haggis.'

'Battered haggis?' said Matt, a little too enthusiastically. 'They do that at the chippy in Hawes as well, you know. Love the stuff. And you really need to try the battered Wensleydale cheese.'

'No, I don't,' Harry replied. 'I've seen it on the menu, even witnessed people order it, but think I'll be giving it a miss.'

'You don't know what you're missing.'

'I do.' Harry focused again on Jen. 'Sorry, you were saying?'

Jen took a moment to twig, clearly distracted by Matt's sudden focus on haggis.

'What? Oh, right ... So, the chippy, yes, plus there's mention of lots of other little details, because these are postcards, right? And if you think about it, what you put in postcards, well, it's details about where you're staying, what you've been up to, that kind of thing, isn't it?'

'This is going somewhere, isn't it?' Harry asked.

'It is,' said Jen. 'Ballachulish, to be exact.'

'Never heard of it.'

'Doesn't matter. It's a little place, just past Glencoe village, which is where Gordy grew up, you know.'

'Did she?'

'Yes,' said Jen.

'She talked about the Highlands a lot,' said Harry. 'And I thought she was going to head back there more than once, but I never realised it was her actual birthplace.'

'You learn something every day,' said Jen.

'But it's a little far away for us to go knocking on doors, isn't it?' said Harry.

'For us, yes, but for Police Scotland, no.'

Harry frowned.

'This is really good, Jen, and I do mean that, but I'm not sure we can just phone Scotland and ask the local police to go and knock on every door in the hope of finding our Mr Heath to tell him his warehouse burned down, that we found a body inside, and to ask why he won't answer he's bloody phone!'

'They won't need to,' said Jen. 'Ballachulish isn't very big. There are only so many cottages rented out as holiday lets. I don't know if I got them all, but it doesn't matter now, anyway.'

'What? Why?'

Harry was beginning to feel like he was being given a lesson in detective work by someone many years his junior and with considerably fewer years on the force.

'Because I've got an address, Harry,' Jen said. 'That's why. I know exactly where Adam Heath is staying.'

Harry couldn't believe what he was hearing.

'And you've done all of this from those postcards I gave you?'

'I have,' said Jen. 'Not saying it was easy, but I know where he is.'

'I'm ... I'm speechless.'

Harry could see the beginnings of a smug grin on Jen's face. And it deserved to be there, too, he thought.

Jen said, 'So, if you're happy with all that, am I okay to call Police Scotland and ask them to go and see if he's in? I've got the number for the Fort William office.'

'I was called in to help with another case up that way a while ago,' Harry said, recalling a helicopter trip that, even with his history in the Paras, had his knuckles go white. 'Can't remember exactly when. A missing kid, if memory serves.'

'Was that one of those times where you told us you'd be away for a bit, disappeared, then came back, and said nowt about what you'd been up to?' Jen asked.

'Yes,' said Harry, without elaborating on the case itself. 'I briefly met one of the DCIs working with the Major Investigation Team out of Inverness; Logan. And by briefly met, I'm not even sure we spoke to each other.'

'What was he like?'

'Angry,' said Harry. 'Looked it, anyway.'

'And you didn't speak?' Matt asked.

'I was there to pick up the kid, that was it. It wasn't a social call where you exchange phone numbers and photos of your family.'

'Not a word, though? Nothing at all?'

Harry could see that Matt was having trouble accepting this, and Jen also looked a little baffled.

'I think we maybe nodded at each other. I flew there in a helicopter. He met me there, I took the kid, that was it.'

'Networking isn't one of your strong points, is it?' said Jen, then added, 'Can we do that now? Fly there by helicopter, I mean. That would be awesome, wouldn't it?'

'Not a chance of it,' Harry laughed. 'Anyway, you phoning is a lot quicker and quite a few quid cheaper, so do that now, if you could.'

'On it,' said Jen, and hung up.

The screen on Harry's phone turned dark. He shook his head in disbelief and looked at Matt.

'Whatever that was, it was genius,' he said. 'All she had was postcards, Matt; postcards!'

Matt was given no chance to respond as a large white van pulled up behind Harry.

'SOC team are here,' Matt said, as Harry turned around to see the van come to a stop. 'What do you want to do?'

'Head back to the office,' said Harry. 'By the time we've arrived, Jen might have even more good news for us.'

SIXTEEN

Harry couldn't believe what he was hearing. Having spoken with Jen before driving back to Hawes from Bedale, he'd been close to what he would regard as a good mood. That didn't mean he was all smiles, just that he was calm and didn't feel as though his next course of action would have to involve ripping a door off its hinges just to make himself feel better. Now, though, having listened carefully and calmly to what Jen had just said, it was all he could do to not grab a table and throw it through a window.

What he and Matt had found in the house in Bedale was certainly confusing, and he'd spent the journey back up to Hawes mulling it over and talking it through with Matt. It bothered him that what the house presented didn't seem to quite add up.

On the one hand, it seemed to be a complete pigsty, and by all accounts was occupied by someone with a drug problem. But on the other, there was evidence of someone who was neat and tidy, who stacked takeaway containers and washing up, who had bleach in a bathroom even if that bathroom was rotting around them. The confusion around all of that had, however, been balanced out by Jen's sleuthing in finding out where Adam Heath was staying in the Highlands. And all from postcards, too, which had been not just surprising but damned impressive.

When Harry had last spoken to Jen, she'd been about to call Police Scotland to see if they could send someone from Fort William to knock on the man's door. It should've been one of the Uniforms, but a Detective Constable Tyler Neish, who was down from Inverness, had been sent around instead. Apparently, he'd been heading out that way anyway, to follow up on something to do with a case he was involved with as part of the Major Investigations Team. Harry had never met Neish, but he doubted he'd ever forget his boss, Logan. Few people he knew had a stare on them that could match his own, but Logan? In spades...

Neish's journey from Fort William to the address in Ballachulish had tied in very neatly with Harry and Matt's own journey from Bedale to Hawes, and they'd arrived just a few minutes after DC Neish had turned up at the address they had for Adam Heath. And it was from that point on that everything had gone from high-fives to horseshit in a heartbeat.

Harry sat himself down, slowly, deliberately, calmly. It took quite some effort, considering what Jen had just told him.

'Run that by me again,' Harry said, and watched Jen's eyes flick from him to Matt. 'And slowly. I need to take it all in, just to make sure I'm not in some bad dream right now, because it certainly bloody well seems like it.'

Jen coughed to clear her throat.

'DC Neish said there was a fire. At the house in Ballachulish.'

'A fire,' said Harry. 'At the house where our Mr Adam Heath is supposedly staying.'

'Yes.'

'And when was this fire?'

'Last Friday. So, five days ago.'

'And we're absolutely sure it's the same house? You're positive about that?'

'Yes,' said Jen, and Harry could tell she really didn't want to, the weight of that one word like an anvil slamming into the office floor. 'DC Neish apologised for not realising.'

'Not realising what?'

'That it was the same house. A couple of the uniform officers had been called out to it. Neish knew about it, but it hadn't clicked until he arrived on the scene.'

Harry rubbed his eyes, suddenly tired. He was moving into a new house in a few days, had things to sort out, to check, and yet here he was dealing with an investigation that was very quickly spiralling, but into exactly what, he didn't even want to guess. Whatever it was, his gut was telling him they were already a long way past it being good.

'Fair enough,' Harry said, and with all the effort he could muster, encouraged Jen to continue with what she was saying. 'I know you've told me it all already, but I really need to hear it again, Jen, just so I'm clear.'

'The fire was reported late in the evening,' said Jen. 'Emergency services were called, the fire dealt with. As I've just mentioned, a couple of the Uniforms from Fort William were in attendance. Once the fire was dealt with and the property investigated, a body was found. The crime scene has been processed, and the body is now with the pathologist.'

'And we think it's Mr Heath?' Harry asked.

Jen shook her head.

'As yet, they don't know. It looks that way, for obvious reasons; he's down as the person staying in the cottage, after all. No ID was found on or near the body, and nothing has come back yet from the pathologist.'

'Did DC Neish say when they were expecting to hear from the pathologist?' asked Matt.

'Early afternoon today apparently,' said Jen. 'There's been a delay, bit of a backlog something. He also said ... No, it doesn't matter.'

Jen clammed up.

'What doesn't matter, Jen?' Harry asked.

'What DC Neish said.'

'If he said it, I want to know it,' said Harry. 'Out with it, Jen, right now.'

Jen opened her mouth, closed it again.

'Jen ...' Harry said, his voice low, his eyes narrow.

'Okay,' said Jen. 'He said that the time difference might mean we get it little a bit later than he said.'

Harry did a double take.

'The what now?'

'Time difference,' said Matt.

Harry gave Matt enough of a hard stare to have him mouth an apology, albeit one nearly invisible due to the barely concealed smirk on his face.

'Scotland's a different country, but it's not like it's on the other side of the planet!' said Harry, his eyes on Jen.

'I pointed that out,' Jen replied.

'And what did he say?'

'Something about having to fly if you want to get to England, so there must be a time difference. Apparently, that's obvious.'

Harry decided it was best not to try and make sense of that, but instead to focus on where the investigation was heading. And right now, that looked likely to be up in Scotland. It was years since he'd last been north of the border. He doubted the place had changed much; mountains, rain, midges, rain, haggis, rain, more mountains and a lot of moorland and bogs, and of course, rain.

Harry checked his watch. The time was just creeping past one-thirty.

'It's early afternoon now, isn't it?'

Both Matt and Jen checked their own watches and nodded in agreement.

'Mind you,' Harry added, 'we need to take account of that time difference, don't we? So, shall we say it's three?'

Harry was frustrated. Waiting was not a skill he had ever really honed with any degree of success. And yet, here he was, with little choice but to do exactly that.

They were waiting on Jadyn and Dave, to hear if they had anything to report from a round of knocking on doors or from the

CCTV. He didn't expect them to come up with much from either, but he was doing his best to be hopeful.

They were waiting on Sowerby and her team, not just from what they had found at the warehouse, and anything on the body discovered in the ashes, but also what they might uncover at the house in Bedale.

There was Jack, or who they assumed was Jack, now in hospital, and they'd not be getting anything from him until he was in a fit enough state to answer questions about just what the hell had happened.

And now, they were waiting on forensics from a fire in Scotland where the owner of the burned warehouse had been staying, and at which another body had also been found.

'Matt,' Harry said, looking now at the DS and thinking a distraction might be useful. 'I meant to have us stop at a chippy on the way back, but I forgot.'

'Is that a subtle hint?' Matt asked.

'Subtle? No.'

'Hungry?'

'Very. And I can't think straight if my stomach's interrupting.'

Matt was already at the office door.

'Any requests?'

'Do you know anything by Britney Spears?' Jen asked.

Matt looked thoughtful for a moment, then said, 'No, but I do a fantastic rendition of Heaven is a Place on Earth, by Belinda Carlisle.'

Then he was gone.

'That's already an image I can't get out of my head,' said Jen.

'Serves you right for letting him put it there in the first place,' said Harry, pushing himself up and out of his chair to go and make a fresh pot of tea while they waited on Matt to return. 'You want one?'

'I'll sort it,' said Jen, and she started to walk over to the small kitchen area, but as she did so, and came towards Harry, he noticed something.

'You're still feeling it, then?' he asked. 'The race?'

Jen was filling the kettle.

'No, I'm fine,' she said. 'Really. And I think calling it a race is a bit of a stretch. More of an experience.'

'That why you're walking like someone's filled your shoes with pins, is it?'

'It's better than it was.'

'Is it...'

'Ish.'

Jen grabbed a couple of mugs.

'How's the house move going?'

'You're changing the subject.'

'I could ask how your running is going instead, if you like?'

'And I can answer both questions at once,' said Harry. 'Just fine.'

'Fine?'

'Yes, fine.'

'Fine's a bit of a non-word, isn't it?' said Jen. 'One of those noncommittal, doesn't really say much, wishy-washy words, if you know what I mean; the kind of word you say through pursed lips or gritted teeth, or with just enough edge to make sure the person asking the question shuts up.'

Harry smiled.

'It didn't work, then, did it?'

'No.'

The kettle boiled and Jen made them both a mug of tea.

'How's Jim?'

'I don't think he's in the best of places right now,' said Harry, taking his mug and sitting down again. 'But he'll be alright.'

'He wasn't himself at all yesterday,' said Jen. 'Not seen him like that before; thought he was going to lamp the bloke.'

'Violence is never the answer,' said Harry.

At that, Jen's laugh came out sharp like the bark of a dog.

Harry did his best to look hurt by what he knew that laugh implied.

'What?' he said.

'Nothing,' said Jen. 'Something caught in my throat, that's all.'

'Really? And what's that, then?'

Jen wasn't given time to answer as Matt entered the office.

'I come baring gifts,' he said.

'By which you mean pies and cakes from Cockett's, I hope,' said Harry.

'I do.'

Matt handed Harry a white paper bag dotted with spots of grease and for the next few minutes, they sat in relative silence, munching away.

By the time Harry had finished, a quick glance at his watch told him it was now gone two.

'Wonder if I should ring this DC Neish,' he said.

'Give him till half past,' said Matt. 'Just to be on the safe side.'

Harry stood up.

'Think I'll get some fresh air,' he said, walking over to the office door. 'I'll be just out the back, so if he calls, come and get me.'

Outside, Harry took a short stroll into the small car park sandwiched between the rear of the Fountain Inn and the community centre. The air was cool, damp, and sweet, and he breathed deep, as he allowed his eyes to rest on the vista before him.

As views went, Harry thought, the very modest car park was unduly blessed. With pastures dipping down to the rush of the Ure, he cast his eyes up past the distant slate roofs of Hardraw to Stags Fell, the road leading to Buttertubs Pass cutting a thin, grey line across its craggy slopes. Looking left, he could rest his eyes on the distant vale of Cotterdale, and if he looked right, the long trench of Wensleydale beckoned. The peace of the place was not one of pure silence, and Harry took a moment to just stand and listen to lambs calling for their mothers, a kite cutting through the air in search of prey, the distant thrum of a tractor taking feed to the flock, and the river high and bouncing.

Sending a quick message to Grace, just to check in, Harry was about to give her a call, if only to hear her voice, however brief the chat, when Matt shouted for him.

Harry turned away from the view and went over to the DS.

'Jadyn's called, says they've had no luck with either knocking on doors or the CCTV.'

'No surprise really,' said Harry.

'Except,' said Matt, 'that the CCTV cables looked like they'd been cut, and fairly recently, too.'

'Well, now that is interesting,' said Harry.

'Also, DC Neish just called,' Matt continued, and Harry noticed a change in the tone of his voice, a hesitancy almost. 'He's just sent through what they've got. Pathology, crime scene report, photographs, the usual.'

'And?'

Matt said nothing, just stared back at Harry. And there it was.

Something heavy sunk hard and fast in Harry's stomach.

'What is it, Matt?' Harry asked. 'What's happened? What's wrong?'

'It's not Heath,' Matt replied.

'What?'

'The body in the house, the one we thought Adam Heath was staying in? It's not him, it's not Adam.'

'Then who the bloody hell is it? And where the hell is Adam?'

'They don't know.'

'Bollocks!' roared Harry, not at what Police Scotland had told them, because he had nothing but confidence in that, but at the fact that no matter where they looked they kept coming up against yet more stuff that made no sense, not one single bit of it. Every part seemed to have absolutely no connection to any other part, and yet he knew it was all connected, because of course it was. But how, that was the problem.

'Harry,' Matt said, 'you took the word right out of my mouth.'

SEVENTEEN

'And you have to go right now?'

Harry could tell that Grace wasn't happy. And he couldn't blame her either; he wasn't exactly bouncing with enthusiasm about what he had to do, either.

He was standing in the kitchen at Grace's house in Carperby, leaning against the worktop, with Grace standing opposite. Most of the cupboards and drawers were empty, much of the house, like his own, packed away in boxes. Smudge was leaning against his leg; she knew he was leaving and was clearly not happy about it either. Harry would miss her as well, which still surprised him, because he would never have believed before that a dog could become so important in your life.

After Matt had delivered the news from Scotland, about what had been found at the house in Ballachulish, he'd run through everything that had been sent to them by DC Neish. It had been enough, once he'd stopped swearing, to have him ask Jen to find accommodation in the area for that same night. Matt had tried to persuade him to give it a day, but Harry was impatient to keep things moving, worried that with so much up in the air, if he stopped, he'd lose sight of some of it.

They had a burned-out warehouse and body number one, what

looked to be a violent burglary, three missing persons of interest, and now another fire and body number two at the address one of those persons of interest, the actual owner of the destroyed warehouse, was supposed to be holidaying at. There was no getting away from the fact that this second body was directly linked to the investigation, so whoever it was, and whatever had happened to cause this second fire, it meant that Harry had to head north.

'The sooner I go, the sooner I'm back,' he said. 'Sorry, Grace. And I really do mean that. Sometimes, this job ... Well, you know.'

'It's not your fault, I know it's not,' Grace replied, and he could see in her eyes that she genuinely meant that, despite the irritation in her voice. 'I'm just concerned, that's all.'

'There's nothing to be concerned about.'

Grace stepped across the kitchen, close enough for Harry to kiss, but he stayed where he was.

'There's everything to be concerned about,' she said. 'You do know that's how relationships work, right? You look after each other; that's what you do.'

He did know that, yes, but it was still taking some getting used to.

'I just don't want you worrying unnecessarily,' said Harry. 'It's a long journey, I know, but Jen's sorted out somewhere to stay, and everyone's favourite constable, Mr Jadyn Okri, is coming along with me. And very excited about it he is, too, I might add.'

'Well, that's something,' said Grace. 'You can share the driving.'

'Exactly. Plus, Jadyn's very good at not knowing when to stop talking, so as annoying as I'm sure it'll be at points, at least he'll keep me awake when it's my turn behind the wheel.'

Grace laughed, and the sound was enough to make Harry's stomach flip. Then she leaned over and kissed him.

'If I'm ever in a coma, come in and do that,' he said, 'and I'll be awake in a heartbeat.'

'What? Laugh?'

Harry returned Grace's kiss.

'If only you knew,' he said.

A horn sounded from outside the front of the house.

Harry checked his watch.

'Fingers crossed we get there before midnight,' he said.

'Where are you staying?'

'There's a hotel in Ballachulish itself,' said Harry. 'Sits right on the loch. View should be nice, anyway. And no doubt the breakfasts will be huge.'

'Jen was lucky to get you both a room each.'

'It's a quiet time of the year,' said Harry, walking into the hallway to open the door, Grace behind him, Smudge at his side. 'Give it a couple of months, and there'd be no chance, not at such short notice.'

'I'd come with you,' Grace said, 'but this house won't pack itself.'

'There's not much left to do, though, is there?' said Harry, opening the front door.

Jadyn waved from his car.

'Let me know when you arrive.'

'Of course,' said Harry, and he gave Smudge a head rub, then stole a final kiss from Grace, which lingered a little longer than he'd expected. He then left the house and jumped in next to Jadyn, throwing a small bag with a change of clothes over his shoulder into the back seat.

'Ready?' Jadyn asked.

'Not in the slightest,' said Harry, shuffling about to get himself comfy. 'You know the way?'

'North, right?'

'That should just about do it. When you see mountains touching the sea, we're there.'

'Really? That's amazing!'

Harry smiled, sent a farewell wave to Grace, then leaned his seat back just enough to make falling asleep a little easier. Late afternoon had already waved goodbye, and evening was just around the corner. He wanted to get a decent kip in as soon as he could, even if he wasn't that tired.

'Wake me in a couple of hours,' he said. 'Or sooner, if you need a break.'

'Mind if I put something on to listen to?' Jadyn asked, pulling the vehicle away from Grace's house and heading back up the dale.

Harry narrowed his eyes at the constable.

'If it's death metal or similar, I'm going to be very unhappy, Constable, very unhappy indeed ...'

Jadyn shook his head.

'Actually, it's a podcast,' he said.

'A Podcast?' said Harry, fairly sure he knew what one was, though he'd never listened to one himself. 'What's it about?'

'Conspiracy theories,' Jadyn explained.

Harry laughed at that.

'You mean like the moon landing being faked, the Earth being either flat or hollow or both at the same time and filled with lizards, that kind of thing?'

'Funny you should mention lizards.'

'Is it? Why?'

'The next one's all about how the Royal family, and how some people think that's what they are.'

Harry frowned.

'Do I need to be worried here?' he asked.

'What? Why?'

'I'm not going to wake up and find you wearing a hat made out of tinfoil, am I?'

'What if they are lizards, though?' asked Jadyn. 'Have you ever thought of that?'

'No, Jadyn, I haven't,' Harry said. 'And you know what? I never will.'

Shaking his head, as much in bafflement as in amusement, Harry closed his eyes.

'Two hours,' he said. 'Then we swap.'

'Two hours,' said Jadyn.

And for some reason, as Harry drifted off, all he could think about was a nice evening walk through Hawes with Grace and

Smudge, and a couple of pints at the Fountain Inn. Absolutely bliss.

WHEN HARRY AWOKE, he felt like he'd only just closed his eyes, but judging by the view through the window, that was very much not the case. Instead of little stone cottages and the green fells of Wensleydale, all he could see was traffic, and plenty of it. The outside world was bright, artificially so, thanks to the head-lights keeping the growing darkness at bay.

'Where are we?'

Jadyn leaned forward as though not entirely sure himself.

'Glasgow,' he said, his tone less than convincing.

Harry sat up.

'You're positive about that?'

'Well, if it's Edinburgh, I definitely took a wrong turn at some point.'

Harry shook his head.

'Of course it's Glasgow,' he yawned. 'But that's not two hours from when we set off, is it? How long have you been driving?'

'Just over three hours,' said Jadyn. 'I didn't want to wake you.'

'What? Why?'

Harry was groggy from his longer-than-expected nap, and a little annoyed that Jadyn hadn't done as he'd ordered.

'Actually, I did try to a couple of times, but you were having none of it. Kept right on snoring.'

Harry's annoyance was swiftly replaced by embarrassment.

'I was snoring? I don't snore.'

'How would you know?'

'Grace would've told me.'

'I wouldn't worry,' said Jadyn. 'It was fine. Not very loud at all. Hardly noticed. More like a cat purring.'

Harry rubbed his eyes, yawned, stretched.

'A cat purring? I'm going to pretend you didn't say that.'

'Me too,' Jadyn agreed.

'Any problems?'

'None,' said Jadyn. 'Sailed through actually; this is the busiest it's been. That's why I kept driving; wanted to make the most of the clear roads.'

'Well, as soon as you can find somewhere to stop, do so; I'll do the next leg.'

'I don't mind, really,' said Jadyn.

'Well, I do,' replied Harry. 'Anyway, I could do with a toilet break.'

'Actually, so could I,' said Jadyn. 'I've been holding on because I didn't want to disturb you.'

'Just so long as you've not had an accident.'

'Not yet, I haven't,' said Jadyn, then pointed at a sign ahead for motorway services. 'There we go, we'll stop there.'

The stop at the service area was brief enough for a toilet stop and to grab a snack, but also long enough to horrify Harry with the clattering cacophony of the place. Not just the cars either, filling the air with irritated horns, the squeal of breaks, and the stink of exhaust, but the crowds. There was a grumbling sea of people washing in and out of the service area, returning to their vehicles with the flotsam and jetsam of modern society on the road carrying over-sized coffee cups, burgers in paper bags, and carrier bags of snacks.

Harry was pleased not only to be leaving the service area, but to be driving, and soon had them back with the river of traffic flooding north, crossing the Clyde on the Erskine bridge to break apart on the opposite side. He declined Jadyn's offer to listen to more of his podcast, instead opting to have the window down despite the chill in the air. Then, as dusk closed its eyes and the darkness of the night drifted across the sky, the still, black surface of a loch rolled up to the roadside to greet them.

'Loch Lomond,' said Harry. 'Been years now since I last drove along here.'

The road thinned and became the twisting body of a giant grey snake, its tarmac skin glistening in the moonlight as it followed the shoreline. Further along, to their left, the land was of woodland and rock, around which shadows wrapped themselves like cloaks, and rivulets spun watery threads across the road, silver in the gleam of the headlights. Harry saw thick moss on the trunks of trees, with new life bursting from branches.

'Was that a holiday?' Jadyn asked.

Harry laughed at that.

'What's so funny?' Jadyn asked. 'People do go on holiday you know.'

'Can't remember when it was, but I was up here for winter skills training or whatever it was called, back in the Paras. So, definitely not a holiday, not by any stretch of the imagination.'

'Really? What was that like?'

'Cold,' said Harry, the memories floating to the front of his mind with ease.

Ahead, a newer section of the road seemed to bow out over the edge of the loch, giving Harry the odd sensation that he was flying rather than driving.

'What did you do?'

'Fieldcraft, a lot of tabbing, jumping in and out of helicopters, that kind of thing,' Harry said. 'If you could ignore the cold, the discomfort, the fact that everything was soaking wet, the food, it was all rather exciting at points.'

'Tabbing?'

'Tactical advance to battle,' said Harry, the words tripping off his tongue like he still used them every day. 'Basically, a fast march carrying your gear.'

'Fun?'

'Like I said, we were wet and cold, and the march had our feet in bits, every muscle hurting, the weight of the gear rubbing our shoulders raw, no sleep, living on rations...'

'That's a no, then.'

Harry gave a shrug, the corner of his mouth daring to hint at a smile. He closed his window, the cold wind blowing in baring sharp teeth keen to bite.

'I loved it,' he said.

Eventually, the road left Loch Lomond behind and in thick darkness Harry drove on, the headlights slicing off bright fragments of the scenery through which they were travelling. Coasting past the edge of Crainlarich, Harry pushed on towards Tyndrum.

'Shame it's so late,' he said, and pointed ahead to petrol pumps and a restaurant with only security lights showing through its windows. 'If I remember correctly, that's the Green Welly, and it serves some of the best filled rolls and pastries I've ever had. Or that's how they tasted, anyway, especially on the return journey to weary soldiers with empty bellies and aching bodies.'

Harry took a right towards Glencoe, and with Tyndrum disappearing in the rear-view mirror, the countryside grew wilder still, and he noticed the wind picking up a little, buffeting the car as they went.

When they came to Rannoch Moor, Jadyn had at last drifted off. Harry was tempted to wake him, but thought better of it. The moors were hauntingly beautiful, their bleakness unbowed by time and humanity's weak and futile attempts to tame them; Jadyn would see them tomorrow anyway, and in daylight, the vastness of their spectacle could really be appreciated.

Speeding over a narrow single-span bridge, the road empty, the night's thick darkness seemed to be swallowed by something ahead which stood darker still. Harry would not have known the name of it had it not been for the postcards Jen had used to find Adam Heath; Buachaille Etive Mor was a vast thing of rock, sitting as an ancient protective sentinel at the gates of the valley of Glencoe.

This last part of the journey made Harry slow down, not just because the road twisted in on itself, but also because even in the dead of night the cathedral-like splendour of the place demanded to be noticed.

As he drove through the valley, he couldn't shift the sensation that the mountains on either side were, as they had done for millennia, quietly watching, observing his passing like that of so many before him.

At last, the hotel came into view and Harry eased the car to a stop.

Jadyn stirred.

'My turn to drive?' he asked, sitting up.

'We're here,' said Harry.

'Dark, isn't it?' Jadyn yawned.

Harry opened his door.

'I suggest we make the most of it and get our heads down as quick as we can. Come on...'

Inside the hotel, bright lights assailed them, but the friendly face of a young woman at the reception desk welcomed them and soon Harry was in a clean room with a view of the loch, its oily surface speckled with stars.

He fell asleep to the sound of wind whipping through the masts of yachts moored in the still, sheltered waters of the bay beside the hotel, and the call of gulls dancing somewhere far and high in the dark.

EIGHTEEN

Thursday morning found Matt unhappy and uncomfortable, standing in a room in white overalls and rubber boots, his mouth and nose hidden behind a facemask. He'd dabbed enough vapour rub under his nose to unblock the London sewers, but he could still smell the place. He knew the insidious stench would follow him as well, that it would seep into his clothes, become at one with every stitch and thread.

'How are you doing over there?'

The question was from a similarly clad figure standing opposite on the other side of a metal slab, which was draped with a white sheet.

'I'm good,' Matt answered, the pungent odour of the mortuary mixing not only with the vapour rub, but the unmistakable smell of burned flesh, like a barbeque that had been left out in the rain.

The room was eerily quiet, but then he would've been considerably more disturbed had it been filled with noise; the dead, at least, were silent.

Bright lights in the ceiling cast everything in sharp relief and Matt felt as though he had walked into a high-definition photograph. All colour was bleached out of the space, and there were no windows to the outside world; he might as well have been miles underground or even on the moon, for all the difference it would've made.

'You were saying Harry couldn't make it, which is why you're here in his place.'

'He's in Scotland,' Matt said, wondering what made someone like Rebecca Sowerby want to be a pathologist. 'The Highlands, to be more specific. That's why I'm here.'

He wanted to ask, to allow his sudden morbid curiosity to pry a little, but decided it was perhaps best to keep quiet.

Sowerby's forehead creased into a confused frown.

'Scotland? Well, that wasn't the answer I was expecting at all.'

'It's a long story.'

Sowerby raised her hands with a shrug.

'Doesn't look like we're going anywhere or have anything better to do.'

Matt wasn't so sure about that last point, and quickly explained.

'Another fire and another body?' said Sowerby, frowning. 'But that's ... Well, I don't know what it is.'

'Weird, that's what it is,' said Matt.

'I'm going to assume Harry's done a lot of swearing.'

'An awful lot, yes.'

'When's he due back?'

'My guess would be as soon as he can. He's the house to move into, as well as all of this to be going on with.'

'That's right, I'd forgotten about that.'

Matt didn't want to say, but he was starting to wish Sowerby would just get on with why he was there. That they were enjoying a chat when between them lay the body of someone burned to a crisp struck him as strange, but then the world of a pathologist was completely alien to him. He had no frame of reference, no way to really grasp what attracted someone to it as an occupation. To Sowerby, though, Matt knew that this was simply a place of work and she was doing her job; a chat in the workplace was no different to himself having a natter in the office in Hawes.

Sowerby reached her hands out and grabbed the top of the sheet.

'Ready?'

Matt was given no time to answer as she lifted the sheet, then very carefully eased it downwards, to reveal what lay beneath.

'Bloody hell,' Matt muttered, staring at what was now lying in full view, instinctively lifting his hand to cover his mouth in shock.

Sowerby glanced across at him, and Matt saw genuine concern in her eyes.

'Like I said, you didn't have to come.'

'I did,' said Matt. 'And you know why.'

Sowerby gave a knowing nod.

'So, it wasn't just because Harry ordered you to, then?'

'No,' said Matt. 'Though he did, but that goes without saying.'

'I can see why you work so well together, then,' said Sowerby, and she reached for a clipboard lying on a trolley to her side to check it over.

'We're not just investigating an event that stands apart from people,' said Matt. 'All crime has an impact. Someone, somewhere, is the victim. Whoever they are, whatever they've been through, they deserve our time and our respect. Even more so when they're gone for good. I need to be here, to let whoever this is know that we're all working to find those responsible.'

'And he certainly is that,' said Sowerby. 'Gone for good, I mean.' The comment was flippant, but her tone wasn't.

'What have we got, then?' he asked. 'Not that we're expecting much.'

Sowerby's eyes widened in mock horror.

'Well, thanks for the vote of confidence,' she said.

'You know what I mean.'

Sowerby was quiet just long enough to make Matt feel uneasy, so he was relieved when she spoke again.

'First of all, I can give you a name.'

Matt wasn't sure he'd heard right. The warehouse had been

pretty much burned to the ground, and the victim little more than an oddly shaped lump of cinder.

'A name? How?'

'Driving licence,' said Sowerby. 'Back pocket. He was found lying on his back on the concrete floor. Despite the heat of the fire and the very obvious damage you can see, the licence was actually very well protected, mainly because it was in this...'

She handed Matt an evidence bag. Inside, he saw something metallic about the size of a credit card.

'And what is that?'

'Radio interference identification or RFID wallet,' said Sowerby. 'Stops people being able to steal your data and then hack into your bank account, that kind of thing. Combine the fact that it's metal with where it was located, resting between the body and the floor, and that was enough to keep the driving licence relatively damage-free. Here...'

She handed Matt another evidence bag.

Matt swapped it with the one containing the wallet.

'Shane Dissall,' he said, reading from the card inside the wallet and getting a close look at the black and white photo. It was a little melted, but he could still make out the image of a man with shoulder-length hair and high cheekbones. He couldn't help that the next thought to enter his mind was that Shane looked exactly like the kind of person who would wear a man bun. His date of birth put him in his mid-twenties. 'Well, that's two down, anyway.'

'How do you mean?'

'The warehouse,' Matt said. 'The coffee business that occupies it belongs to a Mr Adam Heath. He runs it with two staff, Shane Dissall and Jack Moffatt.'

'Which one are you still looking for, then?'

'The owner, Adam, it seems,' Matt said. 'Jack's currently in hospital after what looks like a burglary that took one hell of a violent turn; he's lucky to be alive, I think. And like I said earlier, we thought Heath was in Scotland, but apparently not.'

'Any idea who the other body is?'

Matt shook his head.

'Hopefully, Harry will have something on that later today.' He looked back down at what was left of Shane. 'I'm going to assume it was smoke inhalation that got to him first?'

'A fair assumption, but a wrong one,' said Sowerby. 'There's a hefty whack of drugs in his system.'

'Drugs? What kind?'

'Combination of methamphetamine and cocaine.'

'That doesn't sound like fun.'

'I suppose that all depends on what you're into,' said Sowerby.

'Not that,' said Matt.

'There was enough to knock him unconscious. Plus, the team found traces of both drugs throughout the building, and especially so in the charred remains of some of the sacks carrying the coffee beans.'

'Some?'

'Yes,' said Sowerby. 'Most were just coffee beans, but some were very much more than that.'

'Not sure I understand.'

'What it looks like is the packages containing the drugs were hidden in the middle of the sacks.'

Matt thought about that for a moment.

'Shipping containers can easily carry hundreds of coffee bean sacks,' he said. 'Keep the ones containing the drugs away from the doors and there's probably little, if any, chance that dogs would be able to sniff it out.'

Sowerby said, 'I was looking it up, how cartels use coffee to smuggle drugs; some have even had people hollowing out the beans to fill with whatever product it is they're selling.'

'Bloody hell,' said Matt, trying to get his head that.

'Amazingly, it gets even more interesting.'

Matt was immediately suspicious. He had a strong feeling that his and Sowerby's definitions of that word were poles apart.

'How do you mean, more interesting?'

Sowerby pointed a gloved finger at Shane's left temple.

'Hard to see with all the damage, but he's been shot twice at close range.'

Matt frowned. Yes, the head, indeed the whole body was a mess, but even as he stared at the blackened mess of Shane's skull, he wasn't seeing the kind of damage he would expect for someone to have taken two bullets at close range.

'But I can't see an exit wound,' he said. 'Two shots would cause catastrophic damage as they came out the other side, wouldn't they?'

'Depends on a lot of things, that,' said Sowerby. 'The calibre, the size of the cartridge, range at which the shots were taken. These were .22, close range. Powerful enough to penetrate, to kill, but not to travel all the way through. Both rounds were lodged close to the other side of his skull. Look...' Sowerby held up another bag and inside, Matt saw two small lumps of metal. 'There's not much in the way of deformation.'

Matt stared at the bag.

'So, Shane here was drugged and then shot in the head? Twice? There's being thorough and there's whatever the hell this is.'

'What are you thinking?' asked Sowerby.

Matt remembered what Jadyn had been told by Bob, about how he'd heard what he thought was someone getting hit twice by something. But how had all of this gone from a warehouse fire to two bodies, one of which had a couple of bullets in his head?

'Why use a .22?' Matt asked, the question rhetorical, because he didn't expect Sowerby to have an answer. 'In fact, why drug him, then shoot him? Why was the warehouse on fire? Why did you find drugs in the coffee? Just what the hell is any of this? And how does it all link to another body in a fire in Scotland?'

'A puzzle is what it is,' said Sowerby, and reached for the sheet to pull it back up to cover Shane's body.

Matt stepped away from the now-hidden body, then turned and headed out of the mortuary. Sowerby followed and in the room outside stood with him for a moment, neither of them saying anything. Eventually, Matt managed to gather himself enough to remove the white overalls and rubber boots, the face mask ripped off and thrown in the bin, along with the gloves. The smell, though, was still with him, and he'd be washing everything he was wearing as soon as he returned home after work. Though perhaps washing wasn't enough, he thought, burning might be more effective.

'Well, you've certainly got something to talk to Harry about, haven't you?' Sowerby said. 'Though I don't envy you that.'

Matt squeezed his eyes shut, then rubbed them hard in the vain hope that in so doing he would somehow force everything he'd just learned into a neat line that led directly to the reason behind all of it happening.

'How's the family?' Sowerby asked.

Matt smiled at that.

'Nicely done,' he said.

'What?'

'Change of subject.'

'In a place like this, you learn how to switch off,' Sowerby said. 'Like a television, if you know what I mean? You can't go taking it home with you. And you're no use to anyone if you do.'

'They're fine,' Matt said. 'Thanks for asking.'

'That's good,' said Sowerby. 'Can't be easy though, mixing being a parent with doing what you do.'

'I've learned to switch off as well,' said Matt with a smile. 'But even if I hadn't, when I get home and I open the door, and Joan and Mary-Anne are there waiting? It's all gone. All of it. I don't let the work follow me back. Never have done, though that's not to say it hasn't tried to push its way in.'

'It does try its hardest, doesn't it?'

'Very much so,' Matt agreed. 'But it hasn't got a chance, not against what I have waiting for me at the end of every day.'

Outside, Sowerby followed Matt back to the Land Rover.

'Give Harry my regards,' she said. 'And wish him well with the move.'

'Not sure he'll want them, considering what it is I'll be telling him.'

Matt opened the driver's door and stepped up into the cabin to drop in behind the steering wheel.

'Thanks,' he said.

'Just doing my job.'

'Aren't we all?' Matt replied, and a moment later, was heading back to Hawes.

NINETEEN

The morning was bright and Harry, with breakfast shovelled into his face, was standing out in the sheltered bay beside the hotel. The water was still, and to his amazement, among the moored boats, the brown heads of two seals were bobbing cheerily, both staring up at him as though they were expecting something.

A family arrived, a couple in their early forties, Harry guessed, and their children, two boys with bright blonde hair, all carrying bags, which they quickly unloaded to reveal towels and swimming gear. Their excited laughter at what they were doing caused the two seals to pull their attention away from Harry, but they didn't move away.

A few minutes later, the family was all changed and gingerly making their way to the water's edge. Harry had expected to see them in wetsuits, but instead, and with squeals and howls as they entered the water, the man and the two boys were in swimming shorts, the woman in a swimming costume.

Watching them slip into the water, Harry was reminded of Semerwater, and not just his own first dip in the lake, but Ben's. The memory reminded him of how distracted and depressed Ben had seemed while helping him pack; he'd have to check up on him when he was back, make sure he followed through and talked with Liz when she got home.

'They're mad,' said Jadyn, coming up to stand beside Harry. 'Must be freezing.'

'Don't fancy a dip yourself?'

Jadyn shook his head.

'You should give it a go, though,' said Harry. 'Feels amazing when you get out.'

'It's the getting in that's the issue.'

The seals watched as the family swimmed, and Harry smiled as their laughter skimmed across the water's surface towards an island set out in the loch. Then they all came together, floating in a close circle, and the man revealed a small waterproof camera, attached to what looked like a large, yellow fishing float. His arm out in front of him, he took a photo. Harry knew how much it would be treasured, though couldn't help but notice a faint pang in his chest, the sadness he generally ignored that his own childhood had not been as happy.

'What's the plan, then?' Jadyn asked.

Harry checked his watch.

'We're just waiting, that's all,' he said. 'One of the local team is bringing a file down for us on what they know, and will show us round the house.'

Harry watched the family swim back to land and emerge from the water, skin pink with the cold, all of them laughing as they tiptoed across pebbles to wrap themselves in towels. The woman was first to be dressed and was soon pouring something hot from a flask into plastic mugs. From the smell, he knew it was hot chocolate.

'Any news from Gordy?' Jadyn asked.

'Some,' said Harry, not wishing to share everything the DI had told him, not just in texts either, but phone calls, some of them long enough to require two mugs of tea.

'How's she doing? Can't be easy, after, well, you know...'

'I do,' said Harry, and appreciated Jadyn mentioning Anna's death. 'And she'll be okay, I'm sure.'

Jadyn was quiet for a moment.

'Anna was brilliant,' he said eventually. 'I really feel for Gordy. No idea how you're supposed to deal with something like that.'

'A day at a time, that's how,' said Harry, 'and by leaning on friends and family. No other way.'

Jadyn then turned to look up at Harry. He looked strangely serious, Harry thought, as though in that moment he'd aged a decade or two, and gained the experience that comes with it.

'Well, if there's anything she needs, any help I can, well, you know ... just ask, and...'

Jadyn's voice faded then, and he shuffled awkwardly.

Harry smiled, gave the lad a nod, then tapped him gently on his shoulder with his hand.

'I'll let her know,' he said. 'She'll appreciate hearing it, I'm sure.'

The family were all fully dressed now, though the youngest of the two boys, who was also the skinniest, was shivering through his laughter.

Harry heard footsteps. Turning around, he saw a tall man with broad shoulders heading towards them from around the corner of the hotel. He was wearing a dark thigh-length jacket and heavy boots. Harry noticed how the man's shoulders were rounded forward a little, almost as though he was trying to make himself seem less imposing. Wasn't working at all, Harry thought, not with a stare on him like he had; eyes keen as a hawk's, jaw set firm. He had short black hair, styled, Harry guessed, by a towel and being short on time.

'DCI Grimm...'

'That'll be me,' Harry said, turning to meet the man as he approached, and as he did so, realised something. 'DCI Logan...'

The other man furrowed his brow deeply.

'Aye,' he said, then gave a knowing nod as he stared at Harry. 'Helicopter, right?'

'It was. Couldn't stretch the budget that far this time, though.'

'Knew I recognised the name.'

'Not one that's easy to forget,' said Harry. 'Much like my face.'

Harry saw Logan's granite-like expression crack just enough to show the human beneath.

'Not my place to say, but fair enough.'

'You'd be surprised how many people are convinced it's theirs, though.'

Harry felt sure he saw the hint of a smile at that.

Logan came and stood with Harry, who introduced Jadyn.

'Long way to come,' Logan said, and handed Harry a file.

'We were expecting a uniform,' said Harry.

'Makes two of us,' said Logan, hands now shoved deep into his pockets. 'Most were called away to an incident near Oban. I recognised your name. I was down here, anyway, figured I could do with the drive over and some fresh air.'

'Not a swim, though?' Harry suggested.

The look on Logan's face was enough of an answer.

'Come on,' he said, turning on his heel. 'House is just a walk away.'

Following Logan, Harry, with Jadyn at his side, left the laughing family behind, and crossed the hotel car park. Logan led them through an underpass and soon they were in Ballachulish itself, passing a small supermarket, before arriving in the village and walking alongside the sports field in the centre.

'Football pitch?' Jadyn said.

'Shinty,' Logan replied.

'What's that?'

'Violent,' said Logan. 'House is just up ahead, on the right.'

As they neared the house, Harry flicked through the file Logan had given him. And it didn't tell him much.

'Iain McKenzie,' he said, looking at the scant information in front of him; a grainy photograph, and the briefest of biographies.

'Ring any bells?' said Logan.

'None,' said Harry.

'I had a look myself. No idea why an unemployed oil rig worker from the Fort, with a reputation for violence, petty theft, and drugs, would be shacked up here.' He pointed ahead to a small road that dipped down a shallow hill into a cul-de-sac of single-storey dwellings. 'There it is, or what's left of it, anyway.'

'What's the Fort?' Jadyn asked.

'Fort William,' said Harry.

'It likes to think of itself as a town as grand and important as Ben Nevis, which it sits in the shadow of,' said Logan. 'It isn't.'

'That pie shop still there?' Harry asked.

'Nevis Bakery?'

'That's the one.'

'You've been, then?'

'Years ago.'

The house was a shell, and there was really nothing else Harry could say about it. The roof had collapsed, the windows shattered, and the air was still tainted by the tang of burning.

Closing in on the building, Harry read through what they knew about McKenzie. He was fifty-six, had spent his whole life working on the oil rigs, had a police record comprising to drunken brawls and illegal gambling, divorced, and up to the moment he'd wound up dead in a cottage in Ballachulish, living off disability benefit.

'If he lives in Fort William, then what's he doing here?' Harry asked, still reading.

'Aye, that's a mystery,' said Logan. 'We should have more soon, bank and phone records, that kind of thing. It'll take a while, though.'

Harry wasn't listening. He was reading the cause of death.

'He was shot?'

'Double-tap to the head,' said Logan, tapping his own head with a finger. '.22 calibre at close range. You've seen as well that he had enough cocaine and meth in his system to fly to Mars and back and not know.'

Harry glanced again at the photograph and stared for a

moment at a man with dead eyes, sunk deep in a face weathered and jowly and scarred.

'Anyone been round to chat to folk yet?' he asked.

Logan shook his head.

'Figured you could get on with that,' he said, then glanced at his watch. 'Anyway, I'd best be going. Things to do, bad people to arrest, that kind of thing. Let me know if you need anything. Probably won't be able to help, but it'll make us both feel better if we at least show willing, won't it?'

'Appreciate you coming out,' Harry said, unable to avoid the sinking feeling in his stomach that for the effort of getting there, the time it took, all he'd really gained was more confusion. And he certainly didn't have time to hang around to see what else he could find out.

Logan shook Harry's hand, gave a polite nod to Jadyn. Then, as he made to head off, Harry had an idea.

'About that knocking on doors you just mentioned,' he said, and turned his gaze upon Jadyn.

Logan did the same.

'You thinking what I'm thinking?'

'Something gives me the impression we'd probably do that a lot if we actually worked together.'

'That's a bloody terrifying thought.'

'Isn't it?' said Harry.

TWENTY

With Harry and Jadyn up in Scotland, Jim out and about up and down the Dale, and Matt having taken Harry's place by visiting Sowerby and then taking the afternoon off, Jen had spent Thursday manning the office. And seeing as she was still a little stiff from the run, at least she had a bit of privacy to do a bit of stretching.

The post-run euphoria she had fully expected to experience had yet to truly arrive, and of that she was pleased. Happy she may have been to have even just survived the race, but as yet, she'd not put her name down for another similar event. Jen was happy for things to stay that way for a while as well, and so, when the day had finally come to an end, she'd headed home to set about planning some routes for her training over the next few weeks. She didn't want to lose fitness, but she also knew it would be impossible to maintain the pace and sheer ferociousness of what she'd been doing.

There was also the chance that she might need to go shopping for some new gear. That would mean a trip over to the Castleberg Outdoors shop in Settle. The thought made her grin; the shop was an Aladdin's cave of brightly coloured kit, and she knew how easy it would be for her to justify buying so much. She would have to be careful. Or maybe she wouldn't...

When she'd arrived home, Jen had been greeted by a quiet and still house. Changing out of her work gear, and under the watchful gaze of Steve, she'd then wondered if Jadyn would be popping over when he and Harry finally arrived back from their trip north. It would be late, so, while hanging out some washing in the back garden, she sent him a text, just to say it was okay, and to let himself in if there was no answer because she was in bed. She'd then headed back inside, sat down on the sofa, and immediately fallen asleep.

When she eventually woke up, Jen found the house in darkness, the night having crept up nice and close while she'd been out for the count. She checked her phone, saw that the time was well past ten. How could she still be so tired? What the hell had that running event done to her?

Ruined me, that's what, she thought, aware then of just how cold she felt, and groggy. In fact, she was fairly sure that she felt worse than ever, and was a little annoyed that she hadn't been able to stay awake, because she knew that she probably wouldn't sleep properly that night, which would then have an impact on the following day. And she really did need to get running again, to remind her legs what they were for.

Jen checked her phone. There was a short message from Harry to say he was on his way back and another from Jadyn. Only his reply to her text confused her .

'Not back for a few days. Will keep you posted. Give Steve a hug for me.'

Not back for a few days? But why? As far as she knew, Harry had met with someone from Police Scotland, and as per his text, was now heading back less than impressed with what he'd learned.

Jen replied with a text to ask what was happening. Jadyn called her to explain.

'You're working with Police Scotland, then?'

'Not exactly,' Jadyn said. 'I mean, I've been told I can use their office in Fort William, so that's good, but I'm being left to my own devices, really.'

'Where are you staying?'

'Same hotel you booked us into,' said Jadyn. 'It's not quite the holiday season yet, so they've plenty of rooms going.'

'But what are you actually doing?' Jen asked, shivering at the cold in the house. 'I thought Harry had been given the information about the body in the house.'

'He has,' said Jadyn, 'but he wants me to see if there's anything else I can find out about him, knock on a few doors, ask questions, that kind of thing. There's no one up here to do it ... Well, there is, but they're all busy, and it's our investigation anyway, isn't it?'

Jen couldn't hide the fact she was disappointed she wouldn't see Jadyn for a few days.

'You've no idea when you'll be back, then?' she asked.

'It'll only be a couple of days,' said Jadyn. 'Harry's asked me to keep him up to date with everything. Shouldn't think it'll be more than a couple of days, though.'

Jen noticed something in Jadyn's voice.

'You're enjoying yourself, aren't you?' she said.

'I am! This is like proper detective work, isn't it?' Jadyn said. 'I know I'm just uniform right now, but that won't be forever, will it? This is great practice for whatever I do next.'

'You can be and do whatever you want,' said Jen. 'If you want to stay in uniform, that's fine. If you want to do something else, be a detective maybe, then why not?' She'd always suspected Jadyn was mindful of the career ladder in front of him, and knew it was only a matter of time before he climbed up to the next rung.

'Have you ever been up here, to the Highlands?' Jadyn asked, but didn't wait for an answer. 'It's beautiful. The mountains are amazing. There must be running events up here, mustn't there? You should have a look. Check tonight. And if there is, we could come together, couldn't we? I know it's miles away, takes forever to get here, but it's worth it. You'd love it. And haggis is delicious!'

Jen laughed at Jadyn's excitement, not just for the work he was doing for Harry, but for the trip he was very clearly planning as they spoke.

'We can talk about it when you get back,' she said.

The conversation continued a little while longer, and when it was done, Jen didn't feel so bad about Jadyn being away after all. It was good to miss him, and a trip to Scotland together sounded like a great idea.

Quickly nipping through to the kitchen to grab something for dinner, and still smiling from the conversation with Jadyn, Jen had headed back through into the lounge, only then noticing that the patio doors were still open, she walked over to swish them shut.

Well, that explains why I feel so cold, she'd thought, but as she shut the doors, she noticed something was wrong.

Steve...

Jen glanced around the room.

Steve was usually lounging around on the sofa, but he was nowhere to be seen. And a lizard of his size was next to impossible to hide.

'Steve?'

Jen did her best to ignore the rising panic now reaching up through her stomach to clutch at her chest.

'Steve!'

Jen checked everywhere in the kitchen, then raced around the house, looking in each room, checking under beds, in cupboards.

Steve was gone. That damnably grumpy lizard and his chip on his shoulder about Jadyn muscling in on his territory had done a runner.

Jen's panic ratcheted up a notch as she ventured into the garden.

'Steve!'

She realised that shouting his name would do no good. He knew it, but he'd never been all that keen on responding to it unless he was sitting right next to you, and that in responding, he would be presented with something edible.

Jen ran around the garden, checked bushes, behind the shed.

'Steve! Where the bloody hell are you? Steve!'

The realisation that the lizard had gone walkabout twisted

Jen's stomach violently enough to have her drop to the ground into a crouch. She knew it was patently ridiculous to have so much affection for a creature that generally viewed her with barely disguised disdain, but he was still her lizard, and she wanted him back.

Jen pushed herself back to her feet.

First port of call was the neighbours, and heading back inside the house, she made her way to the front door, only to have a call come in on her radio, which was upstairs in the bedroom.

She raced upstairs and answered it. A few minutes later, and with a couple of quickly written notes stuffed through the letter-boxes of her neighbours to ask them to check their gardens and sheds and garages for Steve, Jen was on her way over to Caldbergh.

It was only when she reached the tiny hamlet itself that she realised, having had the afternoon off, Matt was the one on duty and he should've taken the call. But she was there now, so instead of worrying about it, she climbed out of her vehicle and headed over to the house.

TWENTY-ONE

'Mrs Heath?'

The red-headed woman had opened the door somewhat abruptly, and Jen had found herself staring up into eyes not wide with anger or fear, as she had expected, but indignation and fire.

'I've a fresh pot of tea on, and please, call me Peggy.'

Jen followed Peggy into the house, closing the door behind her with a soft swish across thick carpet. She was worried about Steve, but managed to push that concern to the back of her mind.

He'll be fine, she thought. She just had to hope that someone would stumble upon him over the next day or two, before he made his way into open countryside. If he found himself among sheep, then it would certainly give the farmer something to talk about. She smiled.

In the house, Jen was led up a couple of flights of stairs and into a small office. The walls were lined with books.

'It's like a library in here,' she said, taking a seat.

Peggy clapped her hands together and smiled, also sitting down.

'It is, isn't it?' she said. 'And I do love a good library or bookshop. I've spent some of the happiest days of my life in such places.'

Jen caught sight of some of the titles, all classics, and most looked to be bound in hardback, with a good number sporting gold leaf lettering down their spines.

'Maybe you should take me through what happened?' she said, as Peggy poured out two mugs of tea, then held out some biscuits to which Jen held up a hand in refusal.

'What?' said Peggy. 'You've no more on you than a bird. A biscuit will do you good.'

She has a point, Jen thought; there was only so much healthy food and clean living anyone could do without going a little mad. She reached for a biscuit.

'Two,' Peggy insisted, and shook the biscuits.

Jen took another.

'Now,' said Peggy, 'do you want me to show you where it happened or to tell you about it first?'

'We could do both at the same time,' Jen said.

Peggy clearly agreed, as she was immediately on her feet and at the door.

'Upstairs,' she said. 'Bedroom.'

Jen followed Peggy up another flight of stairs, impressed not only with the house she was in, but the speed at which Peggy moved. This was not someone who spent her twilight years busy doing nothing; she was obviously active and fit.

At the top of the stairs, and past a small bathroom, Peggy led Jen into a room at the front of the house. She saw a dark patch on the carpet, spreading from inside the bedroom, out across the threshold of the door, and onto the landing, which contained two bookcases, a table laden with photographs, and a collection of walking sticks and skis leaning up in the corner.

'That,' said Peggy, pointing at the dark patch, 'was where they were. Gave me the fright of my life.'

'Maybe best if we start at the very beginning,' Jen said, taking out her notebook. 'First, what time was this?'

'I think around ten,' Peggy said. 'Couldn't say for sure, though. There's a few clocks in the house, but none of them are ever right. And I absolutely refuse to go to bed with my mobile phone. Bad for your health, is that, always thinking about it, checking it; impossible to have a good night's sleep with it in the room.'

'You were in bed, then?' Jen asked.

Peggy shook her head.

'I was, but I wasn't. I'd headed to bed early, bit of a sore head, you see, and when I've a headache, often the only way to deal with it is to have a lie-down. So, I'd come to bed at nine, settled down, but then I'd not been able to get to sleep. Figured a hot water bottle might help. I've a kettle in my bedroom as well, what with all these damned stairs and not wanting to be up and down them unless I really have to, so I was up and boiling some water. And the wind! It was rattling my windows terrible, so that didn't help either.'

'What happened then?'

'I filled my hot water bottle, not too full because I'm always wondering if it's going to burst in the middle of the night when I'm asleep, then climbed back into bed. And that's when I heard it.'

'Heard what?'

'Footsteps,' said Peggy. 'And I knew that it wasn't Adam because he's in Scotland, isn't he? And I'm fairly sure he'd let me know if he was popping round, instead of sneaking around the place in the dark.'

'What did you do?'

'My door was closed,' said Peggy. 'I'm not one for leaving doors open at the best of times as it is; nobody likes a draft, and it'll give you a sore neck, too. But I could hear whoever it was climbing the stairs. The only thing I had to hand was the kettle, so I grabbed it.'

Jen yawned.

'Sorry about that,' she said. 'Can you repeat what you just said? Not sure I heard you correctly.'

'The kettle,' said Peggy. 'I sat up in bed and reached out for it. No idea what I was thinking I could do with it, but I wasn't about to scream out and tell them where I was, and neither was I going to be empty-handed if they decided to pop their head round the door.'

Jen jotted everything down.

'So, you're in your bed, you're holding your kettle, and someone's coming up the stairs,' she said. 'Then what?'

'They popped their head round the door,' said Peggy.

'Oh.'

'Oh, indeed.'

'And what did you do?'

Peggy reached for the kettle.

'I flicked on my light to give them a bit of a shock, then threw this at them,' she said, as though it was the most normal thing in the world to do, then pointed at the spout. 'See that? It broke when the kettle bounced off them and hit the wall. Now I'm going to have to buy a new one because I can't use this anymore, can I? It'll dribble all over the place.'

'Then what?'

Peggy put down the kettle and clapped her hands.

'They screamed,' she said. 'The water was still boiling, wasn't it, what with me having just filled my hot water bottle? And after that, I'm not too sure.'

'How do you mean?'

'There was the screaming, and I'm fairly sure that they stumbled backwards out of the bedroom to the stairs. I didn't follow, not right away, but I heard them trip up as they ran. Then there was more screaming.' Peggy rested a hand on Jen's arm. 'You know, I actually felt quite bad, then, about throwing the kettle? The boiling water must've been very painful. But they shouldn't have tried breaking in, should they? That was very silly.'

'Do you have any idea why they were here?' Jen asked.

Peggy shook her head.

'The funny thing is, for the past couple of weeks or so, I've been wondering if there's been other break-ins, but I've always thought it was maybe just my old mind playing tricks, being forgetful, that kind of thing.'

'Not sure I understand,' said Jen. 'You didn't mention this to DCI Grimm or DS Dinsdale.'

'I didn't really think to,' said Peggy. 'Things have been going missing, or been moved about.'

'What kind of things?'

Peggy waved a hand dismissively.

'It's nothing, I'm sure.'

'You've had an intruder in your bedroom,' said Jen. 'And now you're saying that other odd things have been happening; it is very much not nothing.'

'There's been books out of place,' Peggy eventually said, 'but that could be me, couldn't it? Sometimes I've gone to get food I'm sure I've put away only to find it missing, or somewhere else, but then I've probably eaten it or moved it. Sometimes, I get so busy that I can never remember what it is I've eaten.'

'Food?'

'Bread, tins of things, nothing expensive.'

'And how often has this happened?'

Peggy frowned, as though suddenly pondering a very difficult crossword clue.

'I honestly can't say,' she said. 'More than twice, less than a dozen.'

'Is there anything else you can remember or that you need to tell me?'

'Like what?'

'Did the intruder leave anything behind, perhaps?' Jen asked.

'I don't think so, no,' said Peggy. 'The only damage was the water all over the floor and my poor kettle.'

'Did you get a good look at them?'

Peggy shook her head.

'It all happened so quickly,' she said. 'One minute I'm sitting on my bed, gripping my kettle. Next thing, the door's opening, and I've thrown the kettle as hard as I could at their gloved hands.'

'They were wearing gloves?'

'I think so,' said Peggy. 'Yes, they were. Definitely.'

'How can you be sure?'

'There was stitching down the sides. That's a strange detail to remember, isn't it? But I definitely saw stitching.'

'What about what they were wearing? Their hair, maybe, their shoes?'

'I'm afraid it was all a blur after that,' said Peggy. 'Light on, lob the kettle, lots of screaming, the sound of them running away and falling down the stairs as they went, then nothing, just the front door wide open. And then, once I'd calmed down, I called the police.'

Jen read back through her notes.

'I'll need to call someone in,' she said. 'A crime scene investigator.'

'That makes this sound a lot more than it was,' said Peggy.

'You were attacked by an intruder,' said Jen.

'Not so sure about that,' Peggy replied. 'I did the attacking, really, didn't I?'

'The CSI,' Jen explained, 'will look to work out how and where the intruder entered the building, see if they can find anything that might give them some DNA evidence, that kind of thing.'

'Well, if you think it's necessary.'

'I do,' said Jen. 'And by I, I mean the police.'

Peggy turned back toward her office.

'Now, about that mug of tea,' she said. 'It'll have gone cold. I'll pour us another.'

'There's really no need,' said Jen, protesting as hard as she could, but it was obvious that Peggy was ignoring her, so she followed her to her office. 'Are you able to sleep in another room?' she asked. 'It would be best if your room could be left until it was examined properly.'

At this, Jen saw the first flicker of concern in Peggy's eyes.

'I was actually thinking of going to stay with friends,' she said, as she fussed with making the tea. 'Someone in the village, that's all. Would that be okay? I can stay if you think that would be better.'

Jen shook her head.

'No,' she said, 'I think your suggestion is very sensible.'

'Only if you're sure.'

'I am,' said Jen. 'Absolutely.'

Peggy smiled.

'Now, back to more important things,' she said, and held out the biscuits.

'Two?' said Jen, reaching for them.

'You're learning,' said Peggy.

TWENTY-TWO

The journey from the Highlands and back to the Dales started with views that inspired poets and ended with the same, but much of the middle bit Harry couldn't really remember. Or chose not to.

Jadyn had jumped at the chance to stay in Scotland to see if he could find out more about Mr MacKenzie. Harry wasn't hopeful that even if he did, it would be of any use, but it made sense to at least try. And by leaving Jadyn behind, he was freed up to head back down to Yorkshire and push things on there.

Bumping into DCI Logan had caught Harry by surprise. He had a sense that they were as similar as they were different, though knew he would've been hard pushed to explain why, or what that even meant. Regardless, his gut told him that Logan was a man he could probably work with, and Harry said that about very few.

By the time he had sorted things out with Jadyn, made sure he knew what he was doing, and had both accommodation and a route home sorted, Harry hadn't left till well after midday. He'd stocked up on supplies at the Green Welly to keep him going on the drive, and grabbed some shortbread for Grace, and some more for the team.

At the Green Welly, he'd also had a call from Matt, who had then updated him on what Sowerby had found. He quickly told him about the message from Jim, and Matt then passed on a couple of things from Dave, who had been over in Kettlewell dealing with a disagreement between the owner of a pub and the owner of a café. That done, they moved on to the case in hand, with Matt running through his meeting with Sowerby.

'So, in a nutshell, we've got two bodies, both burned, and Adam Heath is still missing,' Harry said once Matt had finished. 'What about Shane's family?'

'That's where I was this afternoon,' said Matt. 'His father's a widower and lives near Catterick. Got the impression their relationship was a broken one.'

'Why?'

'When I told him, his response was, *Ah well*, like it just didn't matter. There were no photos in the house either. I know not everyone's into that like me, but it was odd to see nowt at all.'

'Could he be involved?' Harry asked, knowing the question was bordering on the ridiculous.

'He's on an oxygen tank,' Matt said. 'Not a well man at all. Ex-smoker, I think, didn't really go into it.'

Harry took a moment to consider what they knew so far.

'As well as being burned, Shane and MacKenzie were shot with the same calibre weapon,' he said.

'You think it might be the same weapon, then?' Matt asked.

'Have to wait for ballistics on that,' said Harry. 'Police Scotland are sending what they've got over to Sowerby's team. Hopefully, we'll hear something soon. But I know what my money's on.'

'Don't forget the drugs,' Matt added.

'I'm beginning to wonder exactly what Heath is involved with,' Harry sighed. 'By which I mean, I think we all know exactly what he was involved with, and none of it was good, which is why we need to find him, and soon.'

Harry was very concerned. With two of the three people who worked in the same business now dead, he had no doubt that Adam Heath was either in serious danger, or responsible for what had happened, perhaps even both. But where the hell he was, he had no idea. He'd certainly gone to great lengths to keep his whereabouts secret, right down to those postcards, and Harry suspected that Jadyn would come back at some point with something to confirm this as the reason behind MacKenzie being in the cottage.

'Any idea who this MacKenzie was?' Matt asked, knocking Harry from his thoughts. 'A friend of Heath, do you think?'

'All we know is that he was an unemployed rig worker with a rough reputation from Fort William and that he was, for whatever reason, staying in a cottage in Ballachulish under Heath's name. That's why I've left Jadyn up there to see if he can find out some more.'

'He'll be loving that,' said Matt.

'He certainly seemed even more smiley than usual,' said Harry.

'You think Heath paid him to be there in his place?' Matt asked.

'Hard to come up with another explanation,' said Harry. 'Mainly because we've those postcards sent to his mum, haven't we? Which is one reason I'll need you to speak with Peggy, just to make sure she's certain it's Adam's writing. Also, she needs to be made fully aware of what's happened, about the two lads who worked for her son, and about the body in Scotland. Her son isn't where he's supposed to be, so she might be able to help.'

'I'll do that tomorrow,' Matt said. 'Kill two birds with one stone.'

'Why two?'

'Call came in from Heath's mum about an intruder at the house. She saw them off by throwing a kettle at their head.'

Harry wasn't sure he'd heard right.

'A kettle?'

'Yep, a kettle,' Matt confirmed. 'It should've been me heading out to see her, seeing as I'm on duty, but there was a cock up with the call and it was put through to Jen. She just went into autopilot, I think. Next thing I know, she's calling me from Caldbergh about it all. I managed to persuade her to head home, and Mrs Heath is currently staying with friends. I'm meeting a CSI there in the morning. So, I can talk to her about it all then.'

'You'll be knackered,' said Harry.

'We're all knackered,' said Matt. 'We're not only missing Liz, but with Gordy now gone, we're a little stretched. Dave's popping in to do the early morning and will head back at midday tomorrow. That'll give me a chance to get my head down.'

'I've explained all this to the DSupt,' said Harry. 'She understands.'

And Walker did, or at least she gave that impression, but Harry knew her hands were tied. If there wasn't the money, then there wasn't the money, and they'd just have to suck it up.

And that had been how the conversation had ended, on a low, setting Harry's mood for the journey. He was thankful, then, that Loch Lomond was able to lift him a little as it floated by, the road slick from water trickling down the hillside. Then the Erskine Bridge had loomed ahead, and Harry had rolled through Glasgow as the city itself was shifting from day to evening, workers spilling out of offices and shops and cafés to block up the roads as they tried to get home.

A break at the Tebay Services gave Harry a chance to go to the loo, stretch his legs, and wonder why all motorway services weren't this good, the food at the restaurant proving too tempting in the end. A good serving of cottage pie, and he was back in his vehicle and grabbing a kip.

The next leg of the trip was painless if slow, the traffic heavy, and Harry had the impression he was trapped in a flow of metallic lava, as he drifted with the masses further south.

Another stop and a nap, and he woke to darkness, eventually turning off the main roads to head towards Wensleydale, driving first through the small town of Sedbergh, before narrow, twisting roads pulled him onwards, the gleam of his headlights bouncing between drystone walls like glow worms trapped in a jar.

Arriving in Carperby, Harry was met at the door by Smudge, Jess, and Grace.

'You must be knackered,' Grace said, standing back as Harry almost fell through the door.

'Tired and wired,' Harry said. 'I think I've drunk a little too much coffee. Here you go, a present from Scotland.' He handed her the shortbread he'd bought at the Green Welly.

Grace took the biscuits, then stood back and Harry walked through to the lounge. Little was left of the room, but the sofa was still there, and the television was now parked on top of a box.

'Hungry?'

Harry shook his head, yawned.

'What about a whisky?'

'Not sure I need to answer that,' said Harry.

Grace left the lounge, followed by Jess, while Smudge snuggled up next to Harry's leg, her soft mouth resting on his legs.

Stroking Smudge's head, he realised he'd not checked his phone since leaving the Highlands. Yes, it had buzzed a few times, but there had been no calls, so he'd ignored the messages and focused instead on getting home. The chat with Matt had got him up to date on everything as well, so he felt fairly confident that he knew what was happening and where.

The first message was from Jim to say that he wanted to discuss the possibility of going part-time.

Sensible lad, Harry thought.

The second message was from Matt, asking if he fancied going to a pie and pea supper in a couple of weeks in the back room at the Fountain. This one would be a bit different, he'd explained, as, for some strange reason, it also involved a palm reader.

Harry agreed, because why the hell not? he thought. It would be a fun night out, and Grace and he would probably need it after moving in together and unpacking everything.

The third and final message was a quick text from Ben asking if Harry could give him a call. No reason given, which only served to make Harry worry.

Grace returned with a large whisky and Harry took a deep and warming slug, the aroma of peat filling his nose as the liquid slipped down his throat.

'I've some news,' Grace said.

Harry glanced up over the rim of the glass.

'Good, I hope.'

'We get the keys at the start of next week. That good enough?'

'Well, I'll raise a drink to that,' said Harry, taking another gulp of whisky. 'Bloody brilliant news!'

Tomorrow he'd be pushing on with the investigation, waiting on news from Jadyn, trying to piece things together, maybe even chatting with Jack Moffatt, assuming, of course, that he was able to take visitors. This news was more than good enough to see him through all of it.

He finished his whisky, then leaned back into the deep cushions of the sofa. His phone buzzed again. Another message.

'Who's that?' Grace asked, as Harry read the message.

'Gordy,' he said.

'And how is she?'

Harry turned his phone screen so that Grace could see what Gordy had sent, which was a photo of her in a pub somewhere, smiling over a pint of what he assumed was cider, and sitting next to her was someone they both recognised.

'Is that Jameson?' Grace asked.

Harry laughed.

Jameson was an old friend, a detective who, more than anyone else, had helped him to deal with the darkness he lived with, and to focus enough to not just join the police, but become a DCI. He'd even visited the Dales a while ago to attend a conference about becoming a private investigator now that he was retired and, sadly, widowed.

'Looks like she's got some help to settle in,' said Harry.

'Any idea what he's doing with himself?'

'He's a civilian advisor to the police.'

'He'll be working with Gordy, then? That's good.'

Harry gave the photo one last look, noticing that although Gordy was smiling, there was something missing in her eyes.

Jameson will keep an eye on her, he thought, and sent her a 'thumbs-up' emoji, something he still felt foolish doing, as though emojis were very much not for someone his age.

Grace yawned.

'Bed?' Harry asked, finishing his whisky.

'Bed,' agreed Grace, and they headed upstairs.

TWENTY-THREE

With Liz and Jadyn missing from the office Friday morning, and Gordy no longer a part of things, Harry noticed that the room seemed empty.

He'd arrived early after a good night's sleep and an early morning walk with Smudge, who had come with him to Hawes. First to arrive, he'd got the room set up for a meeting around the board, and messaged Jadyn to see if he could join in on his phone.

Next to arrive was Jen, and Harry saw concern written in lines on her face.

'Morning,' he said. 'Tea?'

'Coffee,' Jen replied, the word almost erased from existence by a yawn.

Smudge padded over to nuzzle Jen's legs as she slumped down in a chair.

'Long night, I hear,' Harry said, sorting Jen a coffee. 'I spoke with Matt, heard about what happened over at Caldbergh.'

'What? Oh, right, yes, that,' said Jen, clearly distracted by something else.

Harry walked over with a coffee and the shortbread he'd bought back from Scotland.

'That's the good stuff,' he said, pointing at the shortbread. 'You can tell, because the packaging is tartan.'

Jen laughed, then opened one of the packets and demolished one of the biscuits.

'You're not wrong,' she said, and reached for another.

'Matt says he's meeting a CSI out there this morning.'

Jen simply replied with a nod, then sipped her coffee, both hands clasping her mug.

Harry wasn't used to seeing her look so worn out. He knew that the race had been a hell of a challenge, but there was something more going on. Was it Jadyn? It couldn't be though, surely, mainly because he was still up in Scotland. Perhaps they'd had a falling out?

'Something up?' Harry asked, deciding it was for the best to pry.

Jen gave a shallow nod, then said, 'Steve ... he's missing...'

For a moment, Harry had to work hard to remember who Steve was.

'You mean your massive lizard?'

'None other.'

'And he's missing? How?' Harry was confused. Steve was huge. The idea of him somehow finding a route out of Jen's house didn't make sense.

'My fault,' said Jen. 'I left the patio door open. Didn't realise until it was too late. No idea where he is.'

'You've asked your neighbours?'

'Yes. I mean, I posted notes through their doors last night before I went to see Peggy, and it was too late by the time I got back last night to go knocking on their doors.'

'What about this morning?'

'Too early. I'll give them a call in a bit.'

Harry looked at Smudge, who was now curled up at Jen's feet. He loved that dog, soppy lump that she was. And he wasn't sure how well he'd do if she went missing.

He stood up.

'Right,' he said, 'finish your coffee and shortbread and get yourself back to Middleham.'

Jen lifted tired eyes to Harry.

'What? No, I'll be fine. I'm sure he'll turn up.'

'If I lost Smudge, I'd be tearing the Dales apart right now to find her,' Harry said. 'You won't be finding Steve if you stay here, will you?'

'There's stuff to be doing,' Jen yawned. 'Honestly, Harry, it'll be fine.'

Harry folded his arms.

'Fine? I don't do fine. And neither should you.'

'Not sure I understand,' Jen said.

'Fine ... it's an acceptance of things being just okay, isn't it? Of whatever you're doing or are involved with being nothing more than satisfactory, perhaps not even that. It's fatalistic, and I've no time for that. So, you're going to get back to Middleham, and you're going to find Steve.'

'But ...'

'No buts,' Harry said. 'Matt's on with the CSI, as I've just said, Jadyn's busy in Scotland, and with myself, Jim, and Dave, we can easily cover everything else. Go.'

Jen hesitated.

'Don't think I won't hoof you out of here if you don't go of your own accord,' said Harry, his voice harsh, but the faintest hint of warmth in the almost smile now on his face.

'Only if you're sure...'

'You've known me long enough now to know the answer to that, Jen.'

Jen rose to her feet, stretched.

'Thanks, Harry. But if there's anything you need me to do, just let me know. I'll do a search, knock on the doors of all my neighbours, make sure everyone's keeping an eye out for Steve, then I'll be free. I can't spend the whole day looking.'

'Go find Steve,' Harry said. 'Before he terrifies the town, and we start getting reports of some prehistoric creature roaming the streets!'

As Jen headed out of the door, the rest of the team started to arrive. Jim was first, with Fly at his heels. Spotting Smudge as they entered, the dog ran over to pounce on her, and Harry and Jim both watched on as they wrestled. Following Jim was Dave, who entered the room with enough force to almost rip the door off its hinges.

'Woah, there,' said Harry, as the door swung shut behind Dave.

'Sorry about that,' said Dave, removing his coat. 'How was Scotland?'

'As beautiful as it was frustrating,' said Harry.

Dave joined Jim over in the kitchen area, then Matt arrived, carrying an old biscuit tin under his arm.

'Here we go,' he said, opening the tin and placing it on a table. 'Something for breakfast. I couldn't sleep, so I ... er ... baked these.'

Harry looked in the tin to see a pile of small cakes.

'And what are they?' he asked.

'Breakfast muffins,' said Matt. 'Maple syrup and bacon.' He grabbed one, unwrapped it, and handed it to Harry. 'Trust me, they're really good.'

'Still warm, too,' Harry said, and took a bite. 'Bloody hell, Matt ...'

Matt's eyes went wide.

'What's wrong? You don't like it?'

'The opposite,' said Harry. 'Those are dangerously good.'

Soon, the team was all gathered around, and Matt's muffins had greatly decreased in number. Harry told them all where Jen was as well, and though concerned, the consensus was that Steve going walkabout was very funny, and that they all figured Jen would no doubt find him in a neighbour's garden as much to his own surprise as theirs.

'Right,' Harry said, wiping crumbs from his mouth, having now consumed three of the muffins, 'we're all here. Even Jadyn.'

From a laptop that Matt had placed next to Harry, Jadyn's grinning face was staring out into the room.

'Where shall we start, then?'

'With me, if that's okay, Boss,' Jadyn suggested. 'Then I can get cracking.'

'The floor's yours,' said Harry.

Jadyn quickly ran through what he was doing for the day, which was to find out as much background as he could about MacKenzie, speak to people who knew him, knock on some doors, and see if he could work out how the man had ended up staying in the house in place of Adam Heath, and how the postcards had been sent to Adam's mother, Peggy.

'I'll let you know as soon as I have anything,' he said.

'What about CCTV?' Dave asked.

'There isn't any,' said Jadyn. 'Not in Ballachulish anyway.'

'No big brother at all?'

'Nope. But then it's not exactly London, is it? I'll check to see if anyone has their own security cameras, though, just in case.'

'Can you check on that ballistics report as well?' Harry asked. 'Make sure it's been sent to Sowerby's team; I know it looks more than likely that the same weapon was used, but I'd prefer to know for sure.'

'Will do,' said Jadyn. 'Can I go?'

'You can,' said Harry, and with a cheery salute, Jadyn's face disappeared.

Harry shut the laptop.

'Strikes me that he's enjoying himself up there,' said Matt.

'You don't say,' smiled Harry. 'You want to go next?'

Matt ran through what he'd told Harry the day before about what he'd learned from Sowerby, and then what had happened over at Caldbergh.

'I'm meeting a CSI there at ten, and will be talking to Peggy about everything, as we've already discussed,' he said, and glanced at Dave. 'I'll need you with me to go and speak with neighbours, find out if they heard or saw anything. And also to deal with those journalists if they turn up again.'

Harry thought about that for a moment.

'I know it's a long shot, but see if there's anything else she can tell us about where Adam might be. Places he visits a lot, anything, really. And there's the postcards as well, like I said last night; have her confirm they're definitely from Adam.'

'She was sure he was in Scotland,' said Matt. 'No reason for her to think anything else under the circumstances.'

'I know, but there may be something else. I don't know what, but right now, I'll take anything.' A thought crossed Harry's mind. 'Maybe we should head this off at the pass as it were; Might help with finding Adam Heath as well.'

Harry saw a frown fold itself onto Matt's forehead.

'How do you mean?'

'I'll provide a written statement. Just something brief about the fire at the warehouse and to say that we are trying to contact the owner, that kind of thing. No mention of Scotland or anything else. Might be enough.'

'If you use the word exclusive, Askew will munch it down for sure. But what about the other one, Bryony White?'

'I'll stick with Askew. Like you said, he'll love the exclusive angle. Anything else?'

Jim raised a hand.

'What do you want me on with?' he asked.

'You're going to be managing the office,' Harry said. 'Need someone here as a point of contact for the rest of us, plus to deal with anything else that comes in not to do with the case. Have a look through the Action Book as well, see if there's anything that needs chasing up.'

'What about the other thing?'

Harry knew Jim was talking about him going part-time. He'd not really had time to think about how it might work.

'Probably best we park that for now,' he said. 'But we'll definitely discuss it and see what works best. That suit?'

'Yes,' said Jim.

'Good,' said Harry, and rose to his feet. 'I'm going to check up on Jack Moffatt at the hospital. I've already called, and he's awake and is good to take visitors, so that's probably me for the day.' He remembered then what Jen had said to him as she'd headed off to look for Steve. 'That intruder at Peggy's,' he said, looking over at Matt. 'If they were covered in boiling water, then there's a good chance they'll have needed medical help, isn't there?'

'Maybe,' said Matt.

'It's another long shot, I know, but I'll ask Jen to check with local doctors' surgeries to see if anyone's turned up with burn injuries. Pharmacies, too. And I'll ask at the hospital. We've all got things to be getting on with. Let's keep in touch, not just with each other, but with Jim, here, who can jot things down on the board if needed.'

'Jadyn won't like that,' Jim said, smiling. 'The board ... he's very protective about it.'

'Just so long as you don't leave the lids off his pens, then I think we'll be okay,' Harry said. 'Anything else anyone want to raise?'

The rest of the team stayed quiet.

'Excellent,' said Harry. 'Then let's crack on, shall we, and see if we can't find Mr Heath.'

TWENTY-FOUR

With the team off to get on with the various jobs divvied up at the meeting, Harry set to putting together a statement for Askew and sent it. There was enough detail in it to make the man feel like he was getting special treatment, and Harry hoped that it would be enough to keep him quiet.

As for the other reporter, Bryony White, he wasn't too concerned about what she did or didn't know. Matt had dealt with her, and Harry suspected she was in touch with Askew anyway, and he'd prefer to keep his communication with the journalistic community as limited as possible.

He also sent a message to Jen about investigating possible burn injuries, while also wishing her well in finding Steve, and told her there was no rush in getting back to him, just to let him know where she was with it when she got the chance.

Arriving at the hospital, Harry managed to eventually find a parking space, the process one of becoming increasingly frustrated as he drove around the car park, and a crescendo of swearing which surprised even him.

Inside the hospital, Harry navigated the warren of corridors, ended up going the wrong way half a dozen times, but eventually found himself in the right location.

The ward, like every other one Harry had ever been on, was a place of strange smells and odd sounds, the air vibrating with muted chatter, bleeps, and blips, and the rhythmic whoosh of a ventilator or two. It was so bright, he wondered how conducive it was to one's recovery, having glaring lights crashing into you from every angle. Some of the patients were watching television, the sound piped through headphones, while others stared off into the middle distance, snoozed, or worked as well as they could to smile and chat with family and friends.

A nurse approached, his face clean-shaven, his eyes keen.

'Can I help?'

Harry's answer was to show his ID first, then say, 'Jack Moffatt's here, yes?'

The nurse glanced at Harry's ID, frowned, and stepped back.

'I'm afraid he's asleep.'

'Then wake him up.'

The nurse's eyes widened and Harry wondered why he was being so short suddenly. He'd never liked hospitals, but then who did? Who in their right mind would wake up and think, *yes, brilliant, I'm going to hospital today, my favourite place*? No one, that's who, Harry thought. Then a memory hammered into him. The room he was standing in shifted and shimmered like a heatwave on a beach, and he was back in that waiting room with Gordy. He saw Gordy fall apart in front of him as her world crashed, heard her heart break, and was then hit by a wave of his own grief at the tragic loss of Anna.

'I'm sorry, what?'

Harry was back in the ward with the nurse, the memory of that moment with Gordy gone as quickly as it had arrived.

'Do you know when he'll be awake?'

'He's not on a timer.'

Harry gave the nurse that; he must have to deal with a lot of awkward visitors, and here he was not making things any easier.

'Tell you what,' he said, 'I'll head to the café, then pop back here in half an hour or so, how's that?'

The nurse considered the suggestion, then said, 'Go for a coffee, and I'll come and get you when he stirs.' He turned to go, then stopped and added, 'Avoid the soup.'

'I wasn't about to have the soup.'

'I'm just saying, that's all,' said the nurse. 'It would be remiss of me not to warn you.'

And with that, he left Harry.

After managing to get lost once again, Harry eventually found his way to the hospital café. He ordered a coffee, avoided the soup, grabbed a brownie, and sat down. Then, thinking back to what had just happened in the ward, and the photo he'd received from Gordy the night before, he opened up his phone and sent her another quick message. He didn't say much, just enough to make sure that Gordy knew the team was thinking about her, that everyone hoped she was okay, and that if she needed anything, all she had to do was ask.

Message sent, Harry sipped the coffee. The liquid was a deep brown, but that was where any similarity to what he had ordered ended. The drink redefined the word insipid, and even a nibble on the brownie did little to improve things.

His phone rang, and he answered without even checking the number.

'Grimm...'

'Harry? It's...'

The voice at the other end cut out.

'Hello?'

'Ha—'

Harry recognised the voice.

'Gordy? Can you hear me?'

The line went dead.

'Bloody hell!'

Harry headed quickly outside, and as soon as he'd found some-where with enough signal, he called Gordy right back.

'Gordy?'

'Hi, Harry,' Gordy replied. 'Thanks for the message.'

Harry heard the distant call of the Highlands in her voice, but also an emptiness, that spoke to the brokenness inside her that she just couldn't fix. Or didn't want to. Perhaps both.

'You okay?'

Gordy didn't reply.

'Something up?'

'No, I'm fine,' Gordy said at last, her voice quiet. 'How's the team?'

'They're good. Always asking after you, that's for sure.'

'I hear from all of them, you know. Quite regularly, too.'

'That's good.'

Harry knew something was bothering Gordy, otherwise, why would she have called him? But he didn't want to press, to push her to say something she didn't want to, so just allowed her to guide the conversation.

'How's the house move going?' Gordy asked.

'Everything's packed and in a couple of days we'll be in.'

'Exciting times.'

'Indeed.'

Gordy fell quiet again, and Harry allowed her the space to do it, risking another sip of his coffee. Then he headed over to a bare patch of ground and poured the rest away, before chucking the cup in a bin.

'This was the right decision, wasn't it, Harry?' Gordy asked. 'Moving south? I've not done something really stupid?'

'Not sure you had much choice either way,' Harry replied, perhaps unhelpfully, he thought. 'You couldn't really go backing out of a job you'd secured. Not sure that was an option.'

'I'm only here because of Anna, though, aren't I? We were doing this together. I got the job so that I could be with her. And now...'

Harry heard Gordy's voice break.

'Tell me about the team; what are they like?'

'Early days,' said Gordy. 'Still working things out. There's a few changes going on and I seem to have turned up right smack bang in the middle of things. I've met Firbank, though, your old DSupt.'

That made Harry laugh.

'Well, if you see her again, send my regards, though I'm fairly sure she wouldn't want them.'

'Actually,' said Gordy, 'she speaks very highly of you, once she's stopped raging and swearing about how much of a nightmare you were at times.'

'Also, change is good,' Harry added. 'Better to be there in the thick of it as it's happening, than turn up afterwards when all the important decisions have been made.'

'Perhaps.'

'How's Jameson? Great photo by the way. Where were you?'

'Another pub with Fountain in the name,' said Gordy. 'The Lamb and Fountain.'

'In Frome?'

Harry knew of it.

'Not changed in decades, has it?' said Gordy. 'Matt would love it. Jameson, though, he's been a godsend. He's always checking in on me. And talking of Matt, the two are similar in a lot of ways, I think.'

'I can see that,' Harry agreed.

Silence again, and Harry glanced back inside the hospital, aware that the nurse could come down to fetch him at any moment and not be able to find him.

'Look, Gordy,' he began, but Gordy interrupted.

'Harry, I'm thinking of coming back up, just for a couple of days or so,' she said. 'I've not been back since the funeral. I've Anna's ashes, you see, and...'

Harry knew what Gordy was trying to say, even though the words weren't there.

'It would be great to see you,' he said. 'And whatever you need, you only have to ask. Any idea when?'

'This weekend, if that works,' answered Gordy. 'You're busy

with the move, I know, and I'm sure everyone else has stuff on, plus there's work I'm sure, but I was just wondering...'

'Wondering what?'

Another moment of quiet went by while Harry waited, watching visitors come and go, some clearly worn out by the ordeal. One woman left the hospital in such a rush she almost knocked into Harry as she headed over to the car park.

'I need to scatter her ashes,' Gordy said. 'There's this spot down by the river we used to go to; she loved it there. We'd take picnics sometimes, even go for a dip. She wanted her ashes scattered there. The funeral, it was so big, and I felt kind of swamped by it, so this ... Well, it would be me saying goodbye, wouldn't it?'

'Busy I may be,' Harry said, 'but never too busy, Gordy; not for you, not for Anna, and certainly not for this.'

'You're sure?'

'Gordy...'

'I'll see you at the weekend, then?'

'Just let me know when you're arriving, what you want to do, and who you want there. How's that?'

'Perfect,' said Gordy. 'Thank you.'

'Mr Grimm?'

Harry turned to see the nurse at the main doors to the hospital.

'He's awake. I've told him you're here.'

Harry gave a wave of acknowledgement and watched the nurse head back inside.

'I need to go,' he said.

'Same,' said Gordy. 'Thanks, Harry.'

'See you soon.'

'Yep.'

Gordy hung up.

Stuffing his phone into his pocket, Harry headed back inside.

TWENTY-FIVE

Jack Moffatt looked in a bad way, Harry thought, as he sat down at the man's bedside in a chair so low it was little better than squatting on the floor.

The only things he knew about Jack was what he'd been able to learn from the medical staff; thirty-two years old, seventy-five kilos, no next of kin.

When Harry had walked up to Jack's bed, his eyes had been closed, so he'd taken his seat quietly, not wishing to give him a fright. Much better to let him stir naturally.

He was pale, with a thick covering of dark brown hair, buzz cut to a grade two or three, Harry guessed. He looked lean, his bare arms, which were resting on top of the blanket, showed muscles like corded wires threaded with veins, and plenty of tattoos. The build of a climber, Harry thought, or someone who did a lot of bodyweight exercises at the very least, maybe martial arts.

The injuries he'd sustained during the break-in were extensive and Harry was not at all surprised that it had taken him as long as it had to be in a position to talk. Though no bones were broken, he was bruised and cut front and back, and his face, which was bandaged and covered in Steri-Strips as well as stitches, was a multi-coloured mess.

Harry leaned back in his chair and waited.

'I know you're there,' Jack said. 'It's just that it hurts like hell to open my eyes.'

'Looks like you took quite a beating,' said Harry.

'Feels like it, too,' said Jack.

Harry laughed at that.

'I'm Detective Harry Grimm,' he said. 'You happy to talk?'

'I'll do my best,' said Jack, wincing as he did so. 'Can't say that anything I do remember will help you, though.'

Harry took out his notepad.

'And don't worry about having to look at me as we talk; probably better for you if you don't, to be honest.'

'That's an odd thing to say.'

'I've an odd face.'

At that, Jack slowly opened his eyes to look at Harry through the thinnest of slits.

'Ah, I see what you mean.'

'I did warn you.'

'How?'

'IED. Ex-soldier. Long time ago, now. I'm used to it.'

Jack scrunched his eyes shut again for a moment, and Harry said, 'Just start where you want to, no rush.'

Jack pushed himself back into his bed, the mattress lifted to provide support.

'It's hard to remember exactly what happened.'

'Not a surprise,' said Harry, and asked, 'How long have you worked for Adam?'

'Four months.'

'What were you doing before that?'

'Bar work.'

'Local?'

Jack shook his head, then squeezed his eyes shut.

'Sorry, thought I was going to throw up just then.'

'Just keep yourself still, no sharp movements,' Harry advised. 'So, you're not from round here, then?'

'I fancied a change,' said Jack. 'Worked lots of bars all over, helped pay for the travel. Got tired of the late nights, no social life.'

'So, you moved into coffee?'

'I've been a barista, so I know what I'm on about when it comes to beans and grinds and all that. Made sense for me to come and help Shane with all that; he's done a lot of work to get that up and running.'

'I didn't even know a coffee subscription was a thing,' said Harry. 'You learn something every day.'

'Shane had worked on that a lot,' Jack explained. 'Adam gave him free rein to see if he could grow that side of things. The business used to be mainly supplying cafés and shops, that kind of thing, and just having it available to purchase on the website. It made sense to develop things.'

The fire at the warehouse had happened on Monday night, so Harry asked, 'Can you remember when you were attacked?'

'Tuesday night,' Jack said. 'It was my day off and I was knackered, so I stayed in. Work's been very busy, more so than usual.'

'Can you remember anything from when you were last at work?'

'Like what?'

'Anything out of the ordinary,' said Harry. 'Maybe someone hanging around outside, or a vehicle passing the warehouse more times than you'd expect. Anything.'

Jack closed his eyes, opened them again.

'No,' he said. 'Like I said, I'm finding it difficult to remember everything. You'd be better off talking to Shane. Why would someone be hanging round outside, anyway?'

Harry had been wondering when the best time would be to bring up what had happened to Shane. Jack had just made that decision for him.

'There was a fire at the warehouse,' he said. 'The night before you were attacked. A body was found inside.'

'What? I don't understand.'

Harry could see when Jack guessed what he was about to tell him.

'We've had confirmation from the pathologist that the body is Shane's,' he said. 'I know this will be a shock, but if there's a link between what happened at the warehouse and your attack on Tuesday night, we might be some way closer to finding who was responsible and why.'

'Does Adam know?'

'We've been unable to contact him.'

Jack looked away, staring out of the window for a moment.

'He's not in Scotland,' he said.

Jack's intonation seems a bit off, Harry thought.

'Did you know, then? Has he been in touch?'

Jack looked back at Harry.

'Know what?'

'That Adam's not in Scotland.'

Jack shook his head.

'No, I meant that if you've not been able to contact him, then where the hell is he? He headed up to Scotland about three weeks ago.'

Harry wondered what else he should tell Jack, and decided in the end it made sense to go in hard.

'Do you know anything about drugs being stored in the warehouse?'

Jack turned back to look at Harry.

'I've never taken drugs in my life. And I never will.'

That didn't match what the neighbours had said, Harry thought, but then a hoodie was all some people needed to think someone was on meth.

'We found traces of both cocaine and methamphetamine,' he said. 'It is our belief that they were hidden in some of the sacks of coffee beans.'

'Drugs hidden in coffee? You're sure? How's that even possible?'

'Drug cartels are very, very clever,' said Harry. 'Believe me.'

'I know they are,' Jack replied. 'And you've really not found Adam?'

Harry shook his head and asked, 'Have you any idea where he might be?'

'I've only ever known him to be at work, at his house in Richmond, or at his mother's place.'

'He's not in Richmond,' said Harry. 'That place is rented out as a holiday let. And we've been round to see Peggy. She also thought he was in Scotland.'

'Doesn't make sense.'

'You're not wrong.'

They both sat quietly for a moment.

'Perhaps you can tell me what happened at your house,' Harry eventually suggested. 'Do you share the place with anyone?'

'God, no,' said Jack. 'You've seen what it's like; it's not the best, is it? I just took it because it was cheap and the landlord didn't want lots of background checks; that stuff always delays things, doesn't it? Just paid my deposit and the first couple of months upfront and in cash, and I was in. Also, I'm not a fan of living with others, really; you never know what you're going to get, do you? I'm better with my own company.'

'Two months' deposit? That's a lot of cash.'

'I have savings. I'm thinking of taking a world trip or something, going travelling again, that kind of thing.'

'How did the attack happen?'

'I was in bed,' Jack explained. 'Like I said, I've been really busy at work recently. I was tired, so I dozed most of the day, then had a takeaway and went to bed. I can't cook because the oven and hob don't work. Something woke me in the night, I went to see what it was, ended up getting the shit kicked out of me.'

The broken oven explained the takeaways, thought Harry.

'You didn't think to call the police?'

'There was someone in the house,' said Jack. 'By the time I realised, it was too late. They attacked me; surprised me actually. Hid behind the door to the lounge or something. Anyway, I tried to fight back, but it was dark. Next thing I know, I'm waking up in an ambulance.'

'Must've been terrifying.'

'It all happened too fast for me to realise what was going on.'

'Any idea why they were there, what they were looking for?'

Jack said, 'I don't own anything worth nicking, not that I'd keep there, anyway.'

'Did you see them? Are you able to give a description?'

Harry was thinking about the break-in at Peggy's; was this the same person? It seemed likely.

'It was dark, like I said,' Jack repeated. 'They had a torch, blinded me with it, before they tried to kick me to death. No broken bones, though, so that's something, isn't it?'

'It is,' Harry agreed.

Jack yawned.

'Sorry,' he said.

Harry slipped his notebook back into a pocket.

'No, you need to rest,' he said, pushing himself to his feet. 'If I have any further questions, I'll be in touch.'

Jack said nothing more, just closed his eyes.

As he was leaving, Harry was approached by the same nurse he had spoken with earlier.

'That's me done,' he said. 'Any idea when Jack will be released?'

'Tomorrow, I should think,' said the nurse. 'We need the bed.'

Harry remembered then about checking to see if there'd been any admissions for burns, and asked who he should talk to.

The nurse advised accordingly and gave him directions, and Harry gave the nurse his contact details.

'If there's any change with Jack, I'll let you know,' the nurse said.

'That would be great, thanks,' said Harry.

'And if I can't get hold of you, should I just leave a message with your colleague?'

Harry frowned at that.

'Colleague? How do you mean?'

'It was a woman. She popped in while you were having your coffee, left me her number,' the nurse explained. 'Didn't catch her name, didn't see the need, seeing as she said she'd be speaking with you anyway. Seemed surprised you were here, though.'

'Can you describe her?'

'Blonde hair, glasses,' said the nurse.

Not much of a description, Harry thought, but one he could place, remembering a conversation with Matt outside Jack's house. No wonder she was surprised.

'And did she say why she was here?'

'Just said it was to do with the case. Why, is something wrong?'

'Yes,' Harry said, pulling out his phone. 'Journalists...'

TWENTY-SIX

Scotland, Jadyn was quickly realising, was an astonishingly beautiful place. A part of him wanted to compare it to the Dales, but what would be the point?

The Dales had an ancient feel to it, but with a history of lives lived over centuries still tattooed on the landscape. Wherever you looked, you were confronted by how people had tamed the place, turned forest into pastureland, built walls and barns and farms, lived. Look deeper, and you could venture into ruined mines, their spoil heaps of grey against the lush green all around, their tunnels still holding evidence of the last feet to tread their dark, twisting, subterranean passageways.

Whereas Scotland was untamed, a landscape which displayed little in the way of what humanity had done to try and bring it under·control. Great mountains and deep valleys, vast, empty moorlands, all connected by the thinnest of threads, allowing people to travel from outpost to outpost.

Fort William, he had discovered, traced its origins to a wooden fort built in the sixteen hundreds. As he made his way through the streets, his eyes were drawn to the loch at the town's side, and the mountains which glared down of it, the most mighty of those the sullen, black hulk of Ben Nevis, he found it easy to imagine what life must have been like for the soldiers who occupied it all those years ago.

Having heard Harry's mention of a certain pie shop the day before, Jadyn had, once his boss had headed off back to the Dales the day before, ventured into the Nevis Bakery. Considering the awe he'd heard in Harry's voice, he'd expected something a little more grand than a pokey place on a grey high street. But then he'd caught a waft of warm and delicious smells slipping out of the door. He'd hurried in and ordered a pie, the ingredients of which were macaroni cheese and haggis. As soon as he'd eaten that first mouthful, he'd understood. He'd immediately sent a photo through to Matt, the one person on the planet he knew would appreciate a good pie.

Beyond trying the best of the local fayre, Jadyn had been busy trying to find out as much as he could about Iain MacKenzie. There'd not been much time left the previous day, but he'd chased the ballistics report, had another read-through of what the pathologist had said, and also got a hold of the crime scene photos. They'd not shown much other than the grizzly scene of MacKenzie's charred remains, an image Jadyn was sure would stay for him for a long while. Today was different. Today he had time. And right now, he was standing outside MacKenzie's address.

The street was away from the loch side and up a slope, far enough for Jadyn to lose sight of the water, and was lined with two- and three-storey, flat-roofed buildings, all of which were apartments. Their stark lines stood out in sharp, angry relief against the rugged vista in which they sat.

Approaching MacKenzie's door, Jadyn took the key from his pocket that the local police had collected from the landlord. He slipped it into the loch, gave it a turn, and heard a voice.

'You'll be looking for that wee shite, MacKenzie, then.'

Jadyn turned to find a squat man with a bald head, wearing a black vest, jogging pants, and sandals. He was carrying a large mug of what Jadyn assumed to be tea in one hand, and clasped in the fingers of the other, was a long, thin cigar.

Jadyn introduced himself, then asked for the man's name.

'Fraser Ross,' the man answered. 'You're English.'

'Yes.'

'Sorry to hear that.'

'Do you know Mr MacKenzie?' asked Jadyn, as he tried to work out exactly what Ross had meant by that.

'Aye,' Ross said, and took a long pull on his cigar, before pushing out a billowing stink of grey cloud, which hid his face briefly before dissipating. 'And I'd never be so polite as to call him "Mr MacKenzie." What's he done now, then?'

'Following reports of a house fire in Ballachulish, Mr MacKenzie's body was later found at the property,' Jadyn stated, keeping the facts plain and simple, and deciding it was maybe a good idea to get out his notebook.

'Burned to death, then? Couldn't have happened to a better man,' said Ross.

Jadyn kept the actual cause of death to himself.

'Can you tell me when you last saw MacKenzie?'

'Maybe just over a couple of weeks ago,' said Ross. 'Did someone finally catch up with him, then, is that it? Taken a while, but he had it coming.'

'Catch up with him?' Jadyn asked. 'How do you mean?'

There had been little in the information he'd been given about MacKenzie to suggest much in the way of run-ins with the police, so what was Ross talking about?

'He used to work on the rigs,' Ross said, sipping his tea. 'Big money jobs, those; hard, lonely work, for the sort who want that kind of thing. Good place to escape to, if you know what I mean.'

Jadyn didn't, but decided to let Ross keep talking and turned to a fresh page in his notebook.

'He'd arrive back home with a thirst on him. Oil rigs, they're dry, you see, no booze allowed. Too dangerous to have workers getting pished while living on a tiny, metal platform standing on stilts in the middle of the North Sea.'

'Pished?'

'You know, pissed, drunk,' Ross explained. He tapped the ash from off the end of his cigar, took another pull on it, then flicked what was left onto the ground to grind it under a shoe. 'Anyways, he'd soon be out in the Fort and bouncing from bar to bar, drink to drink, fight to fight. No' a pleasant man.'

'No, he doesn't sound it,' Jadyn agreed.

'Those fat pay cheques? He'd burn through them in the first few days of being back, so then he'd end up taking on odd jobs for people; bit of gardening, trips to the tip, anything that would pay enough to fill a glass. But it wasn't enough, and soon he edged into dodgier stuff.'

'Sounds like you knew him well,' said Jadyn.

'Everyone knows MacKenzie,' said Ross. 'Mainly, because he's a drunk, but also, and I say this without any hesitation at all, because he was an absolute, raging bastard.'

MacKenzie isn't being painted in the best light here, Jadyn thought.

'You said he was into dodgier stuff.'

'Got into drugs. A bit of dealing here and there. Some proper ratty shites would turn up here. And he's a thick head on him,' Ross added, finishing his tea. 'The kind of head you could ram through a brick wall and not damage. Which was a shame, really, because a few tried, and came out worse for it. Fists like slabs of meat, too. He knew how to use them, and wasn't shy about hiring them out.'

'How do you mean?'

'Debt collection, blackmail, that kind of thing,' Ross said. 'There's plenty of that goes on, nothing written down, just desperate folk needing money, and some git providing it at a high interest. And if they couldn't pay? He'd be round there in that shitty wee van of his to persuade them otherwise.'

'Van?'

'Aye, a brown thing, looked like dinosaur shite, if you ask me.'

'No one ever reported him?'

'No one would ever go to the police about MacKenzie, no' unless they wanted to end up floating in the loch. Always managed to stay under the radar. More people do than you realise, you know; there's some kinds of scum floating about that no matter what you do, you just can't haul in with a net and deal with. He'd disguise it all well enough; offer his services for odd jobs, anything from decorating, to waste disposal, to giving someone a kicking, so long as the price was right. I heard he even did a bit of dog walking for a while, though how he managed to get any dog to trust him enough to let him anywhere near them is beyond me.'

'Do you know if he knew someone called Adam Heath?' Jadyn asked, adding a quick description of him.

Ross shook his head.

'Name means nothing to me.'

So, Jadyn thought, Adam Heath somehow ended up hiring what sounded like a very unpleasant individual to take his place in the house in Ballachulish.

'Is there anything else you can tell me?'

Ross revealed a packet of cigars, pulled from the back pocket of his trousers, unwrapped one, lit it. He then filled the air with a grey plume, and Jadyn had to work hard not to cough.

'Other than my own, no doubt very obvious elation at the sudden and hopefully terrifying and painful demise of that bastard, no,' said Ross, who then flicked his eyes at the door to MacKenzie's flat. 'Oh, and if you're going to venture in there, I'd no' be touching anything if I were you; no knowing what you'll catch.'

Then, without another word, Ross turned and headed back through his own front door.

Jadyn stowed his notepad away and, with disposable gloves slipped on, opened MacKenzie's door. He pushed it open slowly, carefully, then stumbled back as he was hit with a pungent stink powerful enough to rot tooth enamel. The door resisted, and Jadyn was tempted to just let it win, not entirely convinced it was safe or sensible to venture further, but Harry had trusted him enough to leave him north of the border, so he took a deep breath and shoved. The door complained, but moved enough to allow Jadyn to eventually edge inside.

The hallway to the flat was strewn with bin bags. Judging by the stink, and also from what he could see spilling from them, most of the waste was takeaway packaging, frozen pizza boxes, and empty beer cans. A large box was filled with empty bottles of Buckfast wine.

Jadyn scooted past the rubbish, ducked his head inside one door to find a bathroom that was given over to black mould, another that presented a little used kitchen with most of the cupboard doors missing, a third that comprised a mattress on the floor, a chest of drawers, a pile of clothes on the floor, and a stack of adult magazines, and a fourth and final door which led into a small lounge.

The lounge was dominated by a huge television. In front of it sat a three-seater leather sofa. Jadyn circled the room, not really sure what he was looking for, if anything. Really, all he was getting now was a better picture as to who MacKenzie was.

MacKenzie clearly occupied the central seat of the sofa, the cushion here slumped more than those on either side of it. Also, to the right, was a carrier bag filled with something, and to the left, a small pile of what looked like handwritten leaflets.

Jadyn checked the leaflets first, picking one up for a closer look. The writing, which was in thick, black, felt-tip pen, was all capital letters, and everything seemed to be squashed up against the right-hand side: JOBS DUN 4 CASH. NO JOB 2 BIG OR 2 SMALL. GOOD WITH HANDS.

In brackets, after 'good with hands,' MacKenzie had attempted to draw a laughing-face emoji. His phone number was large and at the bottom of the leaflet.

The only other item of interest was the carrier bag. Jadyn reached for it, then jumped back, as the bag moved.

He stared, not sure if he was seeing things, but then the bag moved again, and something brown and furry leapt out of it.

Jadyn stumbled backwards into the television as a rat, at least the size of a cat, landed on the floor, then raced out of the lounge. Jadyn was sure that he saw its tail disappear into the bedroom.

Well, he thought, that's one room I'll not be searching.

The carrier bag, thanks to the disturbance caused by the rat, was now open. Jadyn leaned in for a closer look. To his surprise, it was stuffed full of cash, most of it fifty-pound notes, and all of it not only nibbled and chewed, but giving off the distinct stench of rat piss.

TWENTY-SEVEN

Outside the hospital, Harry climbed into his Rav and grabbed his phone. That he had the number he was about to call in his contacts turned his stomach, but better the devil you know, he thought.

The call rang and rang, and Harry was about to hang up when it was finally answered.

'Askew,' the voice at the other end said.

'Grimm,' said Harry.

There was a pause before Richard Askew came back.

'You've never contacted me,' he said. 'I didn't even know you had my number. And yet, here I am, the happy recipient of not only an email from you earlier, but now a call.'

'You're a lucky man,' said Harry.

'I wouldn't go that far.'

'Neither would I.'

'So, to what do I owe this displeasure?' Askew asked.

Harry laughed at that, despite himself.

'I need the contact details for Bryony White. She was at Peggy Heath's house with you the other day. I understand you both had a little chat with my Detective Sergeant.

'That was not a chat,' said Askew. 'Your DS bullied me.'

'You been taking lessons in stand-up comedy?' Harry asked.

'That's twice you've made me laugh already, and I don't think you've ever managed that even once before.'

'Ms White and I were only doing our jobs.'

Harry thought back to what Matt had told him about finding the two journalists on Peggy's doorstep. Doing their jobs, maybe, but Askew had never gone out of his way to do it in a fashion that people appreciated. Getting in the way, putting noses out of joint, that was his usual style.

Though Harry had used it to his advantage before, most notably when, following the disappearance of a lottery-winning young couple with a huge social media following, Hawes had been full of more journalists than he could shake a stick at. And, as he'd not had a stick to hand, and would've been more inclined to swipe it at their thick heads than just shake it, he'd put Askew in charge, making him the main contact between the police and the journalistic community as a whole. It had worked rather well, too, though perhaps it had inflated Askew's already severely displaced and overblown ego.

'From what I understand, he simply asked you to leave,' Harry said.

'He told me my vehicle was linked to an investigation and would need to be towed!'

'He was just being thorough. It would be ... remiss of him not to investigate something like that, don't you think?'

'But he made it up! My car has never been involved in any crime at all!'

Harry really wanted to get to the point of his phoning Askew. Having a conversation with the man was not what he wanted his day to be about.

'I will check in with him as soon as I can,' said Harry. 'However, if you've heard no more from DS Dinsdale, then I think you can safely assume that no further action will be required.'

'No further action? There was no action required to begin with!'

'Odd, though,' said Harry, 'that you decided to leave Peggy Heath's house so quickly. Suggests a guilty conscience.'

Askew was quiet for a moment.

'No, it was just that I didn't want Mrs Heath to be unduly stressed by what was happening.'

'How very thoughtful of you.'

'Why did you call?' Askew then asked, impatience pinching his words at their corners.

'Bryony White,' Harry said. 'I need her details.'

'Why?'

'Ah, so you have them, then.'

'What? No, I mean...'

'If you didn't have them, your immediate response would be to say *I don't have them*, not to ask why I wanted them, because asking why implies you want a damned good reason to give them to me.'

Another pause.

'Perhaps,' said Askew.

'There's no perhaps,' said Harry. 'You have them. I need them. If you give them to me, then we'll both be happy.'

'We'll both be happy?' Asked repeated.

'Of course,' said Harry. 'I'll have the information I asked you for, and you won't be charged with obstructing a police officer.'

'What? How? I'm not! What are you talking about?'

'Carries a maximum sentence of a month in prison,' Harry continued. 'Might also carry a fine.'

'But I'm not obstructing you!' Askew complained.

'Do you have Ms White's details?'

'She gave them to me, yes.'

'Can I have them?'

Another pause.

'A whole month in prison,' said Harry. 'Imagine the fun you'd have getting to know your fellow pri—'

'Do you have a pen handy?'

Harry pulled out his notebook.

'Go head,' he said, and Askew gave him not only Bryony White's telephone number but her address.

'There we go,' he said, flipping the notebook shut. 'Isn't it so much better helping us rather than getting in the way?'

The phone line was dead.

Fair enough, Harry thought, then punched the Darlington address into his satnav and left the hospital.

The journey to Darlington was punctuated by various examples of terrible driving, a handful of tractors, and on one occasion, a man riding a three-wheeled bike, which was so low, Harry almost saluted his bravery on taking the thing on the road as he overtook it.

Sweeping over a number of roundabouts, Harry arrived in Darlington, and was then shunted through various sets of traffic lights, before seeing the entrance to Darlington Railway Station. The dark opening seemed to gape like a mouth, and it gave Harry the distinctly uneasy feeling that he was driving up its tongue. Thankfully, his route soon took him away from that, and a few minutes later, he was pulling up in a narrow street lined with terrace houses. It reminded him of the street where he had found Jack, except that here, the houses were in considerably better condition.

Locking his vehicle, Harry started to walk along the street, when his phone buzzed. Seeing that it was Jadyn calling, he answered immediately.

'Hello, Constable,' he said. 'Wearing a kilt, yet?'

'What? No,' said Jadyn.

'Well, that's disappointing.'

'You mean you have?'

'Of course,' said Harry. 'A mate in the Paras got married. He was Scottish, we all had to wear them on the stag do. Very comfy. Very breezy.'

'I'll think about it,' said Jadyn. 'Not sure I'll be here long enough to buy one, though.'

'You're ringing me with news, I hope,' Harry said.

Jadyn quickly ran through what he'd learned about MacKenzie

from his neighbour and a clearly less-than-enjoyable exploration of the man's flat. Harry had to work very hard to not laugh at the bit about the rat.

'How much money?' he asked.

'I've not counted it,' said Jadyn. 'I think the rat was using it as a bed.'

'But you've some idea as to how much is there?'

'Looks like at least ten grand,' said Jadyn. 'Give or take.'

'That's a lot of cash to have just lying around, isn't it?' said Harry. 'He probably didn't want to go depositing it into his bank account because that's when questions are asked when the tax man comes knocking.'

'Keep it as cash, spend it carefully, no one will ever know, you mean?' said Jadyn.

'I do,' said Harry.

'The leaflets I found,' Jadyn then said, 'I wonder if Heath found one in a shop pinned to a notice board or something, or pushed through his door. Maybe that's how he found him and he paid him to stay in the house in Ballachulish. Looking at where MacKenzie actually lived, I can see why he'd have jumped at the chance to be somewhere a little nicer.'

'That money in the bag might also have something to do with it,' said Harry.

'But why leave it in the flat?'

'Maybe that's just where he felt it was safest,' said Harry. 'Doesn't want to be carrying around that much cash, does he? Just take enough to enjoy himself, and leave the rest.'

Jadyn also told Harry that he'd chased the ballistics report and that it had definitely been sent through to Sowerby.

'Anything else?' Harry asked.

'I think I'm done,' said Jadyn. 'That's why I'm calling. I don't think there's any need for me to stay here now. Probably best I get myself back home.'

'If you think you're done, then yes, I think you're right,' Harry agreed. 'Enjoy the journey, and don't rush back, either; you were asleep for the last part of the journey up and missed the best bit.'

With goodbyes said, Harry slipped his phone back into his pocket, then got back to the task of finding Bryony White's house. A couple minutes later, he was standing before a neat place with clean windows and a front door of beautifully polished wood.

He knocked.

His phone rang again. This time, it was Jen.

Lifting the phone to his ear, Harry heard someone approaching from inside the house, then locks being rattled free.

'Jen,' he said, as he answered, 'I'm busy. Can I call you back?'

'It's just a quick one,' Jen said. 'It's about the burns you asked me to check up on.'

The door started to open.

'You mean you've found something?'

'Yes,' said Jen. 'Thought I'd get on with it, distract me from worrying about Steve too much. And I struck gold straight away, actually. Figured it'd be best to try the hospital first, you see, just in case, because I thought if there's nothing relevant there, then I'd have to spread my search, wouldn't I? So, I started right at the top of the tree really. And I have a name.'

Harry stared at the woman now looking out at him from inside the house. She had short, dark hair, and tired eyes that registered her shock to see him, and the ID he held up for her to read, standing on her doorstep. But there was something else, too, something almost as unexpected as the hair.

'Let me guess,' said Harry. 'Bryony White.'

'It's Bryo—' Jen went quiet for a moment. 'Wait, how did you know that?'

Harry stared at Bryony, but his eyes were drawn to the bandages on her arm.

'I'll call you back.'

Harry ended the call. 'Hello Bryony ... I think we need to have a little chat, don't you?'

TWENTY-EIGHT

'Well, then,' said Harry, leaning back into the armchair he'd been directed towards by Bryony's healthy arm, 'where would you like to start?'

Bryony had stepped back to allow him inside. There'd been no hesitation in it either, no slamming of the door in his face or attempt at escape, just an acceptance that a police officer was on her doorstep, and she needed to deal with it.

The lounge was small and neat, the furniture and ornaments giving Harry a distinctly Scandinavian vibe, but without the flat pack feel. The room was neither sparse nor crowded, and Harry sensed that Bryony was someone who, rather than buying something to fulfil a need, would instead wait until she could afford exactly what she wanted. The space was also very comfortable, very cosy; this wasn't just a house, it was a home, a haven, a place in which Bryony felt safe.

Harry quietly wished he had a similar sense of style, but then he'd never really had cause to think about it, to fuss over what coffee table went with what chair. Functionality had always been at the forefront of his mind, rather than comfort, and certainly rather than style or design.

Bryony was scrunched up on a deep blue sofa directly opposite

Harry. He had watched her sit down, then slowly, carefully, curl her legs beneath her, reaching then for a blanket with her good arm to cover herself with.

'Sorry,' she said, as she continued to try and get comfortable.

'In your own time,' said Harry. 'Not like I'm going anywhere, is it?'

When Bryony was finally as comfortable as she could expect to be, she took a deep, shuddering breath, exhaled, then rested weary eyes on Harry.

'I know it doesn't look good,' she began.

'That would be a marked understatement,' agreed Harry. 'But let's go with a bit of benefit of the doubt first, shall we, and see where we end up? I'm not one for jumping to conclusions. And frankly, with everything I've got muddled up in my head about what's going on, I'd be lucky to come to one anyway.'

That seemed to cause Bryony to visibly relax, which in turn made Harry think that he might be getting somewhere. He wasn't expecting to come out of this chat with the case sewn up, but he had an inkling that he might have a better idea about where to lay a few of the pieces before having at them with needle and thread.

'I've been investigating links between drugs and coffee for a couple of years,' Bryony said. 'Travelled a bit with it, too. It was the travel that actually got me onto the story in the first place, but I won't bore you with that part. It's part broken-hearted woman goes travelling to heal, and part bad airport thriller. I might write it as that one day, you know, but like I said, I won't bore you with it.'

'So, coffee and drugs, then,' said Harry. 'And you think that's what's been going on at Adam Heath's little warehouse in Leyburn, yes?'

Bryony gave a shallow nod, wincing as she did so.

'I can't disclose my sources,' she said, 'because their lives would be in danger if I did, but yes, that's exactly what I think's been going on.'

'Why?'

Harry knew plenty from his side of things, but he wasn't about to give that information to just anyone. He also wasn't sure how it all tied together, or where it was actually leading.

If Bryony knew something, then he wanted to hear it from her. There might even be a chance that what she knew would help him understand what was going on and maybe even find out who was behind it all, perhaps even what had happened to the still-missing Adam Heath. And on that, Harry was getting the sense that whatever it was, it wasn't good. With two bodies already, he had a horrible feeling that if and when they eventually found Adam, he would most likely make a third; drugs gangs weren't known for their forgiving nature.

'Adam Heath isn't just someone I've seen wandering around the Dales,' Bryony began. 'I bumped into him while I was travelling. I wasn't wearing my journalist hat at the time, if you know what I mean. I was abroad to just get away from things, to escape and to heal. I looked quite different.'

'Considering the description I'd been given, you look quite different from what I was expecting,' said Harry.

Bryony reached for a leather handbag that was on the sofa beside her. As she was using only one hand, she struggled a bit to open it, but eventually managed to flip it open and pull something out to show Harry.

'Blonde wig,' she said. 'A decent one, too; not something you just grab from a fancy dress shop.' She held it out for Harry to have a closer look, but he declined. 'I've not always been a journalist; spent a bit of time as a makeup artist, so I know enough about how to change the way I look, and to do so convincingly.'

Something popped into Harry's mind, pushing its way through everything else that was jostling around in there, vying for attention. 'Shane's house; you were there the other day, weren't you? But Shane wasn't in.'

'I'd reached out to both Shane and Jack,' Bryony said. 'I didn't want Adam to know who I was or what I did or didn't know, if that makes sense. I never heard from Jack, but Shane got in touch, said he wanted to talk about something.'

'You spoke to him?'

'Briefly,' said Bryony, a little hesitantly, like she was keeping something back. 'Just to arrange to meet up at his place.'

'Do you have any idea what he wanted to tell you?'

'He said he had information that might be useful, that's all.'

'About drugs being part of Adam's business? Why wouldn't he go to the police? Why come to you? It's not like you can do much about it, is it?'

Harry was very aware of the edge in his voice and did nothing to dull it, either; a blunt knife was no good to anyone.

'Not everyone trusts the police,' Bryony said. 'Something like this, it's big and dangerous. Go to the police with it and suddenly you're in the middle of an investigation, your life's turned upside down, you're worrying about the safety of family and friends. But tell someone like me, keep it vague enough to make sure it can't be traced? That's different.'

Harry wasn't convinced, but decided to move things on a bit.

'You bumped into Adam abroad, then; how, exactly?'

'Like I said, I was escaping, and, well ... I did a few things I shouldn't, took a few things I shouldn't, if you know what I mean. I saw him with one of the girls I bought something from.'

Harry was suddenly rather impressed with Bryony. She was, for whatever reason, being very open about what she had done. That didn't mean she was being honest, though. Harry had never trusted journalists.

'He was buying?'

'Yes,' said Bryony. 'But not drugs.'

Harry understood immediately.

'But how does that lead you to where we are now?' he asked.

Bryony shuffled herself to try and get comfortable again, though Harry wondered how anyone could be comfortable sitting as she was, and with her arm bandaged up.

'The girl—she was a little loose-tongued is probably the best way to describe her. She'd been ordered to approach him, said men like him were stupid and easy for the people she worked for to target and use.'

'She was a honey trap, then?'

'Yes,' said Bryony. 'It's my belief that Adam was presented with an offer he either couldn't refuse or didn't want to. Perhaps both, though I'm leaning towards didn't want to, considering how easily he slipped into providing his new partners with a route into the UK. Anyway, I didn't really think much more about it, not while I was out there, still escaping. But when I came home and started to get my life back together, and I started writing again, I knew I had a story. I worked on plenty of other things, enough to help me buy this place, but this, it was the big one, the story that would make me.'

Harry sighed.

'You do know there's more to life than getting a story, don't you?' he said. 'Something like this, it's dangerous; you said it your-self, even! It's for the police to deal with, not journalists trying to earn a few quid and an award or two!'

That edge was back in his voice, sharper now, too. But Harry had dealt with drug gangs in the past. He knew how dangerous they could be. If being harsh now saved Bryony more agony in the future, then so be it.

'I know it's dangerous,' said Bryony, hissing with pain as she spoke. 'It's also exciting; why the hell else do you think I'd do some-thing that would end with me in this?' She lifted her bandaged arm, yelping in pain. 'I don't expect you to understand, but there it is.'

'At least you're honest. I can respect that.'

'Honest? Oh, I wouldn't go that far...'

Harry's sharp edge was immediately blunted by the smile that lit up Bryony's face, and he laughed. He then gestured at Bryony's injured arm.

'Putting two and two together, then, I'm going to assume that you were sneaking around Adam's mother's house for something that would help with your story, correct?'

'The gang was communicating with Adam somehow,' Bryony explained, 'but I couldn't get my head around how. I needed to know, otherwise I had nothing.'

'They're hardly going to be open about it, are they?'

'Exactly,' said Bryony. 'You see, I'd followed him enough times to know he wasn't meeting anyone. And no drugs gang was going to be using emails or anything like that, so what was it?'

'Burner phones usually,' said Harry. 'Buy, use once, and dispose, nice and simple.'

'Wasn't that, either. I only ever saw him using one phone, and he'd use that to talk to his mum, to do normal coffee business on, just general everyday stuff, really.'

'You don't expect me to believe you trailed him enough to be absolutely sure he had no other phones.'

'No, of course I don't, but it's the truth,' said Bryony. 'I take my job seriously. I'm thorough. I don't just go ahead and publish something I've not researched properly. I'm not Askew, for God's sake!'

'His reputation goes before him, then.'

'Awful man. But I keep him onside, just in case. He's useful, in a weaselly, sly kind of way.'

Harry said, 'If it's not phones, then what is it? Dead letter drops?'

'Sort of, yes.'

'Really?'

Harry was surprised.

'Not letters, though; books.'

TWENTY-NINE

Something clicked into place in Harry's mind, and like a machine that had been missing the one piece that had been preventing it from working, cogs and gears started to turn.

'You mean Peggy's business? Those books? You're kidding.'

'She's got nothing to do with it,' said Bryony. 'But yes, those books.'

Harry remembered the book Sowerby had shown him, the one found during the warehouse fire, and told Bryony about it. And seeing as Sowerby had popped up in his mind, he sent her a quick message to see if she had anything else to share, hoping for something on the ballistics report from Scotland, at the very least.

'I couldn't work out why the books were even at the ware-house,' he said, 'and then Peggy explained it away. Something about Adam picking them up for her sometimes, and I thought nothing more of it.'

'You wouldn't,' said Bryony. 'And why would you? They're just books, aren't they? Nothing dodgy about books, really, especially second-hand ones, Folio editions, that kind of thing. And with Peggy's business, it's all out in the open, isn't it? She's just happily doing her thing. That's why it works so well.'

'How, though?' Harry asked. 'I've met Peggy. How does what she's doing join up with this?'

'I think Peggy's business does a little bit better than it deserves to.'

'Buyers working for the drug gang?'

'The buyers *are* the drug gang. Not all of them, obviously; Peggy absolutely sells books to legitimate buyers; I know, because I've bought a few from her myself. But a lot of the buyers, they're bogus, and the books contain various coded messages about shipments, that kind of thing.'

'That's actually pretty clever,' said Harry. 'No one's going to suspect someone like Peggy or her business, of being anything other than what it is; a little online shop selling second-hand collectable books, right? But how does Adam send and receive the messages?'

'Simple; he's a buyer, too,' said Bryony. 'He knows what books to bid on and never loses.'

'I can't believe that; he's bound to lose some.'

'If he does, no one's going to be any the wiser; another book is sold to Peggy, and he buys that one instead.'

'They don't contain handwritten notes, then?'

'No. He uses this...'

Bryony reached into her bag again and removed a small, unassuming book with a black cover. She handed it to Harry.

'I found that a few weeks ago,' she said.

'Where?'

'Peggy's. Like most people, she's not great on security; if you hang around long enough, you soon find out where they leave the spare key that they think no one will ever find, and when they're going to be out. I picked that up a few months back,' she said, pointing at the black book. 'I overheard Adam and her talking about a trip out to the theatre in Darlington for her birthday; it was too tempting not to see what I could find.'

'And you found this, just lying there?'

'Not exactly lying there, no, but neither was it difficult to find.'

The story didn't sit quite right with Harry, and then he remembered something else that Peggy had told Jen. She'd suspected she'd had intruders before, because things had been moved or they'd disappeared. She'd thought she was just being forgetful; clearly not.

Harry lifted the code book.

'Why did you go back to Peggy's if you'd already found this?'

'I'm a journalist,' Bryony said. 'I wanted more information for the story. I'd planned to go to the warehouse again, but then when I heard about the fire...'

Harry held up a hand to stop Bryony for a moment.

'What do you mean, again?' he asked. 'And how would you have got into the warehouse in the first place?'

'Shane...'

'But you said—'

'I know what I said!' Bryony snapped back. 'He said he had suspicions, but was nervous about looking into it. I persuaded him to give me the code to get into the building. I'd already used it once before to have a look around, and see if I could find anything.'

So, Bryony had been holding something back, Harry thought.

'Why didn't you tell me that straight away?'

'Because I'm used to keeping secrets, that's why; not in a bad way, just to protect myself, my story, and my sources.'

'You weren't worried about CCTV?'

Bryony laughed.

'CCTV? There isn't any. Well, there are cameras, but the cables were cut months ago by a bunch of kids wanting to do that parkour stuff without getting caught. And they've never been reconnected.'

'Parkour?'

'Running around and leaping and jumping off things, like bridges and buildings and bollards,' Bryony explained.

'What, only things that begin with B?'

'Look it up; it's easier than me having to explain it.'

Harry doubted he would.

'Anyway,' Bryony sighed, 'I tried the night of the fire, but the code had been changed. I got desperate, decided to try and break in. Like I said, I wasn't worried about being caught on camera or anything. But then I saw a van pull up, one I didn't recognise, and I thought it was probably best for me to get the hell out of there before they grabbed me.'

Harry remembered that their witness, Bob Ackroyd, had mentioned something about seeing a large shadow leaving the warehouse the same night, just before the fire.

'This van,' he asked, 'was it really quiet? Odd question, I know.'

'No, it isn't,' said Bryony, 'because it was. I think it was electric. I didn't even hear it approach, and I didn't see it, either, because the driver had the headlights switched off.'

Something else flitted through Harry's mind about what Bryony had just said, a small detail from the night of the fire, but his phone buzzed, and whatever it was popped like a balloon. It was a message from Sowerby asking him to give her a call. He sent a message back, and said he would do so as soon as he was done.

'Bryony, why were you at the hospital?' he asked, putting his phone back in his pocket.

'For this, obviously,' Bryony replied, pointing at her bandaged arm with her good arm. 'It's not as bad as it looks, but I wasn't about to deal with it by dousing it in bicarb and covering it in plasters.'

Harry shook his head.

'No, I don't mean the night when you broke into Peggy's house and she threw a kettle at you; I mean today when I was there to chat with Jack. The nurse thought you were a colleague of mine, mainly because that's what you told him.'

'After hearing about what had happened at the warehouse, I thought I'd see if Jack knew anything. I knew Adam was away, and Shane wasn't picking up, and he wasn't at his place when I went to see him, either. Jack was the next natural point of contact. And the only one as well, really.'

'After Peggy.'

'Yes, after Peggy. But I'd already had that ruined by Askew, hadn't I? He turned up at the same time as me. I've bumped into him before; he's like a bad smell you just can't wash off.'

'But you broke into Peggy's house after you and Askew door-stepped her.'

'Yes, because I had no choice at that point, did I?'

'We always have a choice,' said Harry. 'That's what life is, Bryony; just one choice after another.'

'Yes, and sometimes we make the wrong ones, don't we, or are you Mr Perfect?'

Harry screwed up his face, then pointed at it.

'A few wrong decisions led to this happening,' he said. 'Not that I could've made any other decision at the time, mind.'

'Exactly,' said Bryony, then added, 'How... ?'

'IED.'

'Ah.'

For a moment or two, neither Harry nor Bryony said a word, but it was Bryony who broke the silence.

'I turned up at Jack's place in Bedale, saw what was going on, and followed the ambulance to the hospital. I gave it a day, then went to see if I could speak with him. I'd no idea what I was going to ask him, if I could get him to trust me, or if I could even trust him, but you were there, and I panicked.'

Harry realised then that although Bryony knew about the fire, she had no idea about the body found in the middle of it.

'There's a reason Shane wasn't at his house,' he said, his voice quieter, more solemn. 'We found a body in the wreckage of the warehouse. It's been confirmed as Shane.'

Harry watched Bryony's eyes widen.

'What? Shane's dead?'

'I'm sorry, yes.'

'I ... But that's...'

And again, silence entered the room and sat down between them, this time with a weight to it that Harry wasn't sure how to shift.

At last, Bryony spoke, though her voice was hesitant now, cautious.

'Do you think Adam did it?'

'I'll be honest, Bryony, I don't know what to think,' said Harry. 'This whole thing is going to give me a permanent headache if I'm not careful. Shane's dead, Jack's in hospital, and Adam's missing. Now I've got what sounds like a drug cartel behind it, but that still doesn't mean I'm any closer to finding who's responsible. If anything, it only makes the whole thing even worse.'

Harry decided to keep what had happened in Scotland to himself; there was no need for Bryony to know any of that. More to the point, he was there to find things out *from* her, not the other way around.

'Just out of interest, how the hell did you even drive with your arm like that?'

'With a lot of difficulty and far too many pain killers,' Bryony answered. 'Also, the car's an automatic, so that made it a little more doable.'

'Well, don't go doing that again,' Harry advised.

'Trust me, I won't.'

'Trust you? Really? You've admitted to all manner of things that I should, by rights, arrest you for, and with little to no remorse, either, I might add.'

'Is that why you're here?' Bryony asked. 'To arrest me?'

Harry pushed himself to his feet, scratched the scars on his chin.

'No,' he said. 'I'm not. I think there's a chance that what Peggy did unintentionally when you broke into her house, probably did more than a short spell behind bars would ever have a chance at doing. And really, between you and me, what's the hell would be the point?'

'Bigger fish?'

Harry headed over to the front door.

'Considerably so.'

Bryony moved to get up.

'Don't,' Harry said. 'You'll have done enough damage to that arm of yours as it is, with all your ridiculous driving to chase a bloody story. So, why don't you take a little bit of advice from someone who's been carrying a lot more scars around with him for over half of his life, than you could ever wish for?'

'Who the hell wishes for scars?' Bryony asked.

'My point exactly,' said Harry. 'Stay home, heal, and have a serious think about your choice of career, because from where I'm standing, it doesn't appear to be doing you much good, does it?' He got up, turned toward the door, and looked down at the book he was still holding. 'And,' he added, glancing over at Bryony and catching her eye, 'I'll be keeping this.'

Harry let himself out and marched back to his vehicle, pulling out his phone to call Sowerby as he sat behind the steering wheel, but as he did so, a thought crossed his mind and was immediately T-boned by another driving straight into it. Something Bryony had said about her breaking into Peggy's place, and what Peggy herself had mentioned about intruders. Something didn't add up.

He put the book in the glove box, stowed his phone, got out of his car again, and jogged back over to Bryony's house. He knocked, tried the door, found that it opened, and pushed in.

Bryony hadn't moved. She looked up at him, somewhat despairingly.

'You've changed your mind, then, is that it? Here to arrest me, after all?'

'No,' Harry said, staying over by the open door. 'You broke into Peggy's house...'

'Yes,' said Bryony. 'But I've already told you that.'

'How many times?'

'What?'

'How many times did you break into the house?'

'Twice,' said Bryony. 'First time, I found the notebook in the cellar, and the second time, well, we all know what happened, don't we? Why? What's the problem?'

'Something Peggy mentioned,' said Harry. 'She said she

thought she'd had other intruders because things had moved or gone missing. She thought it might be just her being forgetful.'

'Sounds like the most plausible reason,' said Bryony. 'I was only there twice, and I didn't move anything, and the only thing I took was that code book.'

'She said it was bread, tins of food.'

'Nothing to do with me. I wasn't there for some bizarre late-night supermarket sweep.'

'Why food, though?' Harry said. 'Why that? Why would someone break in and take just a few tins and some bread?'

'Because they were hungry, maybe?' Bryony suggested.

Harry's eyes widened.

'Exactly! It's exactly that, isn't it? Because they were hungry! Of course! Bloody hell! Thank you,' Harry said, then he was out of the door, phone to his ear as he dropped into the driver's seat. But he wasn't calling Sowerby; whatever she'd messaged him about earlier, it would have to wait.

'Matt?'

'Harry? What is it? You sound in a rush.'

'How soon can you get to Peggy's?'

'Caldbergh? Half an hour at the most? Why, what's wrong?'

'And you can go right now?'

'I can,' said Matt. 'Harry, what's wrong? What's happened?'

'I'll explain when I get there,' Harry said. 'Whatever you do, don't go inside. Wait for me, okay? In fact, park up outside Cald-bergh and send me your location, then we can go in together.'

'You're being very mysterious, Harry.'

'I know,' Harry replied, hung up, stuffed his phone in a pocket, and sped away from Bryony's house, half wondering if he was reading too much into it, or seeing it for exactly what it was...

THIRTY

Spotting Matt's vehicle exactly where he'd said it would be, Harry pulled over and realised that he remembered nothing of the journey from Darlington. The whole thing had been done on automatic, while his mind jostled everything around from the last few days, trying to make sense of it. And he still couldn't, not yet, but this next bit he felt damned sure he was right about. If he wasn't? Then he was losing his touch, and it would be time for a career change. Though what he would change to, Harry hadn't the faintest idea.

He clambered out of his vehicle to meet Matt by the side of the road. He'd been a soldier, a police officer, a detective, and those ways of life were in his DNA now. Change? He didn't fear it, he simply couldn't see it happening.

'Now then,' Matt said, as Harry walked over.

Matt was leaning against the side of the police Land Rover.

'Been waiting long?' Harry asked.

'Not really; gave me a chance to stretch my legs. You going to tell me why we're here? Well, not here, exactly, because this is just a layby at the side of the road, isn't it? Not very interesting, really, but the view's decent.'

'You're rambling.'

'I'm waiting for you to explain.'

Harry leaned himself up against the Land Rover beside Matt.

'I don't know everything,' he said, 'not yet, but with this, I've become more and more certain that I'm right.'

'About what?'

'Adam,' Harry said. 'And where he is. Not, I hasten to add, where he's been, or what he's been up to, but where he is, right now.'

Harry watched a frown creep across Matt's face.

'You think he's alive?'

'I do.'

'I thought—'

'That Adam was behind it all?' Harry said, finishing Matt's sentence. 'I've not said that it isn't. It could be Adam, trying to clean house and escape. It could be whoever's been shipping the drugs through his business, too, because they've been compromised somehow. All I've said, is that I think I know where he is. And that's why we're here.'

'He's in Caldbergh? But that doesn't make any sense!'

'We thought he was in Scotland, and it turned out that he wasn't,' said Harry. 'We don't even know if he was there at all, do we?'

'No, I suppose we don't.'

'So, if he wasn't in Scotland, and if he's not yet turned up dead, then where else could he be?'

'Hiding, I should think,' said Matt. 'Assuming he's not dead, which he may well be, and we've just not found him. Or we're not meant to.'

Harry pushed himself away from the Land Rover.

'I'll see you in a few minutes outside Peggy's, okay?'

'But she's already told us she thought he was in Scotland, Harry; she's been getting those postcards, remember?'

'Which were fake.'

'Yes, but they made her think Adam was there, didn't they? That was the whole point of them being sent.'

'Like I said, see you outside the house.'

With nothing else to say, Harry dropped back into the Rav, pulled out and drove past Matt, then carried along until he was in Caldbergh. He parked up opposite Peggy's house, and a moment or two later, Matt pulled up behind.

Harry met Matt as he dropped down out of the Land Rover.

'I still don't understand why we're here,' he said.

Harry gestured towards Peggy's house with a nod of his head, then set off across the lane and up the path to rap hard knuckles against the door.

The door opened, and there was Peggy.

'Oh, Mr Grimm,' she said, her eyes flicking then to Matt. 'And ... oh, I can't remember, now ... Dinsdale, that's it.'

'Now then,' Matt said.

'Can we come in, please, Peggy?'

Peggy stepped back and allowed Harry and Matt into her house.

Harry was relieved to see no boxes waiting at the bottom of the stairs to be carried up.

'I was just having a nap in the lounge,' Peggy said, leading Harry and Matt through the house to the kitchen. 'Now that I'm awake, I rather fancy a brew. Yourselves?'

'Later, perhaps,' said Harry, and took a seat at the dining table. 'Just thought it best we come and have a chat,' he continued. 'There's been a few developments.'

Ignoring what Harry had said about tea, Peggy set to filling the kettle, and didn't turn to face Harry as she replied, 'Really? Well, that is good, after everything that's been happening.'

Harry knew that Peggy as yet had no idea about what had happened in Scotland. Well, that wasn't quite accurate, he thought; he knew that none of his team had told her about it, and that was different.

'Peggy,' he began, his voice calm, almost kind, 'how long have you known that Adam was in your cellar?'

Peggy said nothing, but Harry saw her shoulders sag a little; was that relief at being asked, he wondered?

'What was that, Harry?' Matt asked, sounding confused. 'Think I must've misheard you...'

'No, you heard right enough,' Harry said. 'Didn't he, Peggy? You've known Adam was in your cellar for a good while now. In fact, I'd go so far as to say you wanted us to know as well, didn't you? That's why you made a point of mentioning how food had gone missing. No valuables, nothing important, just a few tins, some bread; hardly items someone would break into a house for, are they? But they are things you'd want if you were hungry.'

Peggy clicked the kettle on.

'Yorkshire tea alright? I know you said you didn't want one, but I know you'll change your mind.'

'When did you find out?' Harry asked. 'Or have you always known?'

Peggy stared at the kettle, but didn't move.

'Peggy, I need you to sit down and talk to us,' Harry said. 'People have been killed. I don't know what part your son played in it, but this can't go on. Not anymore.'

When Peggy turned around, tears were streaming down her face. Harry felt his phone buzz, checked it, and saw that it was a call from Jim back at the office. Well, whatever it was, it would have to wait, so he ignored it. And Jen was probably available anyway, so if it was urgent, Jim could give her a call instead.

'I'm so scared,' Peggy said at last. 'For us both; what they'll do. I just did what Adam said. It made sense, you see. He was trying to come to the police. That's how this all started.'

Matt asked, 'Peggy, where's the cellar? Is Adam still here?'

Peggy gave the most subtle of nods, then pointed back out of the kitchen.

'Door under the stairs,' she said. 'It's more than a cupboard. There's a trapdoor in the floor. Then stairs.'

'Would you mind calling him for us?' Harry asked. 'He'll trust you, won't he?'

'He doesn't trust anyone,' said Peggy. 'Not anymore, not after the way he's been forced to live.'

Harry stood up and Matt did the same.

'Call him up, Peggy,' Harry said, 'and we'll be waiting. Just tell him we're here and to not do anything stu—'

A clatter and bang came from the hall and Harry swept around to see the rear of a man pelting down the hall towards the door.

'Adam!' Harry called, and charged after him.

The door opened, and the man hurled himself out into the day, but Harry was already after him and, thanks to his on-off relationship with running, and the push that Jen would give him now and again, he was the faster of the two.

Racing out of the garden gate and across the lane, the man turned left, making for a stile in the wall. Ignoring how senseless what he was about to do was, Harry launched himself with such an explosion of power, that he crashed into the man and took him to the ground, landing them both in a charitably soft verge.

'Don't even think about it!' Harry roared, as Adam tried to get up and push himself away from Harry. Matt grabbed him and made it very clear there was no running away.

Harry, after doing a very good impression of a tortoise stranded on its back, pulled himself to his feet and gave Adam a long, hard stare.

'Panicking and buggering off isn't the best of ideas, now, is it? We're the police, Adam; we're here to help.'

Adam said nothing. The man was ghostly pale, not from the exertion of trying to escape, but, he suspected, fear.

'Look,' he said, 'right now I've not a clue what's been going on, not all of it, anyway. So, it would be greatly appreciated if you could clear things up. How's that sound?'

'I … I didn't mean to run; I just panicked, and I know you're the police, but … Oh God…'

Harry couldn't help but feel a little sorry for the man in front of him, so softened his voice just enough.

'Your mum's just made a fresh brew. So, what do you say we

have a nice chat over a warm mug of tea, and no doubt a biscuit or two?'

Adam didn't respond, but for Harry, that was answer enough, and with Matt taking the man's other arm, they led him back across the road to the house.

THIRTY-ONE

Jen was sitting opposite an eighty-six-year-old woman with hair as white as a whisp of cloud on a bright summer's day, and eyes so keen that to hold their stare for any time at all left her feeling oddly exposed.

Edna Scar, a woman who had been Jen's babysitter throughout her entire childhood, was reclined in a large, soft, and very flowery armchair perched at the side of a small fire, and the flames were licking at the chimney gleefully. The room was decorated with this and that, a picture here, a teaspoon rack there, a grey silhouette on the flowery wallpaper from where a large cross had once hung. But that had gone the day her overly religious and over-bearing brother had died. They'd lived together their whole lives, but Jen believed it was only since Eric had died that Edna had started to live.

'Where was he, then?' Jen asked, unable to take her eyes away from Steve.

The lizard, who was somehow on Edna's lap, looked very pleased with himself. Jen couldn't for the life of her work out how he had got there, because there was certainly no way Edna could have lifted him. And the idea that he climbed up there of his own accord was frankly bizarre. His jaw rested lazily on her left shoulder, while the rest of him lay across her at an angle, his tail flopping down to touch the carpet.

'In the greenhouse,' Edna said. 'There's a broken pane that Eric never fixed and I've yet to bother with; I think he must've got in through there. It's nice and warm in there, you see, so I think that's what drew him in.'

Edna had her right arm resting across Steve's body, and with her left hand, she was scratching under his chin.

'Do you have experience with lizards?' Jen asked. 'Only ... I mean, he seems very calm with you, doesn't he? How did you get him inside? Actually, never mind that, how did you get him up onto your lap?'

Edna smiled knowingly, which Jen found a little infuriating.

'I just asked him to come inside, that's all,' Edna said. 'And he followed. As for where he is now, I fell asleep, and when I woke up, there he was; he's very soppy, isn't he?'

She scratched Steve's chin again and Jen could've sworn she saw the damned creature grin a little.

'I've not given him anything to eat,' Edna said. 'Didn't want to upset his stomach, and I'm sure you have a special diet for him, mice or insects or something. But I have given him some water. Filtered, too, you know; bought one of those fancy things a few weeks back, and it really has made the water a lot nicer. Do you have one?'

Jen wasn't really listening, she was still staring at Steve.

'What? Oh, no, I don't,' she said. 'I think I should probably take him back now, if that's okay. I can't thank you enough, though. I was so worried.'

'Oh, I don't think you had anything to be worried about,' said Edna. 'Steve can look after himself, can't you, Steve?'

She turned her head to gaze at the creature, and Jen watched his tail swish side to side like a vine in the breeze.

Jen stood up.

'Well, I'd best take him back,' she said. 'Before he gets too comfortable!'

No sooner had she said the words than she saw Edna's keen eyes lose a little of their sparkle.

'You know, you can always come round to say hello to him,' she suggested, as Edna made no attempt at all to persuade the huge creature to slip down off her lap. 'I'm sure he'd love to see you.'

'And you can always leave him here with me, too, if you ever need to,' said Edna. 'He's really no bother at all.'

'Not as cuddly as a dog, though, or a cat, is he?' Jen said.

'Oh, I'll never own a dog,' said Edna, 'and cats ... they're just too aloof, aren't they? They don't really want to be with you at all. Steve, though, I think just loves a bit of company. Don't you, Steve?'

Steve's tail waggled a little more enthusiastically.

Jen was very pleased that Jadyn wasn't around to witness any of this. He was on his way back from Scotland now, wouldn't be home till late into the night. He'd said he would head straight home to Reeth and see her tomorrow, but she'd suggested otherwise, which had made him laugh, perhaps a little too deeply.

Reaching over to take hold of the huge Lizard, Jen was stopped halfway by a phone call. She excused herself from Edna's living room, answered the call, and once it was done, dashed back in.

'Edna,' she said, somehow managing to sound both sheepish and in a hurry at the same time, 'I need to rush off. Don't suppose you'd mind—'

Edna's face lit up.

'What, Steve can stay? Really?'

'Of course,' said Jen. 'I will want him back though, just so that's understood. I'll pop round and grab him when I get back.'

Edna's response was to smile and then shoo her out of the house with a wave of her hand.

Outside, Jen raced over to her vehicle, jumped in, and punched in the address. It had been Jim on the phone, calling from the office to tell her that Bryony White, who she knew Harry had seen earlier in the day, had called to find out where Harry was, and had sounded in a bit of a panic.

Jim had tried Harry and Matt, but hadn't been able to get through. Jen had then advised Jim to send a couple of Uniforms from Darlington around to Bryony's house, to check she was okay, and to keep an eye on her until someone else arrived. So, with Harry and Matt unreachable, Dave otherwise engaged, that someone was Jen, so she turned her vehicle around in the road and headed off, happy at least that Steve was now in safe hands.

BACK IN CALDBERGH, Harry was sitting with Matt at the kitchen table, and opposite them was Adam Heath and his mother, Peggy.

Adam, Harry thought, looked a mess, but then hiding out in a cellar was hardly the Hilton.

'Maybe it would be best,' Harry began, 'if I told you some of what I know, and perhaps even a little of what I think I know, and then you can try and fill in the blanks for me, how does that sound?'

Adam nodded with all the enthusiasm of a small boy told to own up for smashing a church window with his football, and Peggy reached out to tap a comforting, motherly hand on his forearm.

'I'll be as brief as I can,' Harry began. 'Firstly, I know about the drugs; I know that something happened abroad, that you ended up being persuaded, shall we say, to allow your business to be used as a covert way to get drugs into the country, and that your mother's little book business was used as an impressively under-the-radar way for the drug gang or gangs you were dealing with to communicate with you. How am I doing so far?'

'It was a couple of years ago,' Adam said, his voice surprisingly calm.

Harry wondered if finally speaking about what had been going on was a huge relief for him, which was understandable.

'I was abroad, checking out on some small, organic coffee farms, the kind I want my business to be a part of and support, because that's all really good for the brand and the ethics side of things.'

Ethics, Harry thought, and yet he'd ended up in the drug import business.

'What happened, exactly?' he asked. 'If you're out there because ethics is your thing, and like you said, all part of the brand, how does someone like you end up mixed up in drugs?'

'I was approached with an offer I couldn't refuse.'

'By which you mean ...?' Harry asked, but suspected already that he knew the answer.

'I got to keep breathing,' said Adam. 'A young woman approached me, I was flattered, because she was so pretty, and I couldn't believe she would be interested in someone like me.'

'She wasn't,' Harry said. 'You were a mark given to her by her employers.'

'I was naïve.'

'That's an understatement.'

'I went for a drink with her, again naïve, I know, and the next thing I know she's taking me to a bar.'

Harry leaned back in his chair and covered his eyes in disbelief.

'Hell's bells, Adam,' he said, leaning forward again. 'For a start, all of that should've immediately got you thinking, "Hey, wait a minute, am I with a prostitute, here?" Because that's exactly what that sounds like; chat you up, have a drink, tell you of a special place, you follow, you end up in another bar that seems fine, filled with men just like you, lots of pretty girls, then your drink's spiked, you end up in a back room, you're stripped of your belongings, they persuade you to unlock your phone, empty your bank account, and you wake up the next day to a life of flashbacks and crippling shame.'

'I know all of that, of course I do,' said Adam, 'and right now I would swap that entire scenario for this!'

He hammered the point of a finger onto the table to emphasise what he was saying.

Matt asked, 'What exactly happened in the bar, Adam?'

'There was no bar,' Adam sighed, and Harry heard in Adam's voice his horror at what had happened to him, as though the memory was almost impossible to put into words, and it probably was, he guessed. 'I found myself in a room with six men, a chair, and...'

Adam stopped talking, and Harry could see that he was shaking.

'They threatened you, yes?'

A nod from Adam, fragile and terrified still by what he had experienced.

'They tied me to the chair, showed me all these machetes, photos of what they'd done to other people who hadn't done what they'd told them to do, a video ... God, that video! I can still see it now, hear it ... I've never seen anything like it ... it was just...'

Harry stayed quiet and let Adam speak.

'They knew about my business, told me that I was going to do exactly what I was told. If I didn't, it wouldn't just be me in their next video, but Mum. And I believed them. How could I not? I was told someone would contact me as soon as I was back in the UK, and they did, and here we are.'

Harry could see how Adam had had no choice in the matter.

'Not quite,' Harry said. 'Everything you've said, I can understand, and whatever happens from here on in, it'll be down to specialist teams, both here and abroad, to investigate what you've been involved with. But what I can't understand is how all of that ends with a torched warehouse and murder.'

'The stress was at breaking point. I knew what would happen if I didn't do what they said. But I couldn't go on, it had to stop, so I started to collect evidence so that I could go to the police, get protection for me and Mum. And it was all going fine until that bloody journalist turned up.'

'Bryony White, you mean?'

'I've no idea how she knew about any of it, but she did, and she started poking around, talking to Shane, and then to Jack when he was brought on board.'

There was anger in Adam's voice now, the man's emotions all over the place, each vying for attention.

'Then the book went missing. They knew about that soon enough, didn't they, the ones sending the drugs over in the coffee? And I knew it would only be a matter of time before they decided to cut things off here and move operations. And by cut things off, you know exactly what I mean, don't you?'

Adam drew a slow, shaky finger across his own throat.

Matt asked, 'What book are you talking about, Adam?'

'This one, I think,' Harry said, and pulled from a jacket pocket the book he'd picked up from Bryony's.

'You've spoken to her, then?' Peggy asked.

Harry looked at Peggy.

'It was Bryony who broke in that night, and who you threw a kettle at.'

'Well, she shouldn't go poking around, should she?' Peggy replied, an angry fire in her eyes.

'One question,' said Matt, his focus on Peggy. 'Why did you tell Jen about food going missing if you knew it was Adam all along, that he was in your cellar?'

Harry watched as Peggy glanced at her son, tears welling in her eyes.

'I was worried,' she said, her voice cracking a little now, but she controlled her emotions. 'He thought he could keep everything from me, but I knew, of course I did. I'm his mother! I thought, if I dropped a few hints, you might investigate a little further, help us, help him...'

'It was an attempt to send up a flare, wasn't it?' Harry said.

'Something like that.'

Harry looked back at Adam. 'You knew they were on to you, so Scotland was a decoy. Make everyone think you're away, so you can work on everything here in secret; even your mum wouldn't know, would she, what with those postcards you had MacKenzie send through?'

'I'd been to the area on holiday a few times,' Adam said. 'Thought about buying a place up there as well, for a while. One of MacKenzie's flyers was in a pile of leaflets I'd brought back with me some time ago, can't remember when. I just stumbled on it really when I was sorting through a few things, and then a little plan formed. He jumped at the chance to be paid to do nothing for a few weeks, to just house sit.'

Harry realised something.

'You don't know, do you?'

The confusion in Adam's eyes was answer enough.

'Know what?'

'What happened at the warehouse, the same thing happened in Scotland a few days before; the house was torched. MacKenzie is dead.'

Adam's jaw fell open.

'What?'

Harry explained what they knew, and about Jadyn heading north to investigate. As he spoke, Adam's eyes grew ever wider.

'I was right, then, wasn't I?' Adam said, once Harry had stopped speaking. 'They're after me and they're going to kill me! You have to protect me, protect us; please!'

Harry kept his voice calm and said, 'They must've sent someone to check up on you, found out it wasn't you, dealt with it the only way they know how—with deadly violence—then came back to clean out the warehouse of whatever they needed, before torching that, too. Shane must've stumbled in on what was going on, and ended up dead as well. I think they went after Jack as well, but he survived. Just.'

Adam swore under his breath, then paused, looked up at Harry questioningly, and asked, 'What do you mean, survived?'

That caught Harry off guard.

'I mean, that I went round to speak to him and found that someone had given him a good ki—' Another part of the puzzle clicked into place. 'It was you, wasn't it, Adam?'

The nod of acknowledgement was barely noticeable.

'Why?' Harry asked, though the thought that the man in front of him was capable of such violence seemed almost inconceivable.

Adam was on his feet.

'Isn't it obvious? He's one of them, Detective! He's a plant. The bastards didn't tell me. I found out for myself. Too late, as it happens, because Shane sent me a text the night they torched the warehouse, the night they killed him; he'd gone back late that evening to pick up some coffee for himself to take home, a perk of the job, you know? And he stumbles in on Jack and a couple of others with a van, and they're loading up, but not only that, they're spraying the place with fuel, just to help the fire along, because why the hell not, right? He calls me, but it's only a message, and he thinks I'm in Scotland, and I don't even see the message until the next day, and then...'

Harry was on his feet, the chair tumbling to the floor behind him with a clatter.

Adam jumped up to stare at Harry, defiance in his eyes.

'What, you're going to arrest me, is that it?' He tapped the side of his head. 'There's too much up here to just put me away, you know that, don't you? I can expose them, I can do a deal, keep myself and my mum safe!'

'Shut it!' Harry said, jabbing a finger at Adam, his voice so loud it bounced around the kitchen for a moment like it was trying to escape.

'That bastard should be dead for what he's done!' Adam replied.

Harry pointed at Adam's seat.

'Sit down! Now!'

Adam dropped into his chair.

Harry looked at Matt and stepped away from the table.

'We need Uniform at the hospital right now,' he said, leaving the kitchen. 'Tell them I'm on my way!'

'You want me to come with you?'

'No,' Harry said. 'Stay here, and keep any eye on Adam and his mum; I'll be in touch.'

Racing through the house, Harry barged through the front door and was down the path and at the Rav in seconds. Jumping in, he grabbed his phone and rang Sowerby on speaker.

'Nice of you to retu—'

'Ballistics,' Harry said, cutting her off.

'It was the same weapon,' Sowerby said, 'but I was calling about something else—'

'Not important right now,' Harry said. 'I need to get to the hospital. I'll call you back when I'm done.'

'If you're going to see the man you found at the house in Bedale, then it's very important, Harry.'

'What? Why?'

'There's something odd about it.'

'You should've seen the place,' Harry replied. 'Odd is being a tad polite if you ask me; it was an absolute shit tip.'

'I mean the DNA is odd,' said Sowerby. 'We've matched more than enough to Jack Moffatt, and we've also found some on him which is very clearly from his attacker.'

'I've just found out who that is, which is why I'm in a rush right now,' said Harry. 'Jack's the killer, works for the drug gang that's been using the coffee to import their product. Killed MacKenzie and Shane Dissall.'

'But there's DNA from someone else,' Sowerby continued. 'I know it's a house and houses have people in, but it was everywhere, like it's from someone who actually lives there.'

'Yes, Jack lives there!'

'But that's what I mean, it's not Jack, and it's not his attacker; it's someone else. There's even traces of it in Jack's clothing.'

'That doesn't make any sense! Jack lives there! And when I found him, he was even wearing what the neighbours said they'd seen him wear—'

Harry stopped talking.

The neighbours ... they'd described what they'd seen Jack wearing, but that was all. No one had said what Jack actually looked like, Harry realised, remembering something Matt had said about a hoodie being a great disguise.

What if Jack had killed the original tenant of the property and taken his clothes as a disguise? That would be enough to keep the neighbours at bay while he got on with the job he'd been sent to do, and stop them asking questions. Then Harry remembered the flies and an even more chilling thought crossed his mind, but before he had a chance to consider it, Sowerby's voice cut into his thoughts.

'Harry?'

'I've got to go,' Harry said, hanging up. He started the engine, hammered the gear lever into first, and swung the Rav around to head out of the village, just as Matt sprinted out of the house and nearly bounced off his bonnet.

Harry opened his window and leaned out.

'What the bloody hell are you doing, Matt? I nearly hit you!'

'He's gone, Harry!' Matt said, running around to the window.

'Who's gone? Adam? But I told you to—'

Matt shook his head.

'No, Harry; Jack...'

'What? How do you mean?'

'He's checked himself out of the hospital...'

THIRTY-TWO

Harry stared at Matt in disbelief.

'Gone? He can't be! When?'

'Not long after you left, apparently. Half an hour or so.'

'Why didn't someone stop him?'

'My guess, they wanted the bed, and if he was happy to walk out, they probably just let him. Hospitals are busy places, Harry.'

'I saw him, Matt; he was a mess! Adam's not wrong; he really did try to kill him, and that was Sowerby on the phone; they've found more DNA at the house.'

'What?'

'I don't think Jack lives there at all,' Harry explained.

'But that's where you found him.'

'I know, but I don't think he's the actual legal tenant. Remember those flies?'

'The place wasn't exactly clean.'

'Exactly,' said Harry. 'And what if those flies are there for an entirely different reason?'

Harry watched as Matt's eyes widened.

'You don't think...?'

'That Jack disposed of the tenant and took his place?' Harry said, finishing Matt's sentence. 'It's a working theory, but yes, I do.'

'Bloody hell, Harry...'

Harry asked, 'Did the hospital say anything else? Like where Jack's gone? Anything at all?'

'Nothing,' said Matt.

Harry remembered the missed call from Jim. Had that been the hospital, perhaps? Maybe he'd been told more than Matt. It was worth a shot.

Harry grabbed his phone and called Jim.

'It's okay, Harry,' Jim said, before Harry had a chance to speak. 'Everything's sorted. You're not needed.'

'What's sorted? Look, Jim, did the hospital call you?'

'The hospital? No, why would it?'

'Jack Moffatt,' said Harry. 'He's gone.'

'No, this was a call about Bryony White.'

'Bryony? Why?'

Harry couldn't for the life of him think why Bryony would want to speak to him again considering how much she had already told him, and not that long ago either.

'She wanted to know where you were, sounded in a bit of a panic, but it's okay; Jen's on her way.'

'Wanted to know where I was? Why'

'She didn't say,' said Jim. 'I've got a couple of Uniforms heading over to her though, so they'll get there before Jen.'

'And you're sure that Bryony didn't give any hint about what she wanted to tell me, why she was worried?'

'She didn't tell me anything,' said Jim. 'She just asked where you were, and sounded panicky. That's why Jen's on her way.'

'Then tell her to call me as soon as she's there,' Harry said, hung up, and stared at Matt, his jaw set.

'Harry, what's up?' Matt asked.

Harry didn't answer right away; something was twisting his gut into a pretzel. If Jack had been hired by the gang to keep an eye on what was going on at Adam's business, if they'd sent him north to deal with Adam and he'd killed MacKenzie, killed Shane, burned down the house in Scotland, burned down the warehouse, then...

'Bryony called for me, wanted to know where I was,' Harry said, climbing back out of the Rav, all his senses online, scanning the road, the fields, the walls. 'Jim said she sounded panicky, Jen's on her way over there now.'

Matt stepped back as Harry slammed the car door shut.

'Panicky? Why?'

'My guess? Jack; he wants to finish the job.'

'Finish the what?'

Harry grabbed hold of Matt's shoulder.

'Back in the house, Matt, right now!'

Matt froze.

Harry gave him a hard shove to get him moving.

'Shift it!'

Harry didn't give him a chance to complain, and pushed Matt on, forcing him into a run.

They crashed in through the front door and Harry hammered it home behind them, the sound loud enough to shake the house.

'What on earth are you doing?'

Harry saw Peggy staring at him, wide-eyed with shock.

'Keys, Peggy!'

'What? Why?'

'Just give me the bloody keys!'

Peggy nipped back into the kitchen and returned with the keys, and with Adam. Harry locked the door.

'Right, what other doors are there on the ground floor?'

Adam said, 'There's one at the back, and another onto a small alleyway down the side of the house.'

'Lock them,' Harry ordered, and Peggy ran off to do exactly that. Harry told Matt to go with her and added, 'Call this in; we need armed response!'

Adam asked, 'Armed response? What the hell's going on?'

'I'll tell you what the hell's going on,' said Harry. 'I believe your hired killer of an ex-employee is on his way to finish the job.' He glanced at Matt. 'And I think Bryony's suspected as much, and that's why she's in a panic.'

'You said he was in hospital!' shouted Adam. 'And why are you talking about Bryony?'

Harry ignored the question about Bryony. 'He was, and now he's not, and that beating you gave him, though good, wasn't enough to keep him there, not by a long shot. Back in the Paras, a colour sergeant once told me that if you're going to hit someone, make sure you only need to do it once, so they don't get up and fight back. Well, Jack obviously got back up, didn't he, Adam?'

Fear practically radiated from Adam's eyes.

'But he doesn't know I'm here, does he? No one does.'

'I think you giving him a kicking was enough of a clue that you were back in the area, don't you?' said Harry, incredulously. 'When I spoke to him at the hospital, he said he only ever knew of you being at your house in Richmond, at the warehouse, or here. I told him that the place in Richmond was rented out as a holiday let. Only leaves one option, really, doesn't it?'

Harry watched the cocktail of panic and terror rip through Adam in a heartbeat, and the man stumbled. Harry caught him before he crashed to the floor.

'And we've no time for any of that bollocks, either,' he growled. 'Jack's on his way, and that's a fact I'd happily bet my arse on. We've no idea when help will turn up, but I'm going to go with either "too late" or "in the nick of time," neither of which fills me with glee.'

'Too late?' More panic filled Adam's voice. 'What, do you mean, too late? You think he's going to try and kill us?'

Harry stared at Adam.

'Do I think he's going to try and kill us? Yes, very much so. But succeed? That's something entirely different, isn't it?'

Adam looked both terrified and confused—a look that actually suited him, Harry thought.

'How do you mean?'

'I mean,' said Harry, 'not if I have anything to do with it. Which, I hasten to point out, I do.'

Harry could see that Adam wasn't convinced, which was fair

enough; he wasn't standing in front of him tooled up and ready for war by any stretch of the imagination.

'But how can we stop him if we don't have anything to protect ourselves with? What are we going to do?'

Harry ignored Adam as Matt and Peggy returned.

'All doors and windows on the ground floor checked,' said Matt. 'Now what?'

'We can't just stand here and wait, can we?' said Adam. 'He's a killer! We have to get out of here! And now you've just locked us in? Are you mad?'

Harry wasn't listening; he was experiencing his soldier brain coming back online, waking up from a long sleep, but as ready for battle as it ever was.

'Jack seems to enjoy setting things on fire,' he said. 'Peggy, do you have any fire extinguishers in the house?'

'There's one in the kitchen,' Peggy replied. 'No, there's two; I didn't throw the other one away when it went out of date. Sort of a just-in-case; seemed such a waste.'

'Well, this is your just-in-case,' said Harry. 'Get them; they'll be small, but they're better than nothing.'

Adam was still panicking, pacing around the rest of them, his head clasped in his hands as though he was trying to stop his brain from exploding.

'Why didn't we just escape when we could? We've all got cars! Why lock ourselves in the house? It doesn't make sense!'

Harry couldn't deal with the distraction of Adam's nerves and needed him to calm down. He knew there was little chance of that, so decided it was best to just be clear on why they weren't in a car trying to escape, especially as he was still trying to work out how the hell they were going to protect themselves against a man with a gun and with every intention of using it.

'Because there's a damned good chance we'd have met him on the road, that's why,' he said. 'And I don't know if you've noticed, Adam, but every road around Caldbergh is a single sodding lane, and with Jack being the only one of us with a gun, I wouldn't fancy our chances if we met him coming the other way, would you?'

'We could go across the fields!'

The look Harry gave Adam was enough to make the man realise the idiocy of that suggestion.

'We sit, we wait for help, and we deal with whatever Jack decides to do. And that means you and your mum go upstairs, right now. Go as high as you can. Lock the door. And make sure the only people you let in are either me or Matt. Do you understand?'

Adam's answer was a nod, nothing else.

'Then go!' Harry said, and jabbed a finger up the stairs.

Adam and Peggy raced off, and a minute or so later, Harry heard a door slam.

'That's them out of the way,' said Matt. 'What next?'

'Kitchen,' said Harry, the thinnest of plans forming, and led Matt through. 'Get the hobs on,' he instructed, 'fill every pan you can with water, and the kettle. We need boiling water at every window, every door. And check if Peggy has any flour.'

'Not sure we should be baking at a time like this,' said Matt, holding up a couple of bags of self-rising. 'There's a couple more as well.'

Harry ignored him.

'Empty the cupboard of glasses, start with the most fragile ones you can find, and fill those with the flour.'

'But...'

'Just do it!'

Harry tried to think, what else would work? Anything? This was beyond desperate, but that didn't mean it was hopeless. He was also acutely aware of the law in this kind of situation, the use of reasonable force when facing an intruder. They could protect themselves in the heat of the moment, and that included using an object as a weapon. Things got sticky very quickly, though; carry on attacking the intruder when you're no longer in danger and that was hard to defend in court. And no one looked kindly on planning a trap for someone instead of involving the police. Trouble was, what choice did they have?

We are the police, he thought, and someone was heading over to where they were right now, that someone was undoubtedly armed, and they had the intent to kill, which was backed up by what had happened in Scotland and Leyburn. If getting a few pans of hot water and some makeshift flour grenades together was going to give them a chance of surviving till the cavalry arrived, then he was going to do it. As ridiculous as it was, Harry was certain it was better to be ridiculous and alive, than sensible and dead.

Eventually, with hot water placed around the ground floor close to entry points, along with dozens of glasses filled with flour, Harry gave Matt one of the fire extinguishers.

'If Jack throws something through a window and a fire starts, don't think you can put it out with that; all you're doing is stalling it long enough so that you can get the hell out and survive. Whatever you do, don't use water; there's a good chance anything thrown will be petrol, and all water does is spread the fire.'

'I hear you,' said Matt. 'Now, about the pans and the flour...'

'Here,' Harry said, and handed Matt a hefty-looking walking stick, keeping one for himself. 'Found these in the hall. If Jack gets in, the water will scald him, get in his eyes, disorientate him. Same goes for the flour. If he's wet from a pan of water, and in pain from the heat of it, and he gets hit with that as well, it'll stick to him, and the cloud will blind him.'

Harry could see that Matt didn't believe any of what he was being told.

'You adapt to your environment,' Harry explained. 'That's how you survive. We're making the best of what we have. Now all I have to do is keep him at bay.'

Matt frowned at that, clearly hearing something not quite right with what Harry had just said.

'What do you mean, I? Don't you mean we?'

Harry shook his head.

'No, Matt, I don't,' he replied, and he held the man with a stare that had seen things he knew Matt couldn't even begin to imagine. 'I want you upstairs with Adam and Peggy. Your job is to protect them. My job is to make sure you don't actually have to.'

'Not a sodding chance!'

'I mean it, Matt,' Harry pressed. 'You've a wife and a daughter. I'm a soldier and I'm used to fighting; I know what this is like, I've been in worse and survived it. I can't have you here, have you at risk. That's just not happening.'

'I'm not leaving you on your own, Harry; you know I can't do that.'

'You've done what I asked,' Harry said. 'Your job now is to protect upstairs. Get on the phone, find out how far away the response unit is, keep them updated with everything, tell them what we've done, what we've prepared, how we're protecting ourselves, where you and Adam and Peggy are, the layout of the house, give them every detail you can, but leave this bit to me.'

Matt didn't move.

'Please, Matt,' Harry said, his voice quieter now. 'There's a good chance I'm going to have to do things that I can't ask or expect you to do yourself. But this isn't a request, it's an order. Go, Matt!' Harry's shout turned raw and guttural, and he once again grabbed Matt's shoulder and pushed, this time towards the stairs. 'Now!'

'If something happens to you,' Matt began, pushing back against Harry's shove.

'It won't,' said Harry, through gritted teeth.

And Matt was gone.

A moment later, Harry heard tyres on the road outside. Peeking through a window from behind a curtain, he saw someone climbing out of a van. No doubt the same van Bryony had mentioned, he thought.

'Hello, Jack,' he muttered, then saw the back of the van open and three other men climb out. 'Ah, Shite...'

THIRTY-THREE

Harry was momentarily stunned by what he was witnessing. There was brazen, and then there was this; these were people unafraid of being seen, or even of the prospect of the police turning up, which was bad, very bad.

Harry stayed where he was, watching as they walked up to Peggy's front door. Jack and two of the men were openly carrying pistols. Harry didn't care what type; he was on the wrong side of them, and that was all that really mattered. The third man was carrying what Harry recognised as an enforcer, a specially designed battering ram used by the police and fire services; sixteen kilograms of steel, with two angled handles that would allow anyone using one to smash apart the locks on most inward-opening doors.

But then three tonnes of impact-force smashing into you would have that effect, he thought.

Harry stared at the front door; two locks, one chain, but they wouldn't hold for long. He had to do something to delay what was about to happen.

Shoving the walking stick under his arm, Harry grabbed a large saucepan of the boiling-hot water with one hand, and stuffed the fingers of his other hand into three of the glasses Matt had filled with flour, then raced upstairs. He found the bedroom overlooking the front door, let the walking stick fall to the floor on the landing, then, staying low, crept around the bed to open a window as quietly as he could.

As Harry leaned out of the window just as the impact of the first hit from the enforcer slammed into the door, the boom reverberating through the house like it had been struck by lightning, the sound of it thundering through the building, shaking pictures on walls, causing the windows to rattle.

Harry leaned out further to see Jack and the three other men directly beneath him.

The second strike from the enforcer blasted through the house, and Harry heard one of the locks on the front door give way. He didn't wait for a third strike. He dumped the still-steaming water out of the window and directly onto the bare heads of the four men below. Then, as the water hit, and before the men had any idea what was going on, or where the sudden attack was coming from, he hurled down the three glasses of flour.

The water, as it hit the men, caught the sun like a burst bag of diamonds. They yelled out as much in shock as pain from the scalding heat, and then the glasses hit home. One missed, smashing on the path at their feet, another glanced off a shoulder, but Harry was relieved to watch as the third scored a direct hit, slamming into the head of the man wielding the enforcer, and Jack and the three men he had brought with him disappeared in a billowing cloud of flour laced with vicious glass shards.

Harry watched the men stumble into each other, their heads white with flour, blood seeping through from where glass shards had sliced into them, then he went back downstairs to grab more glasses, before bounding back upstairs to another room at the front of the house. He didn't fancy going back to that first window; there was a chance Jack and the others would expect him there, and he wasn't keen to have his face shot off.

Opening a window, Harry saw the men stumbling around, one of them blindly, blood streaming from various lacerations on his face. He could see that, because of the flour and the glass, they were all struggling to wipe their eyes and see what was happening, so he pressed the advantage and hurled down four more glasses.

Two missed completely, exploding on the path, one connected hard enough with one of Jack's knees to make him buckle under the impact, and the remaining glass took one man hard in the face, busting his nose, and making him howl as blood poured from his nostrils.

Harry heard sirens and knew help was on its way. Whether it would arrive in time was another matter. Then he heard something else; it was the sound of splintering wood as the front door caved in.

With no regard for his own safety, the red mist of battle descending, Harry barrelled downstairs. The front door was hanging off its hinges and standing in its place was a man with the enforcer in his hands. He wheeled around, eyes wide, his face a terrifying mask of ghostly white cut through with rivulets of blood, and lunged for Harry with the deadly metal battering ram.

Harry knew that even one hit from the enforcer would put him, not just out of action right then, but potentially forever. He dodged just in time, the enforcer hurtling past him close enough for him to feel the breeze.

The momentum of throwing the enforcer pulled the man off balance. Harry didn't waste a second, throwing an elbow into the side of the man's head to send him crashing to the floor. The man slammed into it with enough force to knock him senseless just long enough for Harry to check on what was happening with Jack and the others, who were still outside.

Jack stared at Harry, raised his pistol, and fired. Harry, who could still hear the sirens and was willing them to hurry up and arrive already, dived, half expecting to feel the impact of the round slam into him. He landed hard, realised he'd not been hit, rolled, and had himself back on his feet, as much by luck as intent, stumbling a little as momentum threw him into a wall.

Wheeling round, Harry saw the man he'd punched struggling to get to his feet. Regretting leaving the walking stick upstairs, he grabbed a small table that was pushed against the hallway wall beside him and threw it as hard as he could. The table collided with the man's legs, tangling them up, and sending him again to the floor with a sickening thud. The man fell still.

Through the door, Harry saw Jack approaching, the flour having turned him into a ghostly apparition, his face and hands streaked with blood, making him look like the cover of a cheap 1980s horror video.

Opening a door behind him, Harry found himself in the dining room. He grabbed the chairs, one after the other, and threw them at the front door to stall Jack's advance.

Another shot rang out. Again, Jack's aim was off thanks to the flour and the blood, but Harry knew his luck could only last so long. He just had to keep everyone at bay long enough for the armed response to arrive.

Jack was at the front door, kicking his way through the chairs, as behind him the two remaining members of his gang were still stumbling around the garden, blinded and confused and raging.

Harry grabbed another chair and threw it at Jack, then another, followed by a vase covered in a delicate decoration of roses, and it hit Jack full in the chest.

Jack stumbled backwards, saw Harry, and raised his weapon, but he was too unsteady and he fired into the wall, then the ceiling, before falling backwards onto the ground, the chairs wrapping him in their embrace.

Knowing he had no chance against a man with a gun, Harry was already moving. He launched two more glasses he'd grabbed from the kitchen. One soared over Jack to smash into one of the men outside, adding to his agony with more flour and glass, and the other hammered into Jack, smashing against the side of his head and bursting like a firework.

With no place safe for him downstairs, Harry bolted to the first floor and dragged a sideboard from against the wall to block the stairs. It wouldn't do much more than delay, but that's really all he could wish for now.

Seeing the walking stick he'd discarded earlier, and realising it was his only weapon now, Harry listened for the sirens, straining to hear them over the sound of the screams of pain and frustration of the men downstairs, when his phone buzzed. He answered it more out of instinct than anything else.

'What?'

'Harry, it's Jen, are you okay?'

'Jen, I'm a little busy right now...'

'It's Bryony,' Jen said, talking over Harry. 'She's not here!'

Harry heard a car racing up the lane outside the house.

'What, Jen? What was that? Who's not where?'

'Bryony!' Jen replied. 'She called the office, spoke with Jim. He tried you, but you didn't answer. And now I'm here, but she isn't, Harry. She's gone. Is everything okay?'

A screeching of tyres cut into the moment.

Harry sprinted to the bedroom window above the front door.

'Harry?'

Harry stared at the car now parked at the end of the path leading to the house. He'd seen it before.

'I know,' he said.

There was a pause, then Jen said, 'What? How can you know?'

'Because she's here,' said Harry, and killed the call.

THIRTY-FOUR

Harry watched in stunned disbelief as Bryony lifted her right hand in what he thought was a wave, only to realise it was anything but.

The shot rang out, and Harry dropped to the floor, hearing the round slam into the wall behind him, above the bed.

Swearing under his breath, Harry stayed low and dashed back out onto the landing, walking stick in hand. He glanced over the oak railings to see that Jack was still at the bottom of the stairs. The man who had entered with the enforcer was still on the ground and, by the looks of things, wouldn't be getting up anytime soon. Well, that was something, anyway.

Harry took a second to work out what his options were, and quickly realised they were desperate, bordering on non-existent. But those sirens, he could still hear them, and that meant he still had to do something, anything, to keep Jack and his friends, and now Bryony, at bay. Seeing Bryony, though, that had thrown him, because he'd not suspected her at all; just how the hell was she caught up in this?

Well, the only way to find out, is to survive long enough to ask, Harry thought, and with that, he gripped the walking stick in his hand, ignored how completely ridiculous his situation was, and headed to the other side of the landing. There, he pressed himself up against the wall at the top of the stairs, hoping the shadows would cloak him just enough to give him the element of surprise.

For a moment, Harry could only hear the sound of his own shuddering breath as he heaved oxygen into his lungs and forced himself to stay calm. Adrenaline raced through him, heightening his senses, but he had to maintain control if he was to have any chance of getting through this.

Over the sound of his breathing, Harry heard voices; Bryony and Jack were, by the sound of it, hissing at each other, their angered words spat at each other through clenched teeth. But they were the only two voices he could hear, so Harry could only hope that was because the other three heavies were still no use to them.

The talking stopped.

Harry heard footsteps, the wood of the stairs creaking and groaning as someone made their way up.

Pushing himself further into the wall, Harry calmed his breathing further, narrowed his eyes on the space in front of him, watching for movement, for a shadow, waiting for that last moment when he would then attack.

Someone was at the top of the stairs; Harry could hear breathing, then the sound of either Jack or Bryony trying to climb over the sideboard he'd pushed across to block the way.

He saw movement, the faintest change in the light and shadow on the floor at the top of the stairs, and with the walking stick gripped tight in his left hand, whipped it round through the air at what he guessed was chest height.

The stick connected hard with something soft. Harry heard a gasp, then a scream, and as he looked out from where he had been standing, he caught Bryony's eye as she tumbled backwards. Eyes bulging in shock, she fell, firing her gun wildly, the rounds thudding into the ceiling. With her other hand, she reached out for the bannister, caught it with her fingertips just enough to stall her fall, but not enough to stop her completely. She whipped around, lost her footing, and fell face forward into the wall, then down onto her knees, before she tumbled the rest of the way down the stairs, only for her leg to catch in one of the ornately carved posts holding the bannister up. The weight of her falling body snapped her leg easily, and the sound was like a rifle crack. Then the house was filled with her screams.

Harry heard a rage-filled roar from below and ducked behind the wall just as Jack charged up the stairs, firing wildly all the way. When he reached the top of the stairs, Harry whipped around once again with the walking stick, only for it to fly out of his hand and down the stairs as Jack dove over the sideboard, rolled, then bounced back up and onto his feet.

Jack lifted his pistol and pointed it at Harry's face.

'Don't,' said Harry, looking into the bloodshot eyes of a madman, his face a terrifying clown's mask of red blood and white flour.

He raised his hands so that they were at the side of his head and just in front of his face.

Jack pulled the trigger.

Click...

In one smooth, violently fast movement, Harry whipped his left hand across his body and wrapped his thick fingers around Jack's pistol, simultaneously moving and twisting his own torso left and out of the way of any possible shot being fired. He continued to drive the pistol forward and down, pushing it into Jack's gut, preventing him from moving it, pinning it against his stomach. Then, before Jack could work out what was going on, or had any chance to fight back or pull his pistol free, Harry brought his right elbow in hard into the side of Jack's head, once, twice, three times, pushing Jack backwards with every strike. He then dropped his right hand to the pistol and, using both hands, ripped it from Jack's grip, snapping his trigger finger in the process.

Jack dropped to the floor with a gurgling scream, and Harry quickly flipped him over onto his front, before cuffing his wrists behind his back.

Ignoring Jack's scream-punctuated swearing, Harry stripped the pistol and stowed it in a jacket pocket when a burst of heat from behind made him snap around in time to see a fireball explode in the hallway below, sending flames blasting up the stairs.

Harry remembered the two fire extinguishers; one was with Matt, the other was still downstairs in the kitchen, and neither would have much of a chance against what was burning below. But it didn't look like he had much choice.

'Matt!'

No answer.

'Matt!'

Still nothing.

With a last look at the now pathetic form of Jack, whose complaints had turned to a sad whimpering, Harry raced along the landing opening doors until he found the bathroom, all the time still shouting for Matt.

Dashing inside, he grabbed a towel, soaked it under a tap at the sink, and threw it over his shoulders. He then grabbed another, drenched it, then wrapped his head in it as best as he could, making sure to cover his mouth and nose. Then, pushing all thought of what might happen if he couldn't put the fire out, he went back into the hallway and came face-to-face with Matt.

Matt lifted the fire extinguisher.

'Need this?'

Harry grabbed it, and jabbed a finger at Jack on the floor.

'Stay here,' he said, 'and keep an eye on him.'

Leaving Matt with Jack, Harry dashed to the top of the stairs and climbed over the sideboard. He saw Bryony sprawled at the bottom of the stairs, no pistol in her hand, her face white from pain and shock, eyes closed, her clothes singed with the heat from the flames.

Jogging down towards her, Harry dropped to her side to check that she was alright, and was rewarded with a blood-curdling scream. That was a good enough sign for him that she had a fighting chance.

Back on his feet, Harry went into the hallway where the fire was already catching, eagerly licking the walls. On the floor, he saw the man who'd launched the enforcer at him. He was trying to crawl away from the fire. Harry looked outside, beyond the fire, and saw the other two men clambering back into the van.

The heat from the fire was growing more and more intense. Harry lifted the extinguisher. At first, nothing happened. Then it burst into life and spewed out a cloud of dry powder. It wasn't enough, but it did the job just long enough for him to dive through the calmer flames to find the other extinguisher. Then he was back in the hallway, blasting the flames with more powder, the heat scorching his skin, but the wet towels doing just enough to prevent him from igniting.

Sirens...

The sound was no longer far away but directly outside, and through the wisps of clearing smoke, Harry saw blue lights breaking through on a wave of shouting.

The next few minutes were a blur of movement and shouting and to Harry it felt almost like he was in a dream, as armed officers streamed in the ruined front door.

Matt came down the stairs with Jack to have him taken away by one of the armed officers. Another officer came in and took the man from the hallway, while another dealt with Bryony. Outside, the two who had tried to escape in the van had already been arrested.

Removing the towels from his head and shoulders, Harry used them to wipe away some of the sweat and grime from his face.

'Mind if I say something?' Matt asked.

Harry frowned.

'You don't usually ask for permission.'

Matt rested a hand on Harry's shoulder.

'You look bloody awful, Harry. Worse, actually.'

'Thanks.'

'I mean it. You need checking over. The blood...'

'It's not mine. At least I don't think it is. I'm fine, really.'

'If it's all the same with you, I think it's probably best if we make sure.'

One of the officers who'd arrived on the scene was now at the top of the stairs with Adam and Peggy.

'You know, you're actually quite terrifying,' said Matt. 'Kind of makes me glad you're on our side, and not theirs.'

Harry laughed, sending a sharp shockwave of pain through his body, which Matt noticed.

'You're fine, then, yes? Sure you are, Harry, sure you are...'

Harry nodded up at Peggy and Adam.

'This is going to be messy, isn't it?' he said. 'What Adam's been involved with, whether he wanted to be or not, I've got this horrible feeling it's going to be huge.'

Another officer joined Peggy and Adam and they were escorted downstairs, an officer at each side, and led outside to the waiting vehicles.

'You know what I want?' Harry said, every bit of him aching now.

'Hospital?' suggested Matt. 'A doctor, at the very least.'

Harry shook his head.

'A pint at the Fountain.'

Matt gave a knowing, understanding nod.

'In your usual chair, the one in the corner?'

'Where else?'

'I think that can be arranged.'

'The first round is on me,' Harry said, and as he led Matt out into what was left of the day, he couldn't quite believe how lucky they had all been to survive long enough to see it.

THIRTY-FIVE

The last forty-eight hours had been a whirlwind, and Harry still wasn't quite sure how, after everything that had happened over in Caldbergh, he was now standing at the edge of the River Ure, on a cloudless and peaceful Sunday afternoon.

Grace, Arthur, and the team were with him, and Smudge was leaning against his leg. They'd been joined by a few others as well, but by invite-only: Ben; Rebecca Sowerby, and her mum, Margaret; Jim's parents, as well as the parents of both Liz and Jen; a small number from Askrigg church itself, and Phil, whose huge Shire horse had been used at the earlier funeral to pull the simple cart on which Anna's coffin had been carried to the church. Anna's parents were also there, and they were standing with Gordy. A number of them were carrying bags; bringing them and what they contained had been optional, and Harry was pleased to see that the whole team had complied with the gentle and somewhat amusing request.

Everyone had parked up in the village of West Witton to follow Gordy along a narrow path that cut through from the road between a row of houses, before threading its way across the fields and along the remains of an ancient track, its surface still marked with the deep ruts cut into it by narrow wheels. Following it, they had eventually been brought to a stop at a wide, sweeping bend, where the waters, brown with peat, flowed gracefully on.

There's no denying it, Harry thought, Gordy had certainly picked a beautiful spot for Anna's ashes to be scattered.

'How's Ben?' Grace asked, while everyone waited for Gordy to gather herself for why they were all there. 'He seems more himself this morning.'

'He is,' said Harry. 'I called him last night. He's still getting flashbacks of what happened when he was a kid, and I think there's still a lot of trauma he hasn't dealt with yet. Needs to talk about it more.'

'Is he going to?'

'He is, and not just to me. He's chatted things through with Liz, and together they're going to sort him some counselling; it'll do him the world of good.'

'Speaking from experience, there?'

'Very much so.'

Grace gave his hand a squeeze, and he returned the gesture.

'They seem pretty sorted, though, don't they?' Grace added, giving a nod over to where Ben was standing with Liz.

Harry smiled at the brightness on his younger brother's face, and the warmth in the smile Liz was giving him.

'They are,' he yawned.

'Tired?'

'A little.'

The events of the past week, which had culminated in the bizarre and violent events in Caldbergh and had run through the night and into the next day, hadn't stopped Harry and Grace from moving house; everything still needed to be unpacked, but at least they were in.

Everything that Adam was involved with was in the hands of a specialist team from Harrogate, though Harry knew he would still be heavily involved, at least for a while. Adam was now in protective custody, and his mum, Peggy, was in alternative accommodation; not only was her home damaged by what had happened, but with what her son had been involved in, her safety was paramount.

Jack, his three goons, and Bryony White had all been arrested and were now in custody, and the little black book Harry had taken from Bryony handed over.

Bryony's involvement still bothered Harry because he'd missed it completely, but no detective was able to uncover everything in a criminal investigation. That was the point of having a team, and even that was no guarantee of success.

Her story had been good, perhaps too good, he now thought, and he wondered just how much, if any of it, was really true. What he did know was that, like Jack, she had been sent by someone higher up, not simply to find out what Adam was doing, but to make sure Jack did as he was told, then dispose of him and the others once Adam and Peggy were dead because he'd made such a mess of things.

That information had not been uncovered thanks to good police work and intensive interrogation, but gleaned from the venom she'd spat at Jack through the screaming about her broken leg. Evidence had been uncovered to show that the house where Harry had met her had been rented by a shell company.

One good thing, though, was Jen finding Steve. Apparently, when Jadyn had arrived home, he'd answered the door to Edna, who had popped round to return the huge lizard. That she had carried him from her house was in itself surprising, but more so was that she had then simply placed Steve in Jadyn's arms, before giving the lizard a kiss on the snout, and heading home. Jen had come down the stairs to find Jadyn too shocked to move, with Steve not only in his arms, but resting his head on his shoulder.

'You okay, there?'

Grace's voice butted into Harry's thoughts.

'What?'

'You drifted off for a moment.'

Harry apologised.

'It's been quite the week,' he said, then saw that Gordy was walking away from Anna's parents to stand on her own.

A hush fell over the small gathering.

'I won't keep you long,' Gordy began, and Harry heard her voice crack a little. 'Anna was never one for being long-winded, as those of you who heard her deliver a sermon will know. She once told me that her mantra was stand up, speak up, then shut up, so if it's okay with everyone here, I'll be doing much the same.'

Soft laughter, filled with both warmth and sorrow, lifted Gordy's words heavenward, as everyone waited for what Gordy would say next.

'If you're wondering why you're here,' Gordy said, 'by which I mean down here at the river's edge, it was Anna's request; like her funeral, she had everything all planned out. Not because she expected to die, I hasten to add, but because she was organised. Well, in some things anyway, because cooking with her was nothing short of crisis management, with every cupboard, every drawer, every pot and pan and tub and packet and tin, open or used or spilled.'

More laughter, and this time because, as Harry suspected, few there knew this about Anna.

Gordy glanced around.

'This was her favourite place,' she said. 'We'd come here together, but she spent time here alone too, walking, sitting, thinking, swimming.'

Another laugh, though this one was a little more nervous, Harry noticed.

Gordy crouched down and lifted from the ground a simple urn.

'Anna's gone,' she said, 'but she's also here. Not in this urn, but in the memories we have of her, how she lived, what she did with her time, the love she had for everyone.'

With a twist, Gordy opened the urn and Harry watched as she closed her eyes briefly, preparing herself for this final goodbye. When she opened them again, they were bright with tears, and beneath them was a smile born both of the deepest love and the most heartbreaking loss.

'I was going to write a poem,' Gordy said, 'because that's what people do, isn't it, at times like this? But the more I tried, the worse it sounded, so I gave up. And I don't think Anna would've been that keen anyway. She was always more for just getting on with things. So, that's exactly what I'm going to do right now...'

With no warning given, Gordy turned to face the river and, as a breeze drifted past, tipped the urn. The wind caught the contents and snatched them away to twist and twirl and dance across the water.

For the next few moments, everyone watched in silence as Anna's ashes drifted away and were soon nothing but a memory of a soul glittering in the sunshine dappling the river's mirrored surface.

Gordy placed the lid back on the urn and turned back around to face everyone. She then clapped her hands together and, Harry was quite sure, rubbed them together with barely disguised glee.

'Like I said earlier,' she began, 'Anna would come here to walk, to sit, to think, and to do something else, which is why she asked, for those of you who wanted to, to bring a few things.'

Gordy cocked her head to one side and looked over at Harry. He saw mischief in her eyes.

'Something like this,' she said, 'needs someone, quite literally, to take the first plunge. So, Harry, if you would be so kind?'

Harry couldn't help himself and laughed, shaking his head as he swung the bag off his back and started to unpack it.

'I'm not going in on my own though,' he said, and sent a sharp look at everyone else.

Heaving out two large, rolled-up towels, and handing one of them to Grace, Harry saw from the corner of his eye other bags being unpacked.

'You're mad,' Arthur said, a wide smile on his face. 'I'd join you, obviously, I would, but someone's got to look after Smudge and Jess, haven't they?'

A few minutes later, Harry was in his swimming shorts and standing at the edge of the water. To either side, the rest of the team had gathered, along with Gordy, and also Rebecca and her mum.

'You, too, Margaret?' Harry asked, as he tried to ignore the fact that he was already shivering just at the thought of what they were about to do.

'Wouldn't miss this for the world!' Margaret replied. Then she turned to Gordy and grinned. 'Come on,' she said, 'let's give Anna not just a proper sendoff, but a bloody good laugh!'

With a whoop, Margaret grabbed Gordy's hand, and the two of them raced into the water, squealing and yelling and laughing as the chill of the water dashed against them in playful splashes. Then everyone else followed, and the Dales echoed to the sound of joy and laughter in the memory of Anna.

When everyone was eventually back on dry land, and the shivering held at bay by thick towels, warm clothes, and a few flasks of steaming hot chocolate, Gordy approached Harry. Grace was chatting with Jim and his parents, so he was alone with Smudge.

'Anna would've loved that,' he said.

'Well, it was her idea, so I hope so,' Gordy replied. 'How did the move go?'

'We're in, so that's something. And we're set up enough for everyone to come round, like I said.'

'You're sure about that? We can just go to the Fountain.'

'We'll be doing another housewarming once we're sorted, and this was Grace's idea anyway, so yes, we're sure. Plus, we've bought an awful lot of crisps, and various other nibbles, not to mention the drinks, so we need it all gone if we're to have any chance of having space for unpacking.'

Gordy gave a nod, and Harry could tell that she wanted to say something else.

'I had a nice chat with Jim and his parents,' she said. 'He's going part-time, then?'

'The call of the farm has grown too loud.' Harry smiled. 'And we've Dave now, haven't we? Obviously, we've lost you, and I'm beginning to think we'll not be getting someone new. Not that I'm too bothered; you're difficult to replace.'

'Thanks.'

'It's the truth.'

Harry gave Gordy a moment longer to get to the real reason she had come over to speak to him when he was alone, but in the end said, 'So, what is it? Something's bothering you, I know it is.'

Gordy hesitated, then dropped down to Harry's bag and stuffed something inside it.

'That's a little something for you,' she said, then before Harry could ask what it was, she was back on her feet and had turned to chat with Grace, who had come over to join them.

Later that day, with the trip to the river a memory, and the house now quiet after everyone had gone, Harry was sitting on a sofa with Smudge at his feet, and waiting for Grace to return from the chippy; they'd not yet unpacked everything in the kitchen, so they were treating themselves, though Harry had declined the offer of the battered Wensleydale cheese.

Feeling weary, Harry closed his eyes, only to snap them open again as he remembered Gordy coming over to speak to him at the ceremony. With a groan, he heaved himself out of the sofa, found his bag, which was still filled with damp swimming gear, and pulled out what Gordy had slipped inside.

Whatever it was, it was small and wrapped in a plastic bag.

Harry sat back down and tipped the bag onto his lap. A small box tumbled out, and he picked it up and rested it on his palm. A note was wrapped around it and held in place by an elastic band.

Removing the band, Harry read Gordy's note: *I think you might have more need of this than me at some point, and I know Anna would think the same.*

Harry opened the box and there, nestled in burgundy-coloured silk, its diamond catching the light with ease, was a ring.

WANT KNOW how Harry rings the changes in his team while cracking the next blood-thirsty case in the Dales? Scan the QR code below to grab your copy of Blood Fountain, the next book in the DCI Harry Grimm Series, and to start a brand-new adventure with Gordy as she heads down south. You'll also be able to download an exclusive free short story, *Dust to Dust*, and sign up for my VIP Club and newsletter.

ABOUT DAVID J. GATWARD

David had his first book published when he was 18 and has written extensively for children and young adults. *Ashes of Betrayal* is his eighteenth DCI Harry Grimm crime thriller.

Visit David's website to find out more about him and the DCI Harry Grimm books, and his new Mendip Murders series.

 facebook.com/davidjgatwardauthor